The piles of c̶ severed hearts grew

Realizing what was coming, the slaves struggled futilely with their bonds, weeping and begging their captors for mercy.

All but the companions.

Jak, Krysty, Mildred, Doc, and J.B. were staring at Ryan. Their fixed, defiant expressions all said the same thing: we're not going to check out like that. Not like chickens on the chopping block.

The one-eyed warrior nodded in agreement, then he looked away. If they couldn't escape, they could do the next best thing. They could take out as many of the bastards as possible before they were cut down.

Ryan Cawdor withdrew deep into the core of his being, shutting out the grisly sights and sounds around him. He wasn't preparing himself to die, he was preparing to fight and chill to his last ounce of strength. To expend it all, here, now. And when that strength was gone, death could nukin' well have him, ready or not. It took only a moment for him to make the attitude shift. It was like a gate swinging open.

And when it was done, Ryan felt a sense of freedom and power.

**Other titles in the
Deathlands saga:**

JAMES AXLER

DEATH LANDS®

Dark Resurrection

EMPIRE OF XIBALBA
BOOK II

A GOLD EAGLE BOOK FROM
WORLDWIDE®

TORONTO • NEW YORK • LONDON
AMSTERDAM • PARIS • SYDNEY • HAMBURG
STOCKHOLM • ATHENS • TOKYO • MILAN
MADRID • WARSAW • BUDAPEST • AUCKLAND

Special thanks to John Todd, Jr., for the insights he so graciously shared about the geography, history and culture of Veracruz, Mexico, and for his Web site's excellent collection of maps and photographs.

Recycling programs for this product may not exist in your area.

First edition March 2009

ISBN-13: 978-0-373-62595-6
ISBN-10:   0-373-62595-2

DARK RESURRECTION

Every parting gives a foretaste of death;
every coming together again a foretaste of
the resurrection.

—Arthur Schopenhauer,
1788–1860

THE DEATHLANDS SAGA

This world is their legacy, a world born in the violent nuclear spasm of 2001 that was the bitter outcome of a struggle for global dominance.

There is no real escape from this shockscape where life always hangs in the balance, vulnerable to newly demonic nature, barbarism, lawlessness.

But they are the warrior survivalists, and they endure—in the way of the lion, the hawk and the tiger, true to nature's heart despite its ruination.

Ryan Cawdor: The privileged son of an East Coast baron. Acquainted with betrayal from a tender age, he is a master of the hard realities.

Krysty Wroth: Harmony ville's own Titian-haired beauty, a woman with the strength of tempered steel. Her premonitions and Gaia powers have been fostered by her Mother Sonja.

J. B. Dix, the Armorer: Weapons master and Ryan's close ally, he, too, honed his skills traversing the Deathlands with the legendary Trader.

Doctor Theophilus Tanner: Torn from his family and a gentler life in 1896, Doc has been thrown into a future he couldn't have imagined.

Dr. Mildred Wyeth: Her father was killed by the Ku Klux Klan, but her fate is not much lighter. Restored from predark cryogenic suspension, she brings twentieth-century healing skills to a nightmare.

Jak Lauren: A true child of the wastelands, reared on adversity, loss and danger, the albino teenager is a fierce fighter and loyal friend.

Dean Cawdor: Ryan's young son by Sharona accepts the only world he knows, and yet he is the seedling bearing the promise of tomorrow.

In a world where all was lost, they are humanity's last hope....

Prologue

John Barrymore Dix staggered forward under the sickening roll of the tugboat's deck, his stride limited by the steel trace that connected the manacles around his ankles. Rain in wind-driven sheets whipped across his shoulders and back. His clothing was already soaked through, front and rear. Water ran in rivulets down his pant legs and squished inside his boots. His beloved fedora was saturated, as well; moisture steadily leaked through its crown onto the top of his head and peeled over the sides of his face.

A drowned rat in chains.

He wasn't alone.

Jak Lauren and Krysty Wroth lurched a few feet ahead of him. The albino youth and the tall redhead were similarly drenched, similarly hobbled, weaving from side to side as the slow-moving ship wallowed through oncoming seas.

Behind the five-foot-six-inch Dix, and in front of Jak and Krysty, were twenty-seven other prisoners. Their captors had passed a rope through their ankle shackles, so individuals couldn't break ranks and commit suicide by jumping over-board, and thereby avoid being worked to death. J.B. and the others circled around the main deck in a drunken conga line, marching to the beat of the Matachìn coxswain, who sat on a canvas folding chair on the stern. The hood of the pirate's plastic poncho shadowed his face as he pounded on a steel drum with a pair of rag-wrapped hammers.

The rest of the galley slave contingent, sixty souls in all, continued to row in unison under cover of metal, pipe-strut-supported awnings that bracketed the port and starboard rails from amidships to stern. Among the chained rowers were Ryan Cawdor, Dr. Mildred Wyeth and Doc Tanner, who watched from behind their long oars as J.B., Jak and Krysty rounded the rear of the superstructure and stumbled across the heaving deck.

It was leg-stretching time for one-third of the conscripted crew.

Every couple of hours the Matachìn pulled one person off each of the thirty benches, leaving the remainder to row. The pirates forced the chosen to circumnavigate the tug's deck at least a dozen times, no matter the weather or sea state—a regimen J.B. figured had come from years of trial and error. Regular stretching was essential to keep slaves in proper working condition; it prevented debilitating muscle cramps and tears. The object was to wring the most out of the rowers before flinging their spent, skeletal carcasses over the side into the Lantic.

The yawing of the tug caused the horizon to leap and fall wildly, making its two sister ships abruptly vanish and reappear astern. Despite the rain, despite the violent motion, J.B. was grateful for the opportunity to move around. Sitting for hours, pulling at the oars, knotted his back and thigh muscles. The constant ache in his cracked but healing ribs had diminished. The pain still peaked every time he took too deep a breath.

They had been rowing the pirates' massive, oceangoing

tugboat for three weeks, give or take; three weeks since the fall of Padre Island and the Nuevo-Texican defeat. After the first week, it had become impossible to separate one day from the next—such was the monotony of crushing, mindless toil.

Rounding the stern, J.B. faced into the wind and the wet. Sideways-blown raindrops spattered the lenses of his spectacles, partially obscuring his vision. He brushed away the drops with rag-bandaged, manacled hands. Dead ahead was a towering gray cloud that drifted alone like a monumental ship of the air. Its crest loomed high above them, hundreds of feet up into the grim sky, from its bottom edge hung a darker gray, ever-shifting veil. Where veil met sea, the water was pitch-black and boiling from concentrated, torrential rain.

Steadily, inexorably, they were pulling for the very heart of the squall.

A gruff voice crackled through the tug's loud-hailer.

The command was unintelligible gibberish to J.B., but the poncho-clad, Matachìn deck-watch immediately opened a hatch in the stern and started passing out five-gallon plastic buckets to the captives.

Empty bucket at his feet, J.B. once again glanced over at Krysty and Jak. His longtime companions were shadows of their former selves. Krysty's prehensile hair hung down around her shoulders in drenched, lifeless ribbons; her hip bones protruded alarmingly. Jak's dead-white but youthful face had aged: it had become drawn and gaunt. His weather-cracked lips were flecked with dried blood; his ruby-colored eyes had sunk in their sockets, and they burned with a fevered intensity. Standing beside them was the blond Padre Islander boy, Garwood Reed, the same brave, defiant Deathlands fourteen-year-old who'd tried to lead the companions to safety during the assault on the grounded freighter. The pirates had transformed the youngest of their surviving captives into a stick figure with eyes rimmed by dark circles.

J.B. was in as bad a physical state as they were. He had lost a lot of weight, too. Half his teeth were loose, his gums bled, his hands were blistered and split. His mind wasn't right, either. He was having more and more difficulty concentrating, his thoughts continually plunging into a pit of self-directed anger. Even though they had been betrayed in the final moment by that shitweasel Daniel Desipio, a fire talker, he still blamed himself for the capture of his comrades, and for this gruesome outcome.

Even though the galley slaves were fed morning and night, they were wasting away; it was inevitable, a matter of calories burned versus calories taken in. Their morning meal was a ladleful of gummy, weevily corn porridge mixed with molasses. The evening meal was the same gruel sprinkled with flaked salt-dried fish—bones, guts and all. Their food was boiled to mush in a caldron on the stern deck.

Chained to their oars, J.B. and the others ate hog slop while their pirate captors feasted inside the ship's main cabin. Fragrant spice and meat smells drifted out from the galley. Chilis. Cumin. Garlic. Beans. Rice. Slow-roasted pork. Deep-fried, freshly caught fish. The aromas made J.B.'s stomach rumble and his mouth water. Food had some kind of special significance for the stinking bastards.

Holy moley significance.

Their off-key singing and rhythmic chanting at meals never failed to set his nerves on edge. The pirates' religion was as incomprehensible and hateful to J.B. as their gobbledygook language.

Even though the Matachìn deck-watch was outnumbered ten to one, they turned their backs on the captives as they handed out the plastic buckets. It wasn't negligence. It was confidence born of experience and training. The pirates knew the limits of their slaves, both physical and psychological. The captives were always chained to the rowing benches or linked together at the ankles; their wrists were cuffed. Overpowering the guards would require all thirty moving as one, an impossible feat, and not just because of the restraints. Fear of the consequences of failure—either lashings of the whip or agonizing death by machete chops—ensured that most of the prisoners would remain immobile during an attack; their deadweight doomed any mutiny attempt from the start.

As far as J.B. was concerned, the Matachìn weren't just foreign fighters, they were aliens from another world.

After three weeks without a bath, J.B. knew he didn't smell so great himself, but the rank, eye-watering pong of his overseers forced him to breathe through his mouth whenever they stood upwind. Pillaged feminine jewelry—delicate golden bracelets and necklaces—glittered around their boot tops and peeked out from behind the masses of waist-length, moldy dreadlocks. Some of them wore the torn, blood-stained dresses of their victims over the outside of their clothes. Guthook machetes, the standard-issue cutting weapon, hung in canvas scabbards on their hips.

The pirates carried stubby submachine guns, of a design the Armorer had never seen. The blasters had an M-16 type plastic carrying handle/rear sight and a smooth, fixed rear plastic stock. A ventilated plastic front stock/shroud concealed an eight-inch barrel. The bore looked to be 9 mm. The 30-round curved mag was also made of the same high-strength plastic.

During the one-sided battle for Padre Island, the Matachìn had worn mass-produced body armor, something unheard-of in the hellscape. The trauma plate had stopped Krysty's .38 rounds cold. J.B. had seen that with his own eyes.

The seven-ship raiding party had voyaged a great distance and without breaking a sweat had obliterated at least two heavily fortified outposts on the Gulf coast, Padre Island and Matamoros ville. They had taken the few survivors—including J.B. and the others—as replacement galley slaves. Inexplicably, the Matachìn hadn't bothered to loot Padre's beached container ship, which was full of what J.B. and his companions deemed irreplaceable predark spoils; they'd just let it burn.

Up until a month ago, up until a week before his enslavement, J.B. had given little consideration to the wider world outside Deathlands. There had been no reason for him to consider it. The daily battle for food, shelter and safety was a grindstone difficult to see over. And on top of that, making do in the hellscape was something J.B. excelled at and took justifiable pride in.

Though nuclear Armageddon was more than a century in the past, Deathlands had not yet recovered in any meaningful way. There was still no manufacturing to speak of, large or small. Its norm population remained primitively agrarian: hand-cultivated crops were supplemented by seasonal hunting and gathering. Vast areas were made uninhabitable by lingering high levels of radiation from overlapping Soviet MIRV strikes. Travel over any distance was risky because of roaming bands of savage chiller-muties. A ruined road system and a lack of surplus goods limited the possibilities for expansion of trade.

The existing social organization lay in the hands of the

barons, self-proclaimed royalty who controlled their fiefdoms with small, relatively well-equipped armies of sec men. The barons' territories were bounded by easily defensible topographic features: mountains, plateaus, river channels and the like. Because mass communication was nonexistent and individual human settlements so scattered, there was no way to accurately estimate Deathlands survivors, but it was certainly a tiny fraction of the 200 million before skydark. The overall numbers were so reduced and the land area so enormous that wider conquest—or national reunification—by any one of the barons, or an association of same, was simply out of the question.

For more than a hundred years the barons' winning strategy had been to hunker down and hold ground.

J.B. wasn't incurious or closed-minded about the outside world—like most other born-and-bred Deathlanders he was simply dismissive of it. If the United States of America, the most powerful country to ever exist on the face of the earth, couldn't rebuild itself after the nukecaust, then how could the considerably less well-off nations to the south?

A month earlier, while still free, he and his companions had been forced to consider an alternate view.

Beyond the southeastern edge of the Houston nuke-a-thon, in Port Arthur ville they had joined forces with a seagoing trader of renowned skill and legendary savagery. Harmonica Tom Wolf had opened their eyes to the possibility that the basic assumption—that Deathlands was the sole nexus and the pinnacle of human survival and culture—might be 180-degrees wrong.

By the skin of his teeth, Harmonica Tom had escaped capture at Padre Island on his forty-foot sloop, *Tempest*. The companions might have made it to safety, too, if J.B.'s rib injury hadn't held them back. That he had been the crew's weak link, that his infirmity had brought them to such a fate, stuck deep in the Armorer's craw.

The tug lurched so violently to starboard that J.B.'s knees buckled and he nearly fell headfirst over his bucket. Catching his balance, he looked up and saw Ryan and Mildred sitting side by side, hauling back on the same oar. Ryan's dark hair was matted with sweat and tangled in a dense black growth of beard. The patch over his left eye was crusted with white salt, as was the long scar that divided brow and cheek. In three weeks Mildred had lost a tremendous amount of weight, the sinews in her caramel-brown forearms and biceps stood out like cables as she rowed. Some of the white beads in her hair had broken, and the carefully woven plaits had come unbraided; they hung in matted puffballs down her back.

Doc occupied the bench behind them, his lips moving as he muttered to himself nonstop. The Victorian time-traveler looked even more scarecrow and skeletal than usual, his clothes hanging loosely from stooped and shrunken shoulders. Wispy strands of gray beard did nothing to hide hollowed cheeks.

All three bared their teeth as they leaned hard into unison strokes, struggling to make way against the gathering headwind and jumbled seas.

J.B. couldn't count the number of times he and his friends had been taken prisoner, but this time was different. The specific details of being exposed to the elements, starved, beaten, forced to eat, sleep and shit shackled to oars was unimportant. What mattered was, each pull southward took them farther away from everything they knew, from everything they believed in, and brought them that much closer to the truth about their place in the larger scheme of things.

So far the truth didn't look all that promising.

During the companions' multiday voyage east from Port Arthur ville to Padre Island, Harmonica Tom had passed on rumors about pockets of predark civilization thriving in the southern latitudes nearly untouched by nuke strikes. Were the Matachìn pirates a scouting party from a much more advanced, a much more populous culture? Was it possible that a complex, industrialized society had existed side by side with Deathlands ever since nukeday? If that was indeed the case, then J.B. knew he and his comrades faced an adversary with overwhelming advantages, an adversary that could chew them up like weevils in porridge. And there was no guarantee that any of the success strategies hard-won in the hellscape would save them.

The Armorer, who had fought on the winning side in dozens of campaigns and a thousand skirmishes, felt both helpless and insignificant. Being short of stature, he found those feelings particularly grating. The lack-of-size business was something he had lived with his entire life, and he'd come to terms with it by making himself extramean and extraquick. He'd been mean enough and fast enough to hold his own alongside Deathlands's most famous warriors: Trader, Poet and Ryan Cawdor. In fact, Trader had often bragged around the convoy campfire that J.B. was the kind of sawed-off, fearless little bastard who would climb up your chest, stand on your shoulders and beat in your head with his gun butt.

The idea of being swallowed up by distance, technology and scale, of being truly, unutterably lost was no longer an abstract concept to J.B. Now he knew what Ryan had experienced when he had been singled out and spirited off to Shadow World. The lesson Ryan had learned on that over-populated parallel Earth was to keep his head down and wait for an opportunity. No matter how bleak and impossible things looked in the present, to trust in fate that the seam would appear.

The cloud looming before them cast a vast shadow, turning the water beneath it inky-black. Over the coxswain's drumbeat and the steady creak and splash of the oars, J.B. could hear the shrill hiss of heavy rain falling on the sea. As the sound of the downpour grew louder and louder, the headwind shrieked and the air temperature plummeted. J.B. shivered uncontrollably in his wet clothes, clenching his jaws to keep his teeth from chattering.

Then it was upon them, roaring.

An impenetrable curtain of rain swept over the tug's bow. The volume of water was astounding, as was its power. It came down like a waterfall, hammering the metal awnings, flash-flooding the scuppers.

The tug wallowed through steep troughs, pressing deeper into the darkness and the din. Cold rain in a wave slammed down on J.B.'s fedora and shoulders, and again his knees almost gave way, this time from the sheer weight of the torrent. As he struggled to keep his feet, the deck lights above him snapped on.

At least it wasn't chem rain, he thought.

This was drinkable water.

The five-gallon buckets filled in no time. The deck-watch forced the slaves to pass them hand to hand down the file and dump them into the stern's freshwater holding tank. Again and again, the process was repeated, buckets allowed to fill to the brim and handed down the line. When the tank was finally topped off, the Matachìn sealed the hatch shut, then ducked back under an awning to escape the cascade's pummeling.

The conga line had nowhere to go.

The tug didn't immediately turn out from under the cloud and let her two sister ships have a go at filling their tanks. Its course and speed held it stationary beneath the downpour, leaving the linked slaves to flounder and slide, gasping from the concentration of water vapor in the air. J.B. groaned as his feet went out from under him and he hit the deck hard. Though he had cradled his ribs with his arms, trying to protect them, white-hot pain lanced through his torso.

On his knees, fighting for breath, J.B. squinted up at the wheelhouse, two stories above the main deck. He glimpsed the pirate captain leaning out through an open side window, chewing on a stub of fat black stogie as he peered down at them; his dreadlocks were piled high atop his head and laced with golden trinkets. The Matachìn commander reached up to the wheelhouse ceiling for a lanyard.

The ship's horn unleashed a string of mocking blasts as the chained captives flopped on the deck.

Through the shifting veil of heavy rain, against the glare of the deck lights, J.B. could see the stinking bastard was laughing his head off.

Chapter One

The convoy's lead tug rumbled onward through the dead-still night. Diesel engines shook the deck under Ryan's boot soles; thick smoke poured from the twin stacks atop the superstructure, enveloping the stern in caustic particulate. Deep breathing was difficult. The smoke burned his one good eye and it left an awful, scorched petrochemical taste in his mouth.

Way nukin' better than rowing, though, Ryan told himself. He'd had enough rowing to last him the rest of his life.

Oars shipped, the Matachìn were powering toward what he figured was their ultimate destination.

The Lantic had turned black-glass-smooth under a starry, moonless sky. In the distance, on the starboard side, its oily surface reflected a narrow band made up of brilliant points of light—white, yellow, red, green—dotting, demarcating an otherwise invisible shoreline. As the bow crested the widely spaced swells, the lights lurched skyward then abruptly dropped. Landfall, the first in more than three weeks, drew inexorably closer.

The lights definitely weren't from fires or torches or anything combustible; Ryan knew that because they didn't flicker or throb. They glowed steadily.

Which meant electricity.

Massive quantities of electricity.

Power to burn, in fact.

What bobbed ahead of them was no looted carcass of an underground redoubt, no shit-hammered, hand-to-mouth ville, no nuked-out urban ruin. This was a city, as cities were rumored of old, and from more than a mile offshore it looked to be very much alive.

Ryan glanced at the exhausted human forms hunched on the benches around him. In the deck lights, the slaves' filthy cheeks were streaked by tears, their lips trembling, their eyes wide with fear and panic at the prospect of an unknown fate.

Faced with the self-same prospect, his companions had drawn on the last of their physical and mental reserves, turning hard-eyed, resolute, deadly focused. Like Ryan, Mildred, Doc, Jak, Krysty and J.B. were a breed apart, their spirits tempered in the furnace of continual conflict and bodily risk. Unlike their Deathlander fellow slaves, they had little interest in finding a comfortable hole to hunker down in, nor in shouldering leather traces and dragging an iron-tipped plow over rocky soil, nor in crawling through the radioactive nukeglass massifs in search of predark spoils, nor in selling their considerable fighting skills to the highest-bidding baron. They were addicted to the kind of absolute freedom only the hellscape could provide.

Aboard *Tempest,* in what now seemed like another life, when Doc had proposed they join Harmonica Tom on a southern hemisphere voyage of discovery, none of them ever dreamed it would be undertaken in chains and at the point of a lash.

Now the impossible situation in which Ryan and his comrades found themselves trapped was about to change.

Maybe for the worse.

Maybe not.

In the latter they saw a crack of daylight.

Ryan nudged Mildred gently with his elbow, nodded toward the crescent of lights, and said, "So, that's what the world looked like before hellday?"

"Pretty much," she replied.

From the bench on the far side of Mildred, J.B. leaned forward and asked, "Where in nukin' hell are we? That's all still Mex, right?"

"I think it's Veracruz," the twentieth-century, physician freezie said. "Or maybe Tampico. They were the two closest big port cities."

One of the Matachìn deck-watch leaned in under the sheet metal awning beside them. He was tricked out in full battle armor. Hanging by his hands on the pipe strut, he unleashed armpit stench with both barrels. There was spattered blood on the canvas scabbard of his gut-hook machete. It was still wet, and it was most certainly human. Slaves too weak to row routinely got the long edge across the backs of their necks before they were tossed over the side like so much garbage. A crazy triumphant look in his eyes, the pirate spoke rapid-fire down at Mildred. Overhearing the words, the Matachìn idling nearby looked on in amusement.

"What did the bastard say to you?" Ryan asked.

Mildred translated. "He said we're looking at Veracruz City."

"He said more than that," J.B. prompted.

"Yeah, he did," she admitted. "He said next to his world, Deathlands is nothing but shit, and that we Deathlanders will always be shit."

"An assessment that might have carried more weight," Doc remarked aridly from a seat on the bench directly behind them, "had his own hairstyle not been adorned with dried sea gull excreta."

"You're absolutely right," Ryan told the pirate. "We're shit and you're not."

The Matachìn scowled and as he did so his right hand dropped to his hip and the pommel of his braided leather lash. English was beyond him, but tone transcended the language barrier.

Mildred spoke up quickly, putting Ryan's remark into Spanish. Evidently the sarcasm was lost in translation.

With a satisfied sneer, the pirate turned back to his shipmates.

As the ship angled closer to shore, the lay of the coast gradually revealed itself. The curve of a southward-pointing peninsula became distinct from the landmass immediately behind it. The tug beelined for a blinking green beacon that marked the deep channel at the tip of the breakwater. When the ship rounded the bend into the protection of the harbor, they hit the wall of trapped heat and suffocating humidity radiating off the land.

The ship's horn blasted overhead; the sister ships behind chimed in, as well, announcing the Matachìn convoy's triumphant return to what Ryan could only guess was its point of origin.

In the lee of the peninsula, under scattered bright lights on tall stanchions, were the remains of a commercial shipyard—docks and cargo cranes. The scale of the development dwarfed what they had seen at Port Arthur ville. The structures hadn't escaped Armageddon unscathed, though. It looked like they had been slammed by tidal waves or earthquakes. Most of the metal-frame industrial buildings were flattened to their concrete pads. Towering cargo cranes canted at odd angles;

some had toppled into the water. The enormous docks were broken, wide sections of decking were missing; moored to the remnants were a hodge-podge of small trading vessels. Beyond the docks, where the peninsula met the mainland, stood a power plant that was fully operational. Floodlights illuminated clouds of smoke or steam from a trio of tall stacks. Over the noise of the diesels, the complex emitted a steady, high-pitched hum.

The lead tug continued, hugging the inside of the peninsula, passing within a hundred yards of another immense structure—a fortress made of heavily weathered, light gray stone, also dramatically lit. Apparently constructed on an offshore island, it was connected to the mainland by a low, stone bridge. Above its crenellated battlements, at either end of the enclosed compound, were cylindrical observation towers. Huge iron anchor rings hung in a row just above the waterline. In front of the high-arched entrance gate, small motor launches were tied up to mooring cleats. Eroded stone sentry boxes bracketed the gate.

The mini-island fortress was a time-worn anachronism, but it had been built to last; it had survived nukeday virtually intact, whereas the twentieth-century artifacts that surrounded it had not.

"It's an old Spanish fort from colonial days," Doc ventured. "Probably six hundred or more years old. Those massive, triangular blockhouses outside the corners of the bastion walls are called ravelins. They were designed to defend the main perimeter from attack by offering a protected position for flanking fire. In the sixteenth and seventeenth centuries Spaniards used stone forts like that to store gold and silver mined from the New World. It could also defend the city from pirates and foreign invaders—French, English, American."

Even bathed in hard, bright light, evil seem to emanate from the structure, from the very seams in its masonry.

Ancient squatting evil.

A consequence of the uncounted thousands who had died as prisoners in its belly, between its teeth, under its claws.

"The question is, what is it now?" Mildred said.

"Those cannons sticking out of the battlements sure as hell aren't six-hundred-year-old muzzleloaders," J.B. said. "If I had to guess I'd say they're at least 106 mm with mebbe a one-mile range. That means nobody comes in or goes out of the harbor without coming under their sights."

As the tug motored through the sheltered waters of the harbor, past the fort's arched gate, a gaggle of armed men spilled through it, waving and cheering in welcome. They didn't look anything like the Matachìn. No dreads. No battle armor. They weren't wearing uniforms as such, more like insignia. They all had crimson sashes over their right shoulders and opposite hips, and they wore off-white straw cowboy hats with rolled brims. Their shoulder-slung weapons were different from what the Matachìn carried. The wire-stocked, stamped-steel submachine guns were much more compact, like Uzi knock-offs, with the mags inside the pistol grips. Men in crimson sashes continued to pour out of the gate, onto the dock.

"Sec man garrison," Ryan said flatly.

Fireworks whistled from the battlements, arcing high into the black sky, and there exploding into coruscating patterns of green, gold and red.

The tug chugged on, turning left for the nearby mainland.

Looking over his shoulder at the wreckage of the peninsula, Ryan guessed that it had taken the brunt of nukeday tidal waves, in effect absorbing most of the energy before it reached the city on the inside of the harbor.

Off the bow, Veracruz glowed incandescent against the black-velvet sky. The one-eyed warrior could make out individual pinpoints of light from the upper story windows of the tallest buildings. At the edge of the city, a long pier jutted into the water; it was overlooked by a lighthouse.

When the tug came within four hundred yards of the pier, Ryan saw it was packed end to end; thousands of people had assembled and were waiting for them to arrive. Another hundred yards closer and he could see that the overloaded dock was just the tip of the crowd, which stretched unbroken, back into the brightly lit city streets. There was no telling how far back it went. The throng was like a single entity, a vast amoeba-thing in constant, chaotic motion, only kept from spilling out in all directions by the building walls on either side. Between celebratory blasts of the ships' horns, Ryan heard yelling and blaring fragments of music. The din got even louder as the tug pulled alongside the pier. The music—caterwaul singing backed by frenzied fiddle, drums and guitar—boomed down from loudspeakers mounted on the lamp posts.

A sea of sweaty, brown faces greeted them.

The wildly excited citizens of Veracruz waved Day-Glo-colored plastic pennants emblazoned with unintelligible symbols. They held ten times larger-than-life-size papier-mâché heads on long poles, which they jigged up and down. Some of the paper sculptures had flat noses, ornate headdresses and leering mouths lined with cruel fangs. The colors were bizarre instead of lifelike—glistening green or pink skins, pointed black tongues, insane red and purple eyes with yellow pupils. Ryan strained to read the words written across their neckplates: Atapul the First; Atapul the Second; and so on, up to Atapul the Tenth.

They were names, he figured.

Ryan had no clue what the stylized images represented, whether they were gods or barons, but the meaning of some of the other sculpted faces was all too apparent. Bobbing in front of him on pikes were gigantic human heads with a ghastly bluish pallor, bleeding from nose, eyes and mouths. Cheeks and foreheads were speckled with red dots. Their expressions were fixed in rictus agony and terror.

Plague masks.

Plague like the one that had struck Padre Island.

Mildred squeezed his arm hard to get his attention, then raised her manacled hands to point toward the landward, lighthouse end of the pier.

There, not thirty yards away, on the end of a wooden pole, ten times life size, was Ryan's own face, or a close approximation thereof. It was crudely rendered and painted, but all the pertinent details were there: the black eye patch, the scar that split his brow, the dark curly hair, the single surviving eye, the bearded cheeks, the square chin. The only difference was, the patch and scar had been reversed on the sculpture, as if he was staring into a mirror.

There were more of the giant, eye-patch faces spaced here and there among the seething throng.

"What the fuck?" Ryan said.

Chapter Two

Harmonica Tom stood at the helm of *Tempest,* feathering the engine's throttle to maintain a constant safe distance from the row of ship lights in front of him. He ran the forty-foot vessel blacked-out, as he had done every night for the last three weeks, every night since he'd escaped from Padre Island. Finding the pirate convoy after dark was a piece of cake for the seasoned skipper. The six target boats were always lit up, mast, bow and stern; this to help keep them from crashing into one another.

During the day, Tom had to lay back in his pursuit for fear a crow's-nest lookout would glimpse his mast tops astern. The last thing he wanted was for part of the fleet to peel off and double back to check out who was following its wake. The seagoing trader was sure they'd have no trouble recognizing *Tempest:* he'd already used it to kick their asses once. Unfortunately, he'd only managed to sink a single ship, while damaging two others. The fallback in pursuit meant he had to do some zigging and zagging to find the convoy again after sundown.

No problem this night, though.

The Matachìn ships were under engine power; even the slave galley tugs were burning diesel. And they were heading in toward the coast, making for the corona of shimmering lights low on the horizon.

By Tom's map reckoning, it had to be Veracruz.

It was starting to look like the fire talkers' stories were all true. That there really was a wider and more prosperous world than Deathlands, existing invisibly, simultaneously, from nukeday forward.

When he had first heard the tales of civilization's survival in the south, Tom had wanted to get in on the ground floor, to be the first to establish peaceful commerce, to forge trade links with the more advanced culture, and thereby get his hands on some of its fabled material wealth. But after seeing what the dreadlocked emissaries of that culture had done to Padre Island, the entrepreneurship fantasies vanished. Payback had become his single-minded goal.

And payback was his forte.

Like other Deathlands traders, Harmonica Tom Wolf had committed his share of morally questionable deeds over the years—some might even call them "atrocities." It was part of staying in business, and staying alive. He had systematically eliminated rivals trying to encroach on his territory. He had closed deals with hot lead and cold steel instead of smiles and handshakes. He had transported cargos of uncut jolt and high explosives without thinking twice. He had never purposefully messed with women and kids, though. And when he had sent another trader or coldheart on the last train west, it had always been a chill-or-be-chilled situation, and it was usually face-to-face, if not nose-to-nose.

The horror he had seen at Padre had transformed him, and not in a good way. Images of the dead and dying in that shantyville were branded into the root of his brain. Whenever he managed to grab a few winks of sleep, they invariably shook him awake. He came to gasping for air, spitting mad, fingers clawing for the butt of his stainless-steel .45 Smith wheelgun, looking around for someone to chill.

The Nuevo-Texicans' passing hadn't been quick or clean, not like getting shot or stabbed or fragged by shrap. They had disintegrated from the inside out, cooked in their skins by fever, laying helpless in pools of their own bodily waste. These were folks he'd done business with for years. Folks he respected. He even knew their kids by name. Kids who'd died the same awful way. He'd had three weeks to stew over what had happened to them, and why.

From the evidence on the scene it looked like disease had ravaged more than half the population before the pirates showed up. Tom had never seen or heard of anything like it. Of the islanders who were stricken by the plague, no one re-covered. It was one hundred percent debilitating and one hundred percent fatal. And that wasn't the whole story. The outbreak had peaked just in time for the naval assault and invasion.

An unlucky turn of fate?

Harmonica Tom didn't think so.

The Nuevo-Texicans were anything but pushovers. Every man, woman and child older than the age of eight could handle a blaster, and they had plenty of ammo and heavy au-tomatic weapons. Through cagey barter they had accumulated some explosives, too—they had a good stock of Claymore anti-pers mines. For thirty years the islanders had successfully defended their grounded freighter and its stores against all comers. The question was, could a small force of Matachìn have overwhelmed the hardened, battle-tested defenses and superior numbers without help from the plague?

Definitely not, Tom had concluded. The pirates lacked the

manpower to take Padre Island hill by hill, and long-distance shelling alone couldn't do the job.

Disease as a weapon of war, of conquest, of genocide wasn't anything new in the history of the planet. Tom remembered reading about small pox–infected blankets somewhere in his shipboard collection of predark books. Long before Armageddon, they had been handed out to reservation Indians to make them sick and wipe them out. The how of what had happened at Padre was a mystery that might never be solved, but Harmonica Tom was damn well sure the appearance of the plague was no coincidence.

The objective of the invasion by sea hadn't been simple, familiar robbery, either. The Matachìn had blown apart the beached freighter that contained all of the islanders' worldly goods, and having done that, they just left it to burn, as if it held nothing worth stealing. The objective apparently had been the destruction of all life and property. Tom took that as an insult to Deathlands, and to the best of its hard-pressed survivors. Moreover, he took it as a personal affront.

And then there was the matter of Ryan Cawdor and his five companions.

No doubt about it, he had dragged those good folks into a world of trouble and hurt. They'd wanted to head east to offload the 125-pound cache of C-4 they'd snatched, but he'd told them they'd get a better price if they sailed west and dealt with the Padre Islanders. When the shit hit the fan on Padre, things had broken badly for Cawdor and the others. They were still alive when Tom had hightailed it for *Tempest,* but the last he'd seen of them, they were pinned down by pirates who were closing in fast. If they had managed to live through the assault, they would have been taken as slaves for the galley ships. In the three weeks since Tom had made his solo escape, they could have all died at their oars.

Death en route was a definite possibility.

More than once he had come across big-ass sharks lazily schooling around a headless floating torso with flesh hanging from it in a pale, bloodless fringe. Every time he saw the rad-blasted black fins circling on the surface, he'd divert course to see if it was anyone he knew.

Harmonica Tom had a very straightforward rule for survival that had proved itself over the years: when the odds were good, hit; when the odds were shit, git.

No way could he fight the convoy at sea and hope to win. There were too many opposing vessels, and three of them had massive diesels and twice his speed. If he tried to engage them in open water with *Tempest,* he knew he'd be outmaneuvered in no time and once committed to the attack, he'd never escape.

In one sense, the farther south he sailed the longer the odds got; in another sense, they actually improved. Though he had penetrated deep into Matachìn territory, nobody in these parts had ever heard of Harmonica Tom. Off his ship he would be unrecognizable, even to the pirates he had outcaptained and outfought along the treacherous Texican shoals. And if the pirate cities were jam-packed with people like the fire talkers said, that gave him the advantage of invisibility. A man who was careful and quiet could get lost in a crowd.

From the angle of the ship lights relative to the shore, Tom figured the convoy was going to make its first landfall at Veracruz. He backed the throttle to idle but left the engine in gear, then lashed off the helm to maintain a steady course. He'd had three weeks to consider the best plan of action.

What he'd come up with involved taking some big chances, but none of them were new.

It was called going for broke.

He opened and swung back the cockpit door, then turned to the box-fed, Soviet PKM pivot mounted on *Tempest*'s stern rail. Unlocking the canvas-shrouded machine gun from its swivel, he carried it down the steep steps to the cabin. He removed the shroud, then fitted the weapon onto the sand-bagged tripod already set up at the foot of the stairs. He opened the feed cover to make sure there wasn't a round chambered. After angling the barrel up to cover the entryway above and cockpit beyond, he locked the elevation.

Tom scrambled up the stairs and attached the end of a steel trip wire to an eye-screw on the inside of the open door. Descending again, he fed the wire through other strategically placed eyes on the staircase, bulkhead wall and the back edge of the galley table on the far side of the tripod. He tested the run of the wire back and forth for smoothness, then inserted the free end of it through the weapon's trigger guard. He depressed the trigger until the firing pin snapped on the empty chamber. Holding down the trigger, he looped the wire around it, pinning it as far back as it would go. Up the steps one more time, he pulled the cockpit door closed, which released the tension on the wire and allowed the trigger to snap back to ready position. Back beside the machine gun, he set the safety switch to "fire" and cocked the actuator, racking a live 7.62 mm round.

The next time the cockpit door was opened, the wire would draw tight; at the door's full, outward arc, the pullback tension would break the trigger and hold it down. The PKM was a sweet blaster, low recoil, no muzzle climb to speak of. It would continue firing until it came up empty—one hundred rounds down the road. Or until someone shut the door. The chances of anyone doing that were slim, unless they were fucking bulletproof.

Tom buckled his holstered Model 625 revolver around his waist. From the galley table he picked up his pride and joy, a nine mill Heckler & Koch MP-5 SD-1 silenced machine pistol. The compact blaster had no rear stock. It weighed in at 7.5 pounds with a loaded, 32-round mag. He slipped the weapon's quick-release lanyard over his neck; thus suspended, its plastic pistol grip hung even with his belly button. He had traded twenty gold-filled teeth for the mint H&K. Thanks to the widespread practice of dentistry before nukeday and the massive depopulation afterward, abandoned graveyards had become the new Klondike. Gold was slowly being accepted across Deathlands as a universal form of jack.

From a hook on the wall he grabbed a duct-tape-patched, olive-drab poncho and pulled it on over his head. The poncho left his arms free and draped low enough front and rear to keep both blasters out of sight. Though his skin was deeply tanned and weathered, he didn't know if it was tanned enough to pass for native. To keep his face in shadow he donned a sweat-stained, frayed, olive-drab billcap. There wasn't much he could do about hiding his sandy-colored, handlebar mustache, except to cut the damn thing off, and he wasn't about to do that.

Shouldering a preloaded pack, he headed toward the bow, climbing the short flight of steps that led to the foredeck. Back out in the night air, he padlocked the forward companionway door behind him. Then he took a handpainted sign from the pack and wired it securely to the hasp.

Crude red letters on a white background read: *Peligro.*

Danger. The middle of the sign was decorated with a childish skull and cross bones under which was another word: *Plaga*. Plague.

He made for the stern and jumped down into the cockpit. After padlocking the entry door, he hung a copy of the Danger sign on it. Even if the locals couldn't read, he hoped the symbol of death would make them think twice before trying to break in. If not, anyone opening the door was going to get a big—and final—surprise.

The stash of C-4 was stowed in a secret compartment under the cabin's deck. To find it, the surviving intruders would have to tear the ship apart, bulkhead by bulkhead. Tom figured to be back aboard long before that happened. Either that or chilled.

Off *Tempest*'s starboard bow, the last ship in the pirate convoy was rounding the blinking green light marker and heading into the harbor. Tom untied the wheel and goosed the throttle, steering for the marker buoy. He throttled back again as he cleared the light, slowing to take in the harbor and the glowing city on the far side.

Amazing, he thought as he took in the panorama. Fucking amazing.

Distant horn blasts rolled over the water. They came from the pirate convoy, which was about a mile ahead, motoring along the inside curve of the peninsula at a sedate pace. As it passed in front of the battlements of a stone fort, a flurry of fireworks exploded over the harbor.

Tom took the engine out of gear and let *Tempest* coast forward. He looked beyond the bursting rockets, beyond the floodlit fort, beyond the tooting convoy, at a four-story industrial complex just north of the city. Nosebleed-high catwalks, huge, bottle-shaped holding tanks, smokestacks, cinder-block buildings—it was all lit up as bright as day.

The seagoing trader's face lit up, too.

He realized it was a power-generating station, probably of predark manufacture and still going strong after more than a century in operation. Diesel-burning by the looks of the smoke, it had to be the source of the massive quantities of electricity in evidence around him. From his reading of twentieth-century books, Tom knew electricity in abundance was what drove the engine of social progress and material comfort, two things sorely absent in the Deathlands. He also knew that seventy or so pounds of properly placed C-4 could inflict massive damage on the power plant.

Maybe the locals had the technology and skills to fix it, maybe not. If not, it was going to be lights out on Veracruz, forever—every nightfall the murdering bastards would have cause to remember the name of Harmonica Tom.

Inside the harbor, it was much muggier; he found himself sweating bullets under the poncho. Peering through binocs, he saw all the armed men gathered on the stone fort's dock, waving at the convoy. He also saw the cannon barrels sticking out from the battlements. No way was he going to try to motor *Tempest* past them. He had avoided a boarding party so far, and that's how he wanted to keep it. There were no patrol boats in sight, no one to challenge his entering the harbor. That much confidence in their command of the sea made Tom conclude that no one had dared to challenge the Matachìn for a very long time. The other boats under way in the harbor were all moving the same direction he was, but they were more than a thousand yards in front of him, swinging in one by one to join the happy parade following the pirate fleet.

Tom motored closer to the peninsula's shore, looking for a place to tie up as close to the harbor entrance as possible. If everything went right for him and wrong for Veracruz, getting out was going to be a hell of a lot harder than getting in.

He swung in alongside a ruined freighter dock that jutted into the bay. Pools of light thrown by mercury vapor lamps on stanchions revealed clusters of small boats moored to the inside of the pier. They were a mixture of predark, motor and sail pleasure craft converted to commercial use. And there were shit-hammered fishing boats with peeling-paint, plywood cabins. The boats that couldn't find mooring space were rafted gunwhale to gunwhale.

Poking ahead cautiously, Tom could see there was no free dock space, so he had to raft up, too. He tossed out his fenders and pulled in beside a shabby fishing boat, then made *Tempest* fast to its bow and stern cleats.

There was no one aboard the fishing boat; no one on any of the boats that he could see.

Tom shouldered his pack and jumped onto the fishing boat. There wasn't any C-4 in the bag. If he got caught with the blasters, he figured it was no big deal. But if he got caught with high explosives, his captors would want to know what he intended to do with them, and if there was more.

The four-pane woodframe windows in the side of the homemade cabin looked like they had been salvaged from a house. There were sun-faded girly pics stuck to the insides, facing out, so the crew could see them and be inspired. On the far side of the fishing boat a steel ladder was affixed to the pier. He climbed the last few rungs cautiously, poking his head up to take in the terrain.

The dock area looked as deserted as the boats, except for

the rats scampering at the edges of the shadows. In front of him was a wrecked cinder-block warehouse, three stories high. The metal roof had partially caved in, the near wall had collapsed. Someone had started scavenging the fallen blocks, which were stacked on wooden pallets.

When Tom stepped onto the dock, it seemed to move under him. He was still trying to get his land legs when someone shouted at him from the darkness inside the warehouse. Tom saw a pinpoint of light, a tiny red-hot coal. He tugged the brim of his hat down to further hide his face.

A short, stout man in a straw cowboy hat and red sash stepped into view, puffing on a thin black cigar. He held a sawed-off, bluesteel 12-gauge in the crook of his left arm. It was hammerless with a full rear stock and a leather shoulder sling. In the hard light from the mercury lamp Tom could see food stains on the front of the guy's white dress shirt; they were bright orange, like chili sauce.

The sound of the hullabaloo surrounding the pirates' arrival drifted over them. As it did so, the guard's round, brown face twisted into a scowl. He was not a happy camper. He was missing all the fun. Tom caught a whiff of the burning tobacco and it reminded him how long it'd been since he'd had a decent smoke.

The guard addressed him in a guttural growl.

Tom couldn't make heads or tails of what the guy said; the accent was so thick he couldn't even be sure it was in Spanish. His command of that language came from memorizing an old college textbook he'd rescued from a bonfire in the Linas. He had mastered all the grammar and vocabulary, but he had no practical speaking or listening experience.

"Buenas noches," Tom said, turning slightly to the side so

the guard couldn't see him drop his right hand under the poncho. The trader had a choice to make: to either pull out the little leather pouch full of gold teeth and pay the man whatever he wanted to go away, or to reach for the grip of his silenced submachine gun and make him go away forever.

The guard looked both puzzled and irritated, as though he hadn't understood a word of what Tom had said. His scowl deepened as he took a step forward.

"Bue-nas no-ches," Tom repeated carefully. When that still didn't work, in desperation he tried a variation, *"Buen-ass nah-ches."*

The whole language thing wasn't going as smoothly as he'd expected.

Advancing on him with the double-barrel at waist height, his close-set, little black eyes narrowed to slits, the guard barked a command, *"¡Manos al cielo!"*

It took a full fifteen seconds for Tom's brain to convert the Spanish into English. "Hands in the air!"

"Seguro," Tom managed to say at last, but it was too late. The scattergun barrels were aiming up at his chin. It was do or die time.

With fluid, blinding speed, the trader back-foot pivoted to avoid the double barrel and simultaneously fired the stubby MP-5 SD-1 in a triburst out the open side of the poncho. The staccato thwacks of the jacketed slugs slapping into the middle of the guard's chest were louder than the gunshot reports. The guard didn't get off a shot. Eyes squeezed shut, teeth bared and clenched, he dropped as though his strings had been cut, first to his knees, the heavy flesh of his cheeks shuddering from the impact, then onto his face on the dock.

There were no exit holes out his back. The subsonic rounds

lacked the power for through-and-through. Tom grabbed a lifeless arm and turned the man over. There were three small holes in the center of a smudge of burned gunpowder on the white shirtfront. A glistening crimson stain was rapidly spreading out from the entry wounds; before it reached the breast pocket, Tom rescued four of the little cigars.

Working quickly, he removed the shoulder sling from the dropped scattergun. He grabbed a couple of concrete blocks from the nearest pallet and looped the sling through them. He then used the strap to attach the blocks to the dead man's ankles. Seconds later, he rolled the still-warm body off the pier. It splashed into the water between moored boats and immediately sank out of sight. Tom tossed the 12-gauge in, too. He sailed the guard's straw cowboy hat into the darkness inside the wrecked warehouse.

So much for the welcoming committee.

He took one last look back at *Tempest,* then headed away from the water at a fast clip, in search of a road that would lead west to the power plant. He needed to get a close-up look at the defenses, if any, and at the site's structural features so he could parcel out and position the stash of C-4 for maximum destruction.

When he reached the main road, he glanced in either direction. There was still no one in sight. If the parallel rows of tidal-wave-damaged warehouses in the port area were deserted, the festivities in Veracruz had shifted into high gear: horn-tooting, wild music, cheering. Tom turned left, heading toward the power station and the city. He'd traveled about a quarter mile down the middle of the road when he heard a horn honking from behind and the loud backfiring of an unmuffled engine. He half turned and saw a pair of dim yellow headlights bearing down on him fast. It was too late to break for cover. Bracing his feet to stand and fight, he reached under the poncho and took hold of the H&K.

The full-size, beat-to-shit Ford pickup screeched to a halt beside him. The left fender and door were different colors, and both were different colors than the body. The front bumper was held on with baling wire; the hood and sides dented; and the exhaust pipe belched clouds of black oil smoke. There were three well-fed, smiling men in the cab's bench seat. They appeared to be unarmed, and they weren't in uniform. They looked like ordinary guys, but they were more than a little drunk.

The driver leaned an arm out his open window, gestured toward the city and over the engine's thunderous racket said, *"¿Fiesta?"*

Eyewatering joy juice fumes hit Tom in the face. Given what had happened the last time he tried his Spanish, holding his tongue and pretending to be a droolie seemed his best bet. He nodded enthusiastically.

"Entonces, vamos," the driver said, slapping the outside of his door hard, then hooking a thumb toward the pickup bed for Tom to climb aboard.

The rusted-through bed was littered with salvaged lengths of iron pipe and other metal scrap. Before they moved on, the guy in the middle of the bench seat reached back through the cab's missing rear window and handed the new passenger a bottle one-quarter full of a pale yellow liquid.

After sniffing at the contents, Tom didn't hesitate. He took a long, gulping pull. The oily, powerful spirits burned like hellfire all the way down to his belly. Not to be outdone by this show of gracious hospitality, he immediately passed out the dead man's cigars. As he did so he said, *"Ehh? Ehh?"*

His new friends accepted the smokes with delight and everybody lit up.

Language problem solved.

After a bit of gear-grinding protest, the pickup roared off down the road, squeaking and rattling like it was going to fly apart on the next pothole. Harmonica Tom sat with his back against a wheelwell, blowing sweet, pungent smoke at the night sky.

For the moment at least, the belly of the beast didn't seem half bad.

Chapter Three

"It turns out you're famous here, too, lover," Krysty said to Ryan's back. "They've got your head on a stick."

"It's not me," the one-eyed warrior countered. "It's ass backward."

As the lead tug slipped in alongside the pier, with the other two tugs following close behind, raucous, rhythmic music blasted from speakers bolted to the light stanchions. When the crews hurried to tie off the mooring lines and extend the short gangways, the waiting crowd really came unglued; Ryan could hardly hear himself think for all the noise.

Up close, the size and frenzy of the mob gave even him pause. For the first time in three weeks of captivity, Ryan caught himself thinking that maybe they weren't going to make it out of this alive, after all. It was a thought he couldn't come to grips with, and instinctively smothered.

Then the pirates started laying on the lash to make the terrified slaves rise from their benches.

Whipped hard across the shoulders from behind, J.B. lurched to his feet, his face twisted in outrage. For a second, Ryan's old battlemate lost all semblance of control. He jerked at his chains like an animal, trying desperately, futilely, to break free, to get his hands on his grinning, dreadlocked tormentor.

At least J.B. wasn't pissing himself, which is more than

Ryan could say for some of the other slaves around them. The Padre Islander kid, Garwood Reed, looked stunned, frozen like a jacklit rabbit. The companions had done their best to protect him during the torturous journey—though young the orphaned boy had proved himself in battle—but apart from their each giving up a bit of the scant rations to keep him going there was little to be done. "Stay close to me, son," Ryan told the teen. "No matter what happens, stay close…."

Ryan felt it was his responsibility to get the companions clear of this mess, somehow, some way, but as things stood that feat was impossible. Looking at the mob, he knew he couldn't keep his friends from being torn limb from limb, if that's the croaking that fate held in store.

For their part, never had J.B., Krysty and Jak been confronted by so many agitated people at one time. In Deathlands a big crowd might be a couple of hundred souls. Krysty's prehensile hair had drawn up into tight ringlets of alarm. The expression in Jak's bloodred eyes was unreadable; the albino had retreated somewhere deep inside his own head. Mildred and Doc, both born in earlier eras, before Armageddon's large-scale population cull, had experience with masses of humanity. And Ryan who had been kidnapped to Shadow World, a parallel earth where the profusion of people had overrun all other forms of life, was no virgin when it came to mob scenes. However, none of them had ever been the focus of such furious and overwhelming attention.

Flogged until they all got to their feet, the rowers were linked ankle to ankle and then driven toward the waiting gangplanks.

As Ryan and the companions edged forward to the tug's gate, he saw men in red sashes and straw hats pounding back the crowd with cudgels and the metal-shod butts of sawed-off, double-barreled shotguns. The sec men swinging clubs carried fold-stock, 9 mm submachine guns on slings over their shoulders. With brute force, they opened a lane in the packed bodies to three stake trucks that were idling on the pier. The sec men held the path open with difficulty. As spectators surged forward, they had to be beaten back.

When Ryan stepped into view on the gangplank, the mob on either side went crazy, pointing at him, jumping up and down. They started up a chant.

"¡Shi-ball-an-kay!"

"¡Shi-ball-an-kay!"

"¡Shi-ball-an-kay!"

Krysty leaned forward and hollered in his ear, "Didn't I say you were famous!"

"What are they saying? What's it mean?" Ryan shouted at Mildred.

"Damned if I know!" she shouted back. "It's not Spanish!"

A superamplified voice, syrupy-smooth and talking a mile a minute, bellowed through a megaphone mounted atop the roof of the lead truck's cab. The rapid-fire speech was backed by recorded accordion, drums and trumpets gone wild—which competed with the other music pouring out of the pier's speakers.

At blasterpoint, Ryan, his battlemates and young Reed were forced to climb into the back of the first stake truck. Like the other two vehicles, it was aimed toward the city center. When the bed was crammed full of slaves, thirty or so in all, a sec man slammed shut the wooden rear gate. The remaining trucks were likewise loaded and locked.

Red-sashed sec men surrounded the vehicles, laboring to keep the crowd from surging forward and overrunning the prisoners. The companions had automatically moved back to back, in a tight defensive ring. Garwood Reed did as he'd been told: he stuck to Ryan's side like glue.

All three trucks gunned their engines and started honking for the mob to make way. Nobody budged. And there were too many people on the pier for the vehicles to force the issue.

Then the Matachìn started trooping off the tugs and onto the dock. They advanced in a tight, military formation with their commander, the guy with the tallest piled dreads and the most pillaged jewelry, marching in the lead.

When the assembled people of Veracruz saw the pirates in full battle gear and weapons bearing down on them, they made tracks backward. And they did something else that surprised the hell out of Ryan. Those closest to the Matachìn immediately dropped to their knees and pressed their noses and foreheads to the concrete. There wasn't room on the dock for all of the people to prostrate themselves. Those who couldn't bow down retreated as far from the pirates as they could, opening a narrow path for the trucks down the middle of the pier.

The pecking order of the men with blasters was established immediately, Ryan noted. The red sashes standing next to the truck whipped off their hats, knelt, and lowered their heads before High Pile, the Matachìn commander. One of them, probably the most senior-ranking, kneaded the brim of his cowboy hat as he spoke and then pointed up at Ryan. His words were lost in the din, but a smile spread over the captain's greasy face.

High Pile jumped onto the lead truck's running board, reached through the open passenger window and snatched the microphone from a suddenly struck-mute public address announcer.

"¡La guerra está terminada!" His voice boomed over the recorded music tape loop, boomed over the crowd. *"¡Victoria eterna para los reyes de la muerte! ¡Los gemelos heroicos son cautivos!"*

The commander repeated the same words over and over, and with every repetition the mob sent up a louder cheer.

"Now, *that*'s in Spanish!" Mildred exclaimed.

The companions huddled closer to hear what else she had to say.

"He's telling them the war is over," Mildred translated for them. "Eternal victory for the Kings of Death—or maybe the Lords of Death. And the hero twins are captives."

"Hero twins?" Krysty said.

"It could be a mythological reference, from ancient Mayan," Mildred said. "I sort of vaguely remember the term—something to do with their creation story, I think. More than a century ago I did some reading to get ready for an archaeological tour of the major Mayan sites in Mexico and Guatemala. How the phrase applies here and now is beyond me."

The truck and its human cargo began to roll slowly forward. Out in front, the Matachìn phalanx parted the crowd with unspoken threat. Ryan watched as a wave of prostration broke before them. Regular folk and red sashes alike supplicated themselves, pressing their faces into the ground. This wasn't a community of equals welcoming home their best and brightest after a successful military campaign; this was a subject people, paying homage.

The convoy proceeded at a walking pace off the pier, past the lighthouse and into the canyon of city streets. High Pile rode the running board, megaphone-assaulting the seemingly endless throng with his news.

Ryan tried to read the sea of brown faces. Mixed in with the overall jubilance, with the mind-numbing cheers, with the legions of fingers pointing excitedly up at him, he saw here and there flickers of shock and even sorrow. The selection of jigged, giant heads-on-sticks was the same as on the pier: there were kings or demons, plague rictus masks and mirror-images of his own bearded visage.

The convoy crawled through a right turn, proceeded a few more blocks and then made a left.

On Ryan's right, three- and four-story colonial buildings loomed above the narrow street. The wall-to-wall facades were painted in bright pastels—aqua, pink, gold—and draped with spotlighted red banners: stories-long, paint-on-cloth portraits of the array of ferocious kings—or devils. Atapuls I through X varied in skin color and texture, as well as head-dress design and height, width of nose, length of extended tongue, and position and shape of fangs.

From every floor, people hung over the Moorishly arched, pillared balconies; some threw brilliantly colored confetti into the air, which fluttered down onto the heads and shoulders of the Matachìn phalanx. Lights burned in every window. At street level, the buildings opened up into cavelike arcades packed with markets and shops. The sidewalks were jammed with spectators and carts, spill-over retail that included hot food, cold drinks, live poultry, cigars and rack after rack of new clothing.

The other side of the avenue was lined with people and hawkers' carts, too, but there were no buildings, just a row of tall, skinny trees that marked the border of a broad, central park. The park's pavement was made up of checkerboard marble tiles in white, gray and black. On the other side of the square, high above the tops of the trees, stood the floodlit bell tower of a predark cathedral. It dominated the square, glowing in the lights like an ember, fiery red against the night sky.

As the trucks crept forward, Ryan picked up distinctive odors by turns—camellias, spices, incense, fresh-baked bread, charcoal smoke and grilled meats. This was nothing like Shadow World. That place had been stripped bare by insatiable human appetites, like the ruins of a cornfield after a swarm of locusts. Veracruz was the exact opposite of the parallel earth: it was ripe, fecund, teeming with energy.

"Oh, my God!" Mildred exclaimed, pointing toward the ground floor of one of the buildings with both manacled hands.

"What?" Ryan said.

"It's a Burger King!" was her cryptic reply.

Further explanation was interrupted by a barrage of garbage. As the trucks came directly under the balconies, the folks up there stopped throwing confetti and started throwing rotten fruit, to the applause of the surrounding mob. The slaves ducked and covered as overripe mango and papaya splattered the bed of the trucks and their defenseless backs.

The volley let up only after the convoy had crawled out of range.

When their truck rounded a corner, Ryan could see it wasn't the tint of the spotlights that made the cathedral look red; it was painted top to bottom the color of dried blood.

Or maybe it *was* blood.

The mob packing the cathedral steps broke apart before the wedge of Matachìn. The three-truck convoy stopped. High Pile hopped down from the running board and climbed up to the stone altar that blocked the cathedral's main entrance.

Pungent clouds of incense poured from brass censers on either side of the arched doorway.

An old man with a sagging, deeply seamed face waited for him behind the dished out altar. His headdress was made of scrolled posts and cross-members of gold-painted wood. His brocaded, crimson robe didn't hide skinny arms and legs, and a round, protruding belly—he looked like a hairless brown spider playing dress-up.

Ryan noticed that while everybody else retreated with their noses pressed to ground, the spider remained upright, as if he and the commander were equal in rank.

Pirate and high priest conferred head-to-head for a moment in the cathedral's entryway, then with a flourish, the priest unsheathed a long, golden dagger that he held over his head and turned for all to see. The captain shouted an order down to his men. Five Matachìn immediately and gleefully swarmed over the sides of the lead stake truck, jumping down into the midst of the chained slaves.

The pirates booted aside the prisoners, moving with purpose in the same direction, toward Ryan and the others.

"Together now," the one-eyed warrior growled as the Matachìn bore down on them in a blitz attack.

Things happened very quickly in the narrow space between the fence walls of the stake truck—close quarters that temporarily negated the pirates' advantage in mobility and firepower.

The companions' three weeks of fury, suffering and frustration exploded in violence.

J.B. jumped forward, howling, to meet and block the rush of the first of the on-coming pirates.

The much bigger attacker tried to bowl him aside with a well-timed shoulder strike. The strike missed by an inch or two when the Armorer spun away, and the pirate kept coming, stumbling forward off balance.

From behind, Ryan threw his manacled hands over the top of the nasty dreads, pulling the connecting chain down over the filthy face, down around the unprotected throat. Then he crossed his wrists, pulling the chain tight under the man's chin and making links dig deep into his flesh. The pirate tried frantically to buck him off, but Ryan wouldn't allow it. By shifting his weight, he kept the man off balance, even as his face turned darker and darker purple.

Sputtering for breath, the pirate reached to his hip for the handle of his machete. As the long, wide blade cleared its scabbard, Ryan gave the chain a vicious twist. There was momentary resistance to the turn, then the neck snapped and the head lolled over onto the left shoulder. Suddenly, Ryan was supporting the full weight of a twitching body. As Ryan uncrossed his wrists, letting his stinking captive fall, Jak snatched the machete from the dead hand.

Two pirates rushed in from the other side with whips cocked back. Mildred and Doc raised cuffed hands to keep from being lashed across the face, and braced to absorb the punishment and protect the emaciated teen behind them.

"It's the boy!" Mildred shouted to the others over the cheers of the crowd. "They don't want us, they want the boy!"

Jak was already in motion, coiled like a steel spring, the gut-hook machete almost dragging the bed floor as he maximized momentum. The chop when it came was far too fast to follow—an arcing, angled blow that landed behind the nearest pirate's right knee. The machete's edge cleaved deep into bone but the battle armor shin guard kept it from slicing all the way through. The blade stuck fast, and the weapon was jerked free of Jak's hand as the pirate leaped backward. When the man's full weight came down, the weakened bone gave way with an audible crack.

The pirate screamed and fell over backward, clawing at his newly fashioned, blood-jetting stump, and before the second attacker could jump away, Mildred and Doc were on him. Mildred grabbed hold of the end of the whip. Doc smashed him across the face with both hands locked, like he was swinging a baseball bat or an ax. As the man staggered back half a step, Doc seized him around the front of the throat, driving him into the wall of the stake truck. Displaying a reservoir of strength and the bottomless depth of his anger, the Victorian time-traveler lifted the 180-pound pirate up on his tiptoes as he strangled him, two-handed. Doc absorbed the man's frantic punches and kicks, his excellent teeth bared in a terrible, triumphant grin.

The two other pirates closed on the companions with their machetes drawn. Ryan and J.B. met the downward slashes on the chains that connected their wrists, steel scraping on steel. Ryan ripped the machete away, sending it flying over his shoulder and out of the truck. Because of his rib injury, J.B. didn't have the strength to tear his trapped blade away, but it didn't matter. He kept it tied up long enough for Krysty and Jak to join the fray. They shoulder-rammed the pirates off their feet, and when the men landed on the truck bed the payback for twenty-one days of hell began in earnest. Concentrating on the unarmored heads, the companions did their damnedest with bootheels, shattering and scattering jawbones and teeth, sending blood and then skull and brains squirting in all directions.

As the companions regrouped around the Reed boy, the rest

of the pirate phalanx scrambled onto the truck. Ryan and his comrades fought in a frenzy, but hobbled by the bodies of the other slaves they were chained to, overwhelmed by the sheer weight of numbers, it was a lost cause from the start. After a couple of minutes they began to fall, one by one, under the rain of blows. Ryan was the last to drop, struck in the head and neck simultaneously. As more blows pounded him to the deck, he felt the boy torn from his grasp.

In a second he was back on his feet, but the anchor of the other slaves he was chained to kept him from jumping out of the truck in pursuit.

Jak, J.B., Krysty, Mildred and Doc rose bloodied from the stake truck bed. They watched through the wall slats as the Matachìn carried young Garwood fighting and thrashing up the steps to the altar. They pinned him on his back in the middle of the ancient stone slab, his arms and legs spread wide. With one hand the spider priest tore open the boy's ragged T-shirt, the other hand held the golden dagger.

"Lord have mercy," Doc intoned.

But there was no mercy on offer this night.

The priest raised the ceremonial dagger in both hands, poised to strike downward, into the defenseless chest.

Garwood Reed didn't beg for his life; he didn't shame himself. A true son of Deathlands, he reared back his head and spit full in the priest's face. That he could work up the necessary gob of spit under the circumstances spoke volumes as to his courage and his fortitude.

Without bothering to wipe away the spittle, the priest drove home the blade.

The boy went rigid on the altar.

A practiced, circular stroke opened a yawning hole beneath

the sternum, and Garwood's body suddenly relaxed. The boy was already dead when the priest plunged a hand into the cavity past the wrist, rooted around for a moment, and then jerked out a handful of dripping red flesh.

The heart.

The priest raised the gory hunk of muscle to his mouth. He sucked a mouthful of blood from one of its severed vessels then spit it out. He sucked and spit four times, in each of the ordinal directions. Crimson rivulets drooled off his chin.

It was a blessing of some unspeakable kind.

"Why him?" Krysty gasped. "Why did the bastards take *him?*"

"Because he was the youngest of the captured slaves," Mildred said, her eyes brimming with tears. "The young ones are probably the most prized as sacrifices to the demons they worship."

"Or are forced to worship," Ryan said.

Looking around, he saw the stigma of the foul religion at every turn. The color of the church. The sashes of the armed sec men. The robes of the murderer priest. The banners hanging down the fronts of the buildings. When you were outnumbered big-time, organized terror was the only way to control a subject people. Mebbe this place wasn't so different than Deathlands, after all, he thought. The barons enforced their tyranny and extracted obedience with violence and fear. If there was a difference here, it was in scale and sophistication.

"There will be hell to pay for this abomination," Doc swore, his pale blue eyes blazing with fury, his teeth stained red with his own blood. "By the Three Kennedys, there will surely be hell to pay...."

Drenched with sweat from the fighting, Ryan struggled to

catch his breath in the seething, humid air. The red sashes all around the convoy were jumping up and down, waving their clubs, working themselves into a dither over the sacrifice. Their chill frenzy spilled into and infected the surrounding crowds. Pretty soon everyone was jumping up and down, and yelling blue murder.

A civilian suddenly darted through the line of red sashes and jumped into the back of the stake truck before anyone could stop him. His eyes looked bloodshot and squirrelly, like he was strung out on jolt. He had a long, thin-bladed knife clasped between his teeth, the sharp edge pointing away from his lips. Whipping the knife from his jaws, with an animal cry, he charged for Ryan.

The reveller intended to do a little sacrificing himself, maybe grab some of glory of the moment.

Ryan easily deflected the too-slow lunge with his manacled wrists and delivered a cracking head butt. Blood gushed from the man's crushed nose, but it was already lights out, squirrelly eyes rolling back in his skull. Doc, Mildred and Jak seized hold of the attacker's arms and legs and threw him out of the truck. The red sashes swarmed in and pulled the unconscious man away.

They were still beating him into the pavement when High Pile hopped back on the running board and the trucks resumed their slow-speed parade. They drove past a railroad terminal, obviously long-abandoned. From there the convoy followed the road's curve onto the peninsula. Behind them, the mob followed, clogging the street curb to curb. It trailed them for what Ryan guessed was close to two miles. Then the trucks turned off the road and parked on a stone quay between a row of stone buildings and the edge of the bay.

Forty feet away, across the water, was the old Spanish fort. Bright lights aiming down from notches in the battlements illuminated a low, pedestrian bridge that connected the fort to the quay.

The captives were shoved out of the stake trucks and forced to line up beside them. At High Pile's order, the Matachìn disconnected Ryan from the file, pulled him from the ranks and pushed him to the bridge.

It appeared he was the slave of honor.

The far end of the bridge terminated at the point of one of the ravelins. The diamond-shaped projection, three-stories of windowless, weathered limestone block, stuck out from the fort's perimeter. Ryan could see a narrow archway at the bridge's end, and an open wrought-iron gate.

Urged forward at blasterpoint onto the bridge, Ryan glanced over the side. In the lights from the battlements he saw bones. Human bones in the crystal-clear water. The bottom was carpeted with mounds of them. Stripped white, jumbled skulls, long bones, ribs. There were darker blotches, too, and they were moving sideways. Crabs the size of dinner plates crawled over the piles of naked bones, looking for a snippet that the others had missed.

Fat, happy crabs.

Chapter Four

To get a view out the screen in the deck hold's narrow air vent, Daniel Desipio had to press his temple against the ceiling and crane his neck at a painful angle. The twentieth-century freezie and author of twenty-nine published novels could hear the wild victory celebration outside, but he couldn't see any of it. The view out the bug-proofed air vent was entirely blocked by the bow of the tug moored closely behind.

Despondent, Daniel slumped back to the floor of his five-by-five-by-five cell and hung his head in his hands. There would have been no great victory in Deathlands without him, yet no one knew or cared about his contribution to the campaign. His thoughts slipped into a deep, dark and familiar groove.

More than a century earlier, before Armageddon, while still a ghost writer on the *Slaughter Realms* pulp action series, he had often imagined his publisher's holiday office parties: the editors and assistants—English Lit majors all—in cotillion gowns and black tuxedos, consuming champagne punch and finger sandwiches to the strains of live, string quartets. While committees of Lit majors risked broken fingernails fastening paper clips to two-sentence memos, Desipio struggled alone and under poor light with hundred-thousand-word deadlines. While the *SR* editorial staff took latte and croissant breaks, he lived on water and corn dogs. Instead of winter vacationing in the Bahamas, driving company cars, carrying company credit cards, the lowly ghost expeditioned to the corner 7/11 on foot and paid for his hot dogs in loose change. He imagined editorial's sweeping, panoramic view from the tower office block; he had no view at all. In his previous life, he had lived belowground, in a grotty, two-room, basement apartment in the flatlands of Berkeley, California. The concrete floor sweated. The concrete walls sweated. He sweated. His above-ground neighbors, all rich college students and professors, mocked him and called him "the Mole Man" to his face.

All Daniel Desipio really had was his devotion to writing, his Art. To further it, and to break the economic and social bonds that kept him from reaching his full creative potential, he had volunteered for ultrasecret lab-rat duty in the jungles of Panama. This in the hope that the experience would give him something truly original and important to write about, and allow him to stake his claim to fame and wealth.

Long before nukeday's dawn, things had gone very wrong on the remote prison island. During the course of the black box-funded experiments, his blood became infected with an engineered virus of unheard-of and unstoppable lethality, but to which he was immune. He had been offered a choice by the facility's whitecoats: to live out the rest of his life in isolation on the island hellhole or to go into cryogenic sleep until a cure could be found.

When he was reanimated more than one hundred years later, he was shocked to learn that there was still no cure for the virus in his blood; that in the interim the civilized world had blown itself apart and that he was to be deployed as a walking biological weapon by the tenth-generation offspring of the penal colony's original rapists and murderers.

Through the narrow air vent, the clamor of the crowd crescendoed. The pirates had begun their victory lap around Veracruz's central square.

Daniel lowered his forehead to his upraised knees, and then thumped it upon them, hard, over and over again. After all the effort he'd made and the pain he'd endured, what in his life had changed?

He still got no credit for his heroic deeds, only now the body count he created was real, and he wasn't paid a penny in compensation. He still lived in a hole, only now it was under even worse conditions. He had a bucket for a toilet and no toilet paper. He ate with his fingers out of an old tin can. No TV or skin mags for companionship. No showers. Whether imprisoned belowdecks or walking free as a plague vector, he was still looked down upon by everyone he met—everyone except the droolies. He'd always been able to count on the droolies.

Though as far as he knew there were no more novels of any kind being published, though he had no writing instruments or paper, that didn't stop him from attempting to compose great works of destiny in his mind. But unhappily, no matter the starting point, all his epic, original ideas eventually turned into *Slaughter Realms* books. No matter how hard he tried, he couldn't get the series and the characters out of his head. Perhaps it was a function of his having written so many of them? Or perhaps cryogenesis had permanently damaged his creative synapses.

Sooner or later, the characters started to banter and jive like the series' regulars. Instead of the vast, labyrinthine conspiracies he envisioned himself writing, the stories devolved into highly detailed, sword and gun fights, and the occasional extraneous, space-filling sexual romp. Heads parted company with necks; cranial contents Jackson-Pollacked opposing mud-plastered walls and ceilings; bowels tumbled steaming from torsos in fat gray coils; and sweat-lubricated bodies writhed in ecstasy and exploded in impossible joy.

In sum, his 137 years of existence had been nothing less than a classic, wall-to-wall fuck up.

More pain and suffering awaited him because his lifeblood was still valuable to his masters; or to be more specific, the marrow in his bones was valuable. Daniel was the only plague vector who'd survived the Deathlands adventure. All the other fire talkers, gaudy sluts and traveling tinkers had perished, either at the hands of the enemy or thanks to an overabundance of friendly fire. Without *enanos,* their infected ones, the Lords of Death couldn't maintain their stranglehold on the Central American city-states. For their part, the Matachìn didn't care how many of the *enanos* died, or how it happened. The only accounting of casualties came from Commander Casacampo, and he could make up any story that suited him.

A very long time ago, while Tooby was still an ice cube with hair, the Lords of Death were just a band of Matachìn, themselves—simple, brutal seafaring pirates. They had elevated themselves to godhood by being the first to control the plague and then apply it to the battlefield.

There was a roar at Daniel's back; the tug's diesels were starting up. He felt a lurch of movement as the tug turned away from the pier.

The next leg of his long journey about to begin.

The journey back to hell.

Chapter Five

At blasterpoint, Ryan crossed the footbridge and passed through the iron gate, which opened onto a narrow, dank, stone corridor. The passage was lit by a string of bare, dim bulbs draped along the ridge of the ceiling. Ryan guessed the walls were at least five or six feet thick—thick enough to stop a sixteenth-century cannonball.

From behind came the clanks of chains and the sounds of boots scraping on the limestone floor; the other slaves were being hurried along by the Matachìn.

When Ryan, High Pile and their escort exited the corridor's far end, they stepped out into the corner of a huge courtyard. Harsh light from the battlements illuminated the long colonnades on either side. On the left, the structure was faced with red brick; on the right it was naked limestone. Through the room-size arches on that side, Ryan could see the exterior wall and the gated entrance to the fort's dock. The three masts of a large sailing ship were visible above it. Stretching out before them was a grassy sward. A two-story building blocked the far end, its rows of tall windows overlooking the courtyard.

Immense, sculpted stone heads of the various Atapuls guarded the colonnades' entrances, ten heads to a side, glaring across the sward at one another. As Ryan walked on, he saw evidence of other recent human sacrifices. Fist-size gobbets of blackening flesh lay on the ground at the base of each of the idols.

Excised hearts. Twenty of them in all.

Along the left-hand wall were the rest of the remains, torsos in one heap, heads in another.

It smelled like a charnel house, and there wasn't a breath of wind to stir the death stench inside the compound.

A group of eight men awaited them in front of the building at the end of the courtyard. Seven were robed and head-dressed priests, led by none other than the hairless spider himself. Ryan glanced up at the battlements on either side, three stories above. They were lined with red sashes. Close to three hundred of the sec men, he reckoned. All armed. All looked down at the spectacle.

The pirate commander advanced the last twenty feet by himself. Ignoring the priests, he knelt in front of the eighth man, who apparently outranked them all.

At first Ryan thought the guy was wearing an elaborate mask over his face, then he realized it *was* his face.

The one-eyed warrior had seen plenty of disfigurements in Deathlands. Some were accidental; some were battle scars like his own; some were hard punishment meted out for crimes; some were purely decorative. This one was in a league of its own.

A living fright mask.

The corners of the man's mouth had been surgically extended deep into his cheeks, and the lips excised top and bottom, this to reveal inch-and-a-half-long fangs of gold where his canine teeth had once been. It gave him a permanent, awful, stylized grin, like the Atapul heads. Evenly spaced welts of purple, scarified tissue bridged his nose and cheeks, making them look corrugated, like a boar's snout. Unlike the Atapul representations, his tongue wasn't pointed or a foot long. His high-piled dreads were caged in a ceremonial headdress. The breastplate of his gilded battle armor was spattered with drops of fresh blood.

At a hand signal from the pirate captain, the Matachìn pushed Ryan forward, then kicked him behind the knees to make him kneel before their headman's headman.

Fright Mask addressed the audience of pirates, priests, red sashes and prisoners in a booming voice, punctuated by punches thrown at the night sky. Ryan couldn't understand a word of it, but it drew rounds of cheers from the red sashes.

He glanced back at Krysty and the others. They stood helpless, outnumbered, awaiting whatever fate this jabbering asshole had in mind.

Fright Mask shouted something down at him to get his attention.

Ryan squinted up at the hellish mask of flesh. "Speak English, fuckhead," he snarled back.

The bossman called out impatiently to the rest of the gathered slaves. Ryan thought he caught the now-familiar word "Shi-ball-an-kay."

Doc shouted something back in Spanish and was immediately dragged from line and forced to his knees beside Ryan.

"So here we are," Doc said with resignation.

Fright Mask yelled something in Doc's face. As he did so, saliva spilled from the corners of his vast, carved mouth, gooey, yo-yoing strands drooling onto his gilded battle armor.

"This strikingly handsome fellow wants to make certain you know that he's a high muckety-muck," Doc loosely translated. "Governor of the city-state of Veracruz. His name's al Modo, Generalissimo al Modo."

Fright Mask yelled some more, this time at considerable length.

"Apparently," Doc continued during a pause in the tirade, "the governor-general, here, is of the firm opinion that your capture and that of someone he calls Hunahpu, represents the turning point in a war waged by the Lords of Death since the day of creation, itself."

"How worried should I be?"

"Very worried," Doc said. "As should the rest of us. The governor says you will be tried by a duly assembled religious tribunal tomorrow and then executed pursuant to holy writ before the following dawn. What your supposed crimes are, he did not elaborate."

Ryan glowered at the priests he presumed would be sitting in final judgment on him. "Does it really matter?"

"Perhaps not," Doc said. The time-traveler stared him in the eye, his haggard face full of anguish and sorrow. "You and I have come an awful long way to take our leaves in a place such as this," he said, "with our hands and feet bound, and our weapons out of reach."

"Doc, no matter how bad it looks, this isn't over yet," Ryan said. "Don't give up. Don't let the others give up, either."

As Doc was dragged away, he called out to Ryan. "I pray we meet again, my dear friend, if not in the here and now, then somewhere beyond this fucking vale of tears."

"Remember the islander boy," Ryan called to him. "Remember Garwood Reed."

Something slammed into his left temple so hard that it made him see stars. He looked up at Fright Mask, who showed him a balled, metal-gauntleted fist. Ryan was grateful for the blow, which allowed him to focus his anger.

"Unchain me for a minute," Ryan told his captor, "and I'll widen that smile all the way to the back of your head."

The governor-general didn't understand the threat, and so ignored it. He gestured to the pirates, who pulled Ryan to his feet and hauled him off to one side.

Fright Mask had other, more pressing business to attend to. He snapped his gauntleted fingers twice in High Pile's direction.

As the Matachìn commander took a small, dog-eared notebook from inside his armor, the priests started making rhythmic scraping sounds, steel on whetstones. They were touching up the edges on their ceremonial daggers.

High Pile walked over to the line of slaves. Pausing in front of the first man, who was naked to the waist, his back and shoulders blistered and peeling from the sun and the lash, the captain referred to a page in his little book and made a check mark with a tiny stub of a pencil. When he nodded, the crewmen unhooked the captive from those waiting behind him. Before the poor bastard could make a break for it, the pirates grabbed him under the armpits and rushed him toward Fright Mask and the waiting priests.

Though the slave screamed and fought, and tried to dig in his heels, it was to no avail. The Matachìn carried him bodily the last fifteen feet, then flung him to his knees in front of the men in robes. One of the pirates grabbed the prisoner from behind by a hank of hair and pulled his head back; another held his cuffed hands out of the way. A priest stepped forward and expertly dispatched him with a backhanded knife slash across the exposed throat. The slave made a gurgling sound as blood sheeted down his bare chest. After a moment the pirates let their victim slump onto his back. Kneeling, the priest plundered the still-heaving chest for its precious clod of muscle.

No sooner than the gruesome butcher job was done, a second slave was unhooked and bum-rushed to a nearly identical death.

As Ryan watched the next man in line dragged off to meet the point of a knife, he saw the priests were taking turns in the chilling duties, so as not to overtax themselves. All but the hairless spider, who was chanting in a nasal singsong and doing a little shuffle-foot dance behind them. High Pile made another check mark in his little book before consigning a fourth prisoner to the same fate. The courtyard echoed with shrill screams and the cheers of the red sash audience.

Were they going to sacrifice all the slaves? Ryan asked himself. His companions were still a good ways back in the file. For the first time, he saw the possibility that he might actually outlive them, spared from death for another day; and worse, that he would be forced to stand by and watch them all slaughtered.

That was not something he could accept.

He had tested his manacles so many times since their capture that he had worn away the skin of his wrists, but he tested them again, anyway.

Mind working in overdrive, he tried to see a way clear. If he could overwhelm the pair of pirates guarding him, then what? Chill the Matachìn with their own blasters, allowing the slaves to flee? Even if he managed to do that, the only way to get out from under the sights of the red sashes along the battlements was to make it inside the hard cover of the colonnades. But the prisoners were chained together. They'd have to all pass through the same archway, which meant instead of ten exits to cover, the red sashes would only have one. They could concentrate fire. It would be a turkey shoot.

Escape was impossible against these odds on this terrain, Ryan concluded.

As High Pile advanced down the line of the condemned, the piles of corpses and severed hearts grew. Realizing what was coming, the slaves struggled futilely with their bonds, weeping and begging their captors for mercy.

All but the companions.

Jak, Krysty, Mildred, Doc and J.B. were staring at Ryan. Their fixed, defiant expressions all said the same thing: we're not going to check out like that. Not like chickens on the chopping block.

The one-eyed warrior nodded in agreement, then he looked away. If they couldn't escape, they could do the next best thing. They could take out as many of the bastards as possible before they were cut down.

Ryan Cawdor withdrew deep into the core of his being, shutting out the grisly sights and sounds around him. He wasn't preparing himself to die, he was preparing to fight and chill to his last ounce of strength. To expend it all, here, now. And when that strength was gone, death could nukin' have him, ready or not. It took only a moment for him to make the attitude shift: it was like a gate swinging open, and when it was done, Ryan felt a sense of freedom and power.

The hairless spider was gathering dripping lumps of muscle in a wicker basket as High Pile stepped up to Jak, who was next in line for sacrifice. Ryan knew the pirates weren't going to discount the albino because of his size or mutie appearance. Just the opposite. They'd already seen him in action

with a commandeered machete. One of them put a subma-
chine-gun muzzle to the back of Jak's head before they unfastened his ankle chains from the others.

Ryan planned to make his play the moment the pirates
started to rush Jak forward to his doom. When they pulled the
albino youth to the side instead, he held back. One by one,
High Pile ordered the companions released from the file and
moved over to join Jak. They were then rechained together at
the ankles. After J.B. was linked to the others, the next slave
in line, to his surprise and dismay, got the standard dagger
treatment.

The companions glanced at Ryan again, wanting the go
signal.

He shook his head. It looked like they weren't going to be
slaughtered along with the rest. It appeared their captors had
other plans for them, which changed everything as far as he
was concerned.

A pirate approached High Pile with a heavy, blanket-
wrapped bundle. The captain ordered the man to untie it and
lay it out on the ground at Fright Mask's boots. When the
bundle was opened, Ryan saw it held his scoped Steyr longblaster, J.B.'s scattergun and the rest of their weapons.

Trophies of conquest.

Or mebbe objects of ridicule.

Fright Mask got a big laugh over the LeMat. After inspect-
ing it closely, he held Doc's black-powder blaster by the
barrels and swung its butt like a hammer head into his palm—
as if pounding nails was all it was good for. He tossed the
antique pistol back onto the blanket, which the pirate rolled
up and retied.

High Pile waved the blaster-bearer ahead of him, through

a white stone archway toward the dock and sailing ship beyond. Surrounded by Matachìn, Krysty, Jak, Mildred, Doc and J.B. were then shoved in that direction. They looked back over their shoulders at Ryan one last time, still awaiting his signal for them to act.

He shook his head. A final emphatic no.

It was also a goodbye.

The companions disappeared from sight.

Ryan had no clue where they were being taken or why. But whatever fate held in store for the others, the odds had to be better than what they faced here. If they still had a chance to survive, they had to leave him behind and take it.

The sacrificial chilling of the galley slaves continued as his pirate escort spun him the opposite way and forced him to walk under the red brick colonnade. They followed a dimly lit passage that led through the fort's exterior wall, and out the door of a cylindrical guardpost.

In front of Ryan was a floodlit stone bridge, wider and more ornate than the first he'd crossed, and twice as long. This one was painted pale yellow and decorated with stout pairs of pillars at both ends. It led to a separate island, which was completely covered by a ravelin half as large as the courtyard they'd just left. The three-story structure was shaped like a triangle, or an arrowhead, pointing away from the bridge. Above the arched entryway were more crenelated battlements. There were only two windows that Ryan could see. The rest was smooth, featureless stone.

There was no doubt in Ryan's mind that what lay at the far end of the bridge was the epicenter of the bad juju he'd sensed earlier.

A death camp for the ages.

As they mounted the bridge, Ryan considered and rejected his options. Even though it was way easier for one man to slip through a crack than six, the pirates had him cold—at least for the moment. Without a diversion, he'd never get the jump on them, never get his hands on a blaster, never get righteous payback. And trying to swim away chained hand and foot, assuming he could dive over the bridge wall before they caught him, was suicide.

The pirates marched him through the prison entrance and into a stone-walled anteroom. A half dozen red-sashed guards awaited his arrival. Two of them immediately took up long wooden poles, which had metal hoops attached to one end.

While the Matachìn pinioned his arms and two red sashes aimed double barrels at his chest, the poles were extended, front and rear, and the hoops slipped over his head and down past his chin. The red sashes then pulled on straps at the ends of the poles, drawing the steel bands so tight around his throat that he could hardly breathe.

When the Matachìn released his arms, the men holding the poles were in total control of him. The rods were so long, he couldn't reach them with fists or feet. The leverage they offered made it easy for his captors to drive him to his knees, if they wished. And if that didn't tame him, they could tighten the nooses even more and choke him into unconsciousness.

With a pole-bearing red sash in front and one behind, Ryan was simultaneously pushed and pulled forward, through a floor-to-ceiling iron gate. He entered a labyrinth of stone, and stifling heat and humidity. The walls and floors were warped and worn. There were standing puddles of unidentifiable fluid everywhere.

To his left were rows of passages, presumably the cell

blocks, stretching off into the dark. From that direction he heard moaning.

When they passed by one of the cramped cells, Ryan saw it had no bed. It had no water. No toilet. No window to let in air or natural light. It reeked of urine and rotting flesh. A human form lay huddled and hidden under a pile of rags on the damp stone floor. There were rats inside the cell. They were merrily burrowing under the rags, feeding on the dead or the nearly dead prisoner. When Ryan looked farther down the passage, in the faint light he saw rats scurrying in bands of a dozen or more, darting back and forth across the corridor, between the cells.

At that moment he knew that few if any had ever returned from this awful place.

It wasn't just a prison.

It was a tomb.

They continued on until they reached the very heart of the darkness, the place that was the hottest, the rankest, the most oppressive, the core of the man-made hellhole. With double barrels pointed at his head, Ryan was uncollared and booted into an already occupied cell. The iron-barred gate clanged shut behind him. Their work done, the red sashes turned away and left him to get acquainted with his cell mate.

The other prisoner squatted with his back pressed into a corner, his head lowered, his long black hair hanging down over his face. He appeared to be naked except for his chains. The weak light from the single overhead bulb threw him in deep shadow. As Ryan took in the bleak cell, he noticed the stalagmites on the floor, white beestings of calcite that had dripped from the ceiling. When he stepped closer, his fellow prisoner stirred and slowly raised his face to the light.

For the second time in as many hours Ryan exclaimed, "What the fuck!"

His words echoed in the gloom.

Then a disembodied voice whispered in his ear, "Haven't I seen you somewhere before?"

The words seemed to have come from behind him. Ryan whirled, but there was no one there, only the sweating lime-stone wall.

When he turned back, the deadpan expression of his mirror image had transformed into a wide grin.

Chapter Six

Doc Tanner wept as he was force-marched across the stone dock toward the waiting black schooner. He cried without making a sound, tears streaming freely down the seams in his weathered face. Even if he lived forever, he knew he would never see the likes of Ryan Cawdor again. He cried for his brave and noble friend, and for his own accursed helplessness under the circumstances. The unstoppable flow of tears also came from sheer exhaustion, from three weeks chained to an oar and from the all-out brawl they'd just lost in Veracruz.

"We've got to do something," Krysty declared to the others as the iron-hulled ship's gangway was swung out and lowered to the dock. "We can't let these evil bastards chill him."

"Not leave Ryan here," Jak growled in assent.

"And what, pray tell, are our other options at present?" Doc asked, wiping his eyes with the backs of fight-bruised, manacled hands. "We cannot rescue him if we cannot rescue ourselves."

"We need a window of opportunity to turn things in our favor," Mildred said.

"A lowering of the rad-blasted odds would be an excellent start," J.B. added.

"We still have time," Mildred assured them earnestly. "We could—"

"*¡Silencio!*" one of the pirates growled.

High Pile mounted the gangway first and strode onto the aft deck of the black schooner.

There to greet him was a tall, thin man and two short, round women. All of them wore clean, starched white coats. All were as brown as coffee berries. They smiled hopefully as the Matachìn stepped up to them.

High Pile dismissed the trio with an impatient snort. He brushed past the whitecoats without a word, stepped down into the cockpit and disappeared belowdecks.

Doc realized at that moment that whatever the captain's new mission was, he did not particularly relish it.

The whitecoat man waved the prisoners and their pirate escort aboard.

The black ship was much bigger than *Tempest,* easily twice as long, and half again as wide across the beam. The hull was riveted metal plate; the masts and superstructure were made of wood. It was a type of vessel Doc was very familiar with. During his first life in Victorian times, similar oceangoing, commercial sailing ships, barks and schooners, were still plying the world's seas.

When the companions were assembled along the starboard rail, the male whitecoat spoke in soothing tones. He said, *"Soy médico. Mi chiamo Montejo."* He had slicked-back black hair, and a profile dominated by a long, hawkish nose.

Doc translated for the others. "He says he's a physician. Dr. Montejo."

The hatchet-faced man prattled on in Spanish, actually wringing his hands in eagerness, this while the pair of chubby-cheeked whitecoat women beamed up at him with pride.

"The other two are his medical assistants," Doc said, resuming the translation. "He says they understand the terrible ordeal we've all been through, and that their job is to restore us to full health and vigor."

"Do you believe this nukeshit!" J.B. said. "For almost a month they do their damnedest to chill us, now they want to take care of us?"

"The question is why?" Krysty said.

"Whatever the reason for the change of attitude," Mildred said, "we've got to play along with it, at least temporarily."

"I concur wholeheartedly," Doc said. "This presents a golden opportunity to take our own back."

The whitecoats led them down the companionway's steel steps. The Matachìn escort followed behind, their weapons ready. Overhead, generator-powered light bulbs in metal cages faded in and out, from intensely bright to dim. Aft of the stairs, across the width of the stern, was the captain's cabin; in front of them, under a low, sheet-metal ceiling was the ship's mess. A long, metal-topped table was bracketed by bench seats. The floor was worn linoleum. Immediately they were enveloped by cooking smells from the galley—meat, beans, onions, garlic and savory spices.

The aromas made Doc's mouth water and his head swim.

"Good grub," Jak murmured.

"Mebbe the whitecoat wasn't lying about the food, after all," J.B. said.

"See if we get of it any this time," Krysty said.

Beyond the mess, a bulkhead door opened onto a narrow corridor lined with riveted steel doors. Each door had a peephole on the outside so anyone in the corridor could look into the rooms.

At Dr. Montejo's command, the pirates began to separate Krysty and Mildred from the others.

"*¿Que pasa?*" Mildred asked him.

The whitecoat responded to her through a big smile. The expression in his hooded eyes was romantic. An alarming bedside manner, to be sure.

"What did he say?" J.B. asked, glowering at the oblivious man.

"He said," Mildred replied, "you two lovely ladies have been assigned a separate cabin for your comfort and privacy. Each stateroom has its own toilet and sink."

Doc bristled at the idea of their being split up. It grievously complicated what they had to do, which was take command of the ship by force, and quickly. As they were still in chains and controlled at blasterpoint by the pirates, whether he liked it or not there was nothing to be done about it.

While Doc, Jak and J.B. waited in the corridor, Mildred and Krysty were ushered into a room on the right by the female whitecoats and three of the pirate guard. As the doorway was blocked by the male bodies, Doc couldn't see what was going on inside. After a few moments, the whitecoats and pirate guard came out. Dr. Montejo pulled the door shut behind him and shot the slide bolts, top and bottom.

As if there was ever any doubt, Doc thought, this, too, was a prison ship.

Then Dr. Montejo opened a door on the left and waved for them to enter.

Doc stared into a low-ceilinged, windowless steel box, roughly ten by eight, illuminated by a pair of caged light bulbs. There were three built-in bunks along the left-hand wall, and a sink and a low, lidless toilet on the opposite side.

"Beats the rowing bench all to hell," J.B. said.

The pirates roughly pushed them into the small room.

Dr. Montejo ordered the connecting chain removed, but left their ankle and hand manacles in place.

Jak shook his wrist chains in the man's face. "These?" he said. "Like to wipe own butt."

The whitecoat addressed them with open palms, in solicitous, dulcet tones.

Doc translated for his Spanish-challenged comrades. "The good doctor deeply apologizes for the continuing security measures, and assures us from the bottom of his heart they are only temporary. As soon as everything is secure, the ship will be leaving Veracruz, then we will have much more freedom. He says he knows we must be hungry and we will be fed shortly. After that, we will receive a complete physical examination and our wounds will be properly dressed."

The smiling Montejo and the scowling pirates backed out of the cramped room. The door slammed and the locking bolts clacked shut.

"Trust no whitecoat," Jak said. "All lying fuckers."

"You'll get no argument from me on that, dear boy," Doc said. "I'd just as soon see them food for crows, dangling by their overstretched necks from every incandescent light pole…"

"Shh," J.B. said. "Listen…"

They could hear heavy boots moving around on the deck above. Then the sound of the gangway being winched in.

"Count ten, mebbe more, not sure," Jak said.

"If the rest of the bastards got off the ship, our odds are looking better," J.B. said. "How many bodies does it take to crew a tub like this? When the time comes, how many are we going to be up against?"

"If memory serves," Doc said, "even a skeleton crew to run a ship this size would be seven or eight sailors, not including the captain. That would be the minimum, and it would entail hard duty for all around the clock."

The ship's auxiliary diesel engine started up with a rumble. There was a burst of shouted orders from the dock. After a moment, the heavy mooring lines thudded onto the deck above the companions' cell, and then the vessel slowly backed away from the dock.

"Where they take us?" Jak asked.

"Where do they *think* they're taking us, you mean?" J.B. corrected him.

"South," Doc said. "My guess is it has to be south, deeper into Matachìn territory. I can't think of a reason for them to want to ferry us back north."

The time-traveler took a seat on the edge of the bottom bunk and stared at his own blurred reflection in the polished metal wall. Looking closer, he noted that its surface was covered with crude graffiti. Proper names. Obscene phrases in Spanish. Obscene cartoons. All apparently scratched into the soft steel with the edges of handcuffs.

Wherever they were being taken in chains, they were not the first.

Doc saw their situation as nothing short of desperate. They were in unknown territory, they were captives of a culture they didn't understand, and worst of all, they were leaderless. On top of that, Ryan was living on borrowed time, already condemned to death. Who could step up to fill the void left by his absence? Were any of them really capable of honchoing his rescue operation?

Doc knew that as a warrior and a scout Jak Lauren was without peer, but because of his rudimentary communication skills he could never function as their leader. Mildred Wyeth was a trained scientific thinker, but military strategy was an entirely different kettle of fish. Her brand of science was not chess, nor was it game theory. Though Krysty Wroth was a formidable fighter with special powers, she lacked the emotional detachment necessary to take the group into combat. J.B. was good at all things mechanical, but had trouble seeing beyond the parts laid out in front of him.

And then there was Doc, himself.

A dedicated student of American history, he remembered in detail the grand engagements of the Civil War—Bull Run, Shiloh, Appomattox—but he lacked Ryan's facility for thinking on the run, for guerrilla-style warfare, for immediately seeing the opposition's weak point and knowing instinctively how to exploit it.

Doc also knew he was at times stricken by fits of irrationality. They were the consequence of damage inflicted by a double time trawl against his will. Sometimes he raved; sometimes he cried; sometimes he walked around in a daze. The attacks were unpredictable and when they hit, completely debilitating. He knew he couldn't be counted on because of them.

The companions' present limitations, and the consequences of same were all too clear to Doc, even if he couldn't see a way around them. Their short time aboard *Tempest* had in no way prepared them to sail a ship twice its size. They could of course run this huge vessel on engine power, assuming there were no glitches in auxiliary propulsion. Under the circumstances there was no time for mistakes, which meant that somehow they would have to not only overcome their captors, but keep a few of them alive and convince them to follow orders.

From years of observation, Doc knew that Ryan always

advanced his strategies one step at a time. He ignored the array of uncontrollable factors set in motion by the initial action, and concentrated entirely on successfully completing the opening move.

Get free, that was the immediate objective.

The ship picked up speed as it set course for the harbor entrance. From the hiss of the water against the hull, Doc guessed they were making six or seven knots.

"Do you hear someone talking?" J.B. asked. Then he put his ear against the bulkhead wall opposite the bunks. When he pulled his head back he said, "Someone's in the cell next door."

"I hear." Jak nodded. "Not understand."

"This may help in that regard," Doc said. He stood and reached for the narrow air vent set in the wall near the ceiling. He slid back the metal cover on its tracks.

The voices immediately became louder and much more distinct, although they were still distorted and muffled by the steel wall and the engine noise.

At first it sounded like at least three people, perhaps four. One of the voices was familiar, although Doc couldn't immediately place it.

"Why can't you get it through your thick heads," the familiar voice said, "I'm trying to explore the limits of moral responsibility and personal faith in an epical context. Every time you three pop up in the mix, that exploration comes to a screeching halt."

"Stalk this, you unmitigated hack!" said a squeaky voice, possibly male. "You're telling us we're not good enough to flesh out your philosophical digressions, but we were damn good enough to put food on your kitchen table for years."

"Yeah, Alpo and bubblebread."

"Perhaps the fault isn't with us, but rather with you?" The third voice sounded female; it was sultry, with an odd, lilting accent. "After all, we're just stock fictional characters with half-a-page bios. You've always been in control of what we do and say. Empty canvasses. We are what you make of us. Perhaps you, the author, lack the skill, the depth of intro-spection, and the native intelligence to animate us in any other way?"

"Uff da!" a deep, gruff, manly voice protested. "Once again the gorgeous princess is talking through her shapely, buckskin-clad backside! I, Ragnar, am no mere puppet! I am a Warlord of Norseland!"

"Are you looking to get your head *and* pigtails hacked off, Viking?" said the squeaky voice.

"No, please don't! Not again…" begged the familiar moderator.

"Draw your steel, you walking, talking vegetable, and I will chop you into Waldorf salad."

"Advance another step forward, Ragnar," the woman's voice cried, "and I'll have your fire-furred goobers dangling from my cinchwaist."

"Not if I take one of your firm upthrusties for a coin purse!"

"No, stop, stop…" the moderator pleaded. "Can't you see I'm searching for something important, something that will stand the test of time, something eternal, some kind of moral certitude, evidence of a divine hand in all things, the hope and nobility of humankind, and all you want to do is fight…"

Jak hooked a thumb at the wall. "How many locked up in there?" he said.

"Just the one soul, I believe," Doc said. "He's doing all the voices himself. Falsetto. Baritone. Tenor. The Norse and

Native American accents, too. Not a very convincing job, either, I might add."

"Hey, wait just a nukin' minute!" J.B. said. "I know those names. They're from those books Harmonica Tom had lined up on a shelf in *Tempest*. The *Slaughter Realms* series. Remember, I opened one of them and read some of it to everyone. It was so bad Krysty made me stop. It sounds like someone else's got their hands on one of the books and is reading it out loud."

"The excess of verbiage does sound familiar," Doc agreed, "almost as if the author was being paid strictly by the word."

The acted-out melee next door continued, the voices by turns uttering threats and inanities.

Fed up, the albino teen suddenly leaped from his bunk, pounded on the wall with both fists and howled up at the vent, "Shut fuck up!"

A stunned silence ensued.

"Why should I?" came the reply after a moment. "If you are on the other side of that wall, you're in chains, and no threat to me."

Behind the lenses of his spectacles, J.B.'s eyes opened wide in recognition. He hissed the words, "Fire Talker."

Jak drew his cuffed hands across the front of his throat like a knife blade.

Doc gestured for quiet and calm. Indeed, it appeared that the occupant of the neighboring cell was Daniel Desipio—the self-same soulless bastard who had led the Padre Islanders to their awful, rotting doom, and who had betrayed the companions to the Matachìn. And he was separated from them by just few millimeters of scarred steel.

It also appeared that Daniel didn't know who they were.

At least not yet.

"Are you reading from a book?" Doc called up to the vent.

"I'm not reading, I'm composing dialogue out loud," Daniel informed them. "That way the ear can pick up the ebb and flow of natural speech. Besides, I lack paper and pen to set things down in a more permanent fashion."

When the companions failed to react, Daniel added, "I'll have you know I'm an author of considerable repute."

"You mean for *Slaughter Realms?*" J.B. said.

"You know the series, then?"

"Who doesn't know Ragnar and the Ninja Princess?" J.B. replied.

"It ran to more than two hundred and fifty titles, I believe," Doc added. "Not even Armageddon could wipe all the copies off the face of the Earth."

"Most gratifying to know that the body of work still lives on," Daniel said.

On the other side of the wall, Doc and J.B. were laughing up their sleeves. From the void of expression in Jak's ruby-red eyes it was impossible to tell whether he fully understood the joke.

"How did you come to live so long?" J.B. asked Daniel. "Are you a time-traveler?"

"After a fashion. I went into cryostasis before nukeday."

"So you're a freezie."

"Not intentionally. Out of a deep sense of patriotism I volunteered and was chosen to participate in a supersecret experiment. In the course of unforeseen tragic events I ended up in a cryotank."

The ship's almost imperceptible forward passage suddenly changed. Clearing the protection of the harbor's breakwater, the bow began gently rising and falling as it crossed the widely spaced, Lantic swells. The engine kept rumbling; there was evidently not enough wind for the pirates to raise sail.

A point of no return lay some hours ahead of them, Doc knew. A point after which they couldn't reverse course and still make it back in time to save Ryan. They had to act, to overpower the captain and crew and take command of the ship before they passed that critical point.

Meanwhile the joke they were playing on the traitor Daniel had lost a good deal of its edge.

Doc only half listened as the man bragged on and on about his illustrious career prior to the end of the world: his many novels; their complex story arcs and deep characterizations; how his skill had left the other writers in the publisher's stable in the dirt. He said that he was always the editors' favorite because of the quality of his work, and that the other writers were jealous of the size and sophistication of *his* audience. Daniel described a dedicated fan club of eight people who corresponded with him on a regular basis on the worldwide Web; then admitted that before Skydark he had learned, much to his dismay, that two of his most rabid devotees were residents of a maximum security prison located in central California, and that a third was serving hard time in a federal lockup in Massachusetts for impersonating an FBI agent.

The Fire Talker's boastfest was interrupted by the sounds of door bolts being cracked back. Then the door to the companions' cell opened and the plump little whitecoat women entered bearing trays with large, covered ceramic bowls.

Amazing aromas entered with them.

With a flourish, and twinkling black eyes, the whitecoats uncovered the bowls' brimming contents.

Doc gazed down on a thick red stew dotted with islands of little cornmeal dumplings. Was that slow-cooked pork or boneless breast of chicken floating in the broth? Maybe both? Certainly he could see black beans, rice, squash of some sort, chopped up red and green chilis, and what looked like sprigs of cilantro. Sprinkled on top was a pungent, soft and crumbly white cheese.

One of the women handed him his bowl and then gave him a big metal spoon to eat with. In the process, some of the red gravy got smeared on the pink ball of her thumb. She licked it off, rolled her eyes in delight, and exclaimed, *"Sabroso."* Then she giggled most fetchingly.

"You are a true angel of mercy, my dear lady," Doc told her as he tightly clutched his spoon.

Even though the stew was scalding hot, it was difficult to keep from wolfing it down. Doc had to force himself to chew and savor each bite. He had almost forgotten what good food tasted like. There were no squirming weevils to crunch. No gagging threads of black fish guts. No tuberous, rubbery or gristly unidentifiables to gulp down whole. No sharp bones to stick in the back of the throat and choke on.

Beaming with delight, the whitecoats backed out of the room, then closed and rebolted the door.

Jak and J.B. made soft grunts of pleasure as they plowed into the meal.

Watching them chow down, Doc felt a sudden pang of guilt that stopped him from chewing. Guilt for so thoroughly enjoying himself while Ryan endured God only knew what. He prayed with all his might that his old friend was faring as well as they were, then with determination he resumed eating. He needed to regain his strength for the battle to come. They all did.

After a few minutes Jak abandoned his spoon, tipped up his bowl and stuck his face inside to lick it clean.

When Doc was finished, he sank back on his bunk, gasping for breath. Somehow he had managed to pack it all in. It was remarkable how the stomach could stretch. But the weight of the meal left him feeling more than a little woozy. And his tongue felt strange, tingly and thick.

Too much food, too fast, Doc told himself.

Then he burped and felt a little better.

Chapter Seven

Daniel Desipio carefully fished a walnut-size cornmeal dumpling from his stew with the tip of his spoon. He deposited it on his tongue, shut his eyes and let it slowly melt in his mouth. Rapture.

This was the lap of luxury.

A cell with a flush toilet, and a ceiling tall enough for him to stand up in.

A bunk with a mattress to sleep on.

Food that didn't make him gag and then come squirting out his nose.

For an *enano* in the service of the Lords of Death, life didn't get any better than this. And there was an added, extraspecial bonus, which had yet to kick in.

The barrage of questions from the captives next door had stopped as soon as the food was delivered. Daniel knew they had to be Padre Islanders, fresh from one of the Matachìn tugs.

The questions resumed after his neighbors finished eating.

"Where are we being taken?" one of them asked through the air vent.

"I don't know any more than you do," Daniel lied. He was a little miffed that the subject of conversation, post-prandial, had turned away from *SR* and his predark literary accomplishments.

"Why were we chosen?" another man asked. "And all the other galley slaves slaughtered?"

"Sorry, I don't have a clue about that, either." Another lie.

Daniel knew all about the selection criteria. Although he hadn't endured the process himself, he had witnessed it many times. It had been developed over a century of trial and error. The galley slave ordeal removed the weakest from the pool of potential infectees, those who would not survive the rigors of inoculation anyway. That saved time and effort that would have been otherwise wasted on useless corpses. On top of the physical hardiness and resilience necessary to recover from the medical procedure, the chosen *enanos* also had to be convincing as traders, sluts, mercies and the like, convincing enough to infiltrate and infect a target population without raising suspicion. Daniel's next-door neighbors were all English speakers, which meant the target they'd eventually be aimed at would be their own home turf and his—Deathlands.

He heard muffled belching sounds from the other side of the wall.

"Is the food always this good here?" one of the men asked.

"Don't know. This is the first I've had of it."

More lies.

Daniel could have told them the truth about everything, exactly what was going to happen to them, the precise order of events and why. He could have tortured his neighbors with the gruesome details, making them endure the rest of the voyage in horror and trembling dread. But he restrained himself. Knowledge was the only power he had. No way would he give it up for nothing.

Daniel was already beginning to feel the effects of the food. A spreading, delicious warmth and heaviness through his limbs and chest. A dryness in the mouth. Sleepiness. Some difficulty concentrating.

He didn't know what the ship's cooks used—some kind of tasteless, odorless opiate, most likely. A precise dose based on estimated body weight was mixed in with each bowl of delicious grub. Grub that had to be gobbled. Whatever it was they used, the chemical restraint transformed the angry, hostile captives into peaceful and compliant zombies. It forced them to sleep and to rest twenty or more hours a day, and allowed them to rebuild their bodily reserves. This was vital because of the stress of the upcoming inoculation procedure. Only a fraction of plague-carrier candidates actually lived through the entire ordeal, which involved being infected by cells taken from a carrier's marrow.

For his part, Daniel had always enjoyed the drug's effect. He found it made the voyage to Xibalba pass even more pleasantly, as in a dream: doped up with a satisfyingly full belly; a real bed to sleep on; no one trying to chill you; no one abusing you; and no thoughts about the pain and suffering to come. The latter because under the drug's influence there was no way to hold a coherent thought in your head.

Not even one of terror.

And as Daniel knew from long experience, it all went downhill from here, starting with the withdrawal symptoms, but that was later, much later at the end of the journey, at the gates of hell.

He noted that his neighbors had stopped asking their annoying questions. Daniel thought he heard snoring coming through the vent.

Scratched into the wall of his cell beside his bunk were the words *La comida es veneno*.

The food is poison.

Maybe so, he thought as he slowly chewed a last, succulent morsel of pork. But at least it ain't Alpo.

Setting aside the bowl, he curled up to sleep until breakfast.

Flapjacks and bacon with a big ol' side of stupefy.

Yum.

Chapter Eight

Ryan's smiling mirror image stood up from the floor of the cell. His naked body was streaked with caked-on filth. About an inch shorter than Cawdor, he had the same rangy, powerful build and shoulder-length, black curly hair.

Up close and face-to-face, the resemblance was not so startling, Ryan decided.

The man's nose was wider, as were the cheekbones. His chin was narrower and a bit less rugged. The man's skin was much darker than Ryan's, reflecting perhaps some *indio* heritage. Although the black eye patch was similar, the surviving eye he stared into was not sky-blue; it was a deep brown, almost black. The jagged welt of scar that divided the ruined eye socket ran close to horizontal, starting on the forehead above the bridge of the nose and curving down around the top of the cheek; Ryan's scar on the other hand was nearly vertical, slicing straight down from above the eyebrow. In the light of the caged bulb strung on the ceiling, his cell mate's teeth looked very white. With manacled hands, the man played with a small flat pebble of limestone, tumbling it expertly over the backs of his fingers. The back and forth, back and forth was so practiced it was automatic, if not unconscious. He managed the feat without even looking down.

"Who the hell are you?" Ryan said.

"The priests have convinced the red sashes and most of the *campesinos* that I'm the flesh of your flesh, your brother, Hunahpu." The man spoke English.

"You're no brother of mine."

"No, of course not. But it suits the priests and their distant masters if everyone believes they've captured the living embodiment of the fabled Hero Twins, Hunahpu and Xbalanque."

"Who might they be?"

"Part of the ancient Mayan story of the beginning of the world," Ryan's cell mate said. "The original Hero Twins, One-Hunahpu and Seven-Hunahpu, were the third creation of the gods of the universe. They were killed and dismembered by the Lords of Death. Their offspring, Hunahpu and Xbalanque, avenged the murders through trickery and magic, and in so doing consigned the twelve lords and all their subject devils to the underworld, thereby limiting their power to do harm to innocent human beings. A more recent myth, devised by the Atapuls and their priests, claims that nukeday undid the Hero Twins' five-thousand-year-old victory and opened the gates to hell. Since then, so the story goes, the Lords of Death have roamed free on Earth in the form of the Atapuls. They and their devils spread plague, pestilence, war and suffering in their wake.

"The story presents two opposing forces—one offers light to the world, the other darkness. My people believe because the Hero Twins beat the Lords of Death once before, and held them in check for five thousand years they are humanity's last remaining hope. If the Atapul clan and their priests can convince everyone that they have killed the forces of light, that hope is gone. When you and I die in public view, they believe the growing resistance to their rule will crumble. And they will reign unchallenged over humankind forever."

"If you aren't Hunahpu," Ryan said, "then who the fuck are you? And where did you learn to speak English?"

"I'm called Chucho. I've been an outlaw with a price on my head for more than ten years now. I was first imprisoned by priests in Cancun, another of the Atapul city-states, for a crime I didn't commit. They did this so they could rob my family and take everything that was ours. While I was locked away in prison, they killed all my relatives and moved into our house and onto our lands.

"Cancun's prison was full of very bad men who taught me to rob and to murder, and how to do it well. When I had learned all I could from them, I found a way to escape. Within days, I fell in with a dramatic troupe that traveled from town to town along the coast. The actors showed me how to disguise myself, how to throw my voice, how to do magic tricks, how to pickpocket. One of them taught me your language."

Chucho held up his handcuffs for Ryan to see.

"No keyhole," he said, shaking them. "No bolt, either. They are welded shut. There is no lock made that I can't pick. And they keep me naked for a reason."

"Which is?"

"So I can't hide weapons under my clothes. Out on the road, I'd carry as many as five blasters at once, in holsters, pockets, boots, my hat, taped against my skin. The red sashes sometimes got lucky and caught me at a checkpoint or on the street. After collecting three or four pistols, they would give up the search, figuring they had them all. Before they knew it, I'd have a little .22 bellygun going pop-pop-pop point-blank into their heads. I killed six of the bastards and walked away from the stockade of a fortified garrison up north. After that happened, they got smarter.

"I've been caught six times since then, and condemned to death six times, but I always found a way to escape before the sentence could be carried out. And when I returned to their world, I made the bastards pay, and I took pleasure in it. The priests put a bounty on my head in gold, and every year I was free they raised it higher. Even so, no one ever turned me in. The people wrote songs about me instead, and they still sing them in the *cantinas* when there are no red sashes around."

"Songs?"

"Of celebration, because I killed their oppressors, stole treasure from the Lords of Death, and all that I stole I gave back to the people robbed and brutalized by the priests and red sashes. What I did was something the people will never forget. Or the priests or their masters for that matter.

"Last spring there was an uprising in one of the western provinces. The silver miners there went on a rampage, killing the red sashes with shovels and picks, and burning down their garrison. Because I happened to be there and was seen helping in the fighting, the priests blamed it all on me. That's when they started calling me 'Hunahpu' and began circulating the rumors about the Hero Twins coming to life and waging final war on the Lords of Death."

Ryan watched the pebble roll over the backs of his cell mate's knuckles. From the moment Chucho stood, the rolling pebble had never stopped, never even hesitated. His mirror image had amazing finger speed and dexterity.

In the hellscape Ryan had come across plenty of crazy, lying blowhards. They congregated around campfires and on the front porches of gaudy houses, and amused themselves with pissing contests. If Ryan hadn't seen giant papier-mâché models of this man's head on sticks, he wouldn't have believed a word he said. But you didn't get your head waved around on a pole if you were a nobody. Chucho was right up there with the Atapuls and the plague faces that dominated and terrified the people of Veracruz. That he was locked away in the deepest, darkest hole of this stinking shit pit of a prison, that his handcuffs were welded shut, that he was naked, were all testaments to the danger his captors felt he represented.

If there were explanations for the facts on the table other than the ones Chucho had given, Ryan couldn't think of them.

Believing was different from trusting. He had no reason to trust Chucho, even though they were scheduled to die together.

"And you who are not my brother, what is your name?" Chucho said. "What did you do to end up here? You come from Tierra de la Muerte?"

"The name's Ryan. You're right, I come from Deathlands. I got trapped in the wrong place, at the wrong time doing a little trading. Pirates took me and my partners for slaves, made us row down here."

"And you had the terrible misfortune to look like Chucho, only in reverse."

"Some things can't be helped."

"You have traveled down many hard roads. I can see it in the eye you still have left. I see many dead. I see destruction."

"Been blamed for some bad things I didn't do, just like you."

"I think in Tierra de la Muerte the bastards who prey on the weak have nightmares about you coming to visit. So perhaps we are related after all?"

"How long have you been a prisoner here?" Ryan asked.

"Weeks and I still haven't found a way out. This *revellín* is escape proof, so they say. The stone walls are six feet thick.

They can't be tunneled through. The floor is even thicker. It runs straight down into bedrock coral. No one has ever escaped from this prison alive. The dead leave here in wheelbarrows every day. Mebbe if I had another month I might be able to figure a way out, but we don't have that much time. We die before dawn the day after tomorrow."

"What about the trial?"

"If you're thinking you might get justice from these animals, you can forget it. They don't know the meaning of the word. The trial is a sham, a chance for the priests to chant and burn incense and wear their judge hats in public. They want to get the execution over and done with as quickly as possible so I don't slip away again. It's funny, even though they're priests, they don't have much in the way of faith."

"We don't have their stinking religion in Deathlands."

"Not yet, but just you wait. It's been moving up the coast ever since Skydark. The people of Veracruz—the Jarochos—escaped the worst of Armageddon only to be set upon seventy-five years later by the Matachìn. They hit the city first with plague, then with religion and the red sash traitors. The sickness they brought was like nothing anyone had ever seen before. Whole neighborhoods were wiped out. And when the disease was at its peak, the pirates sailed into the bay and flattened the resistance with a relatively small number of fighters. The priests moved in right behind them with images of new gods to worship. They painted the churches the color of blood and told the people if they didn't obey their every command, the Lords of Death, who had been resurrected by the fires of global destruction, would bring back the plague to punish them. From that day forward, everything returned to the ancient ways, at the time of creation, when the Lords of Death ruled the world."

"Wait a bastard minute," Ryan said. "You're telling me that disease was a weapon of war? That it was turned loose on purpose?"

"A terrible weapon, indeed, my friend. The tidal waves of Skydark reduced the population of this city to a quarter of a million people. After the plague struck, the living numbered less than fifty thousand. The killing was indiscriminate and wholesale. Within ten days of the outbreak, the graveyards of Veracruz overflowed. The streets were heaped high with bodies. Because of the volume of corpses, and the effects of the tropical heat, they had to be put in a mass grave."

Having seen what the disease had done on Padre Island, Ryan tried to visualize that many people sick and dying. And he could not. It was a horror beyond imagining.

"We learned later how it was done," Chucho said. "The Matachìn had seeded the target cities with *enanos* of the Lords of Death."

"I don't understand."

"They sent in infected people, plague carriers, in advance of the attack, to weaken the opposition with the sickness and guide the invasion."

"Son of a bitch!" Cawdor swore. "There was this two-faced little bastard on the island where we were captured, where the sickness had struck. When we tried to escape, he turned us over to the Matachìn. He had to be working for them. You're saying he was a plague carrier, too? That he brought all that death with him?"

"I don't think there's any doubt about it."

"He came back with us on the tug," Ryan said. "The pirates kept him belowdecks the whole time. He never saw the light of day, not in three weeks."

"That's understandable. If he'd been allowed out, the disease might have killed everyone aboard."

"And here I thought the Matachìn were keeping the stinking piece of crap down there for his safety, so the people he'd betrayed wouldn't tear him apart," Ryan said, shaking his head.

"No, they did it to protect themselves from what he carries," Chucho said.

"Explain something else to me, then," Ryan continued. "The disease weapon didn't chill everyone on Padre Island. From what you just said, it didn't chill everyone in Veracruz, either. Why?"

"The survivors either had resistance to the sickness or somehow managed to avoid being infected. Once the Matachìn established military control of the city, they and their priests selected red sashes from the fifty thousand who were left. They were picked for their willingness to obey orders and to hurt others. There are less than a thousand of them in Veracruz and outlying areas. The threat of the plague coming back keeps the people in line. No one wants that. Even in the countryside, people obey because of fear. Priests have churches there, too, but they are really just warehouses for collecting valuables—precious ores, fuel and food. Everyone pays a tax to them, otherwise the red sashes come and take even more."

"And you gave the taxes back."

"With interest."

"How are they going to chill us?"

"It won't be pretty, that's for sure. And like I said, it will be in public. Not much point in killing your fabled enemies if no one sees it."

"So the executions won't be here?"

"No, they'll hold the trial here, so the ceremony won't be interrupted. After the guilty verdict they'll take us back into the city tomorrow night for the killing. There will be another big parade, ending at the lighthouse. They'll murder us in plain sight of every citizen of Veracruz. Then it'll be our flesh-and-bone heads on sticks paraded around the *Zócalo*. And the mob will cheer at gunpoint."

"Why at night?"

"It's cooler—they'll draw a bigger crowd."

"So our best chance of escape is after the trial, during the move."

Chucho gave him an amused look. "Our best chance surrounded by a thousand red sashes?"

"You're not giving up?"

"I've worked magic before, I just may do it again."

It suddenly occurred to Ryan that Chucho might not trust him, either. "You don't have supporters on the outside to rescue you?" he asked.

"You mean, take this fort by force? You must be joking. The only access is either by bridge or by water, and both are defensible from the battlements. To try to break in here is suicide."

Whatever hand Chucho held, he was keeping it close to his vest. Ryan didn't see a reason to give him any more information about the companions, how many there were and what they were capable of. By now they were probably miles away, anyway. The odds of their overpowering their captors and returning for him were slim and none.

Ryan felt the stirring of breeze from down the dim corridor, from a distant door opening or closing. It wafted a strong smell of urine.

Out of the corner of his eye, he saw something move just inside the cell's iron bars, a shadow of a shadow, scooting low and fast across the floor.

Without a word, Chucho suddenly whirled and sidearmed the limestone pebble. The rock didn't clatter and ricochet off on the stone. It thunked into something soft.

Chucho stepped over to the bars and picked up the dead rat by the tail. When he held it up to the light its little curled-up front legs were still twitching.

"Have you had your dinner, my friend?" he asked.

Chapter Nine

Harmonica Tom stood in the bed of the parked pickup, bracketed by his three new amigos. They had pulled over to the
shoulder of the road, unable to get any closer to the glow of
the city because of the big parade creeping their way. Tom
could hear the distant music and chanting. Lit by lamps on
tall, steel stanchions, the street around them was already lined
with spectators. Some of the audience waved pennants, some
held big paper heads on poles.

He recognized the plague head from his own nightmares.
It made his skin crawl.

Tom's amigos cracked open a fresh bottle. When he was
offered more joy juice, he politely declined.

The plague face was of a generic dying man, a synopsis of
symptoms rather than an individual likeness. He had no idea
why that horror was being displayed. Or why it was mixed in
with garishly painted, gargoyle heads. Were they in celebration of things honored or feared, or both?

When he saw Ryan's face up there, too, Tom stiffened in
shock. He shifted the unlit stub of his cigar to the corner of
his mouth and clenched it between his teeth. How could these
people possibly know what the one-eyed warrior looked like?
he asked himself. And why for nuke's sake would they wave
his head about?

Tom didn't understand the symbolism of the images on display nor the relationship between them, if any. And he was reluctant to ask his brand-new drinking buddies about it. He barely had the language skills to frame an intelligible question in Spanish, let alone understand the answer if it was complicated or lengthy. And he didn't want to reveal himself as a foreigner just yet.

"Ahí viene el otro gemelo," his driver buddy said thickly, weaving slightly on his feet as he raised the new bottle to his lips.

After a delay of several very long seconds, Tom's brain unscrambled two of the three words that had been spoken to him: something was coming; *another* something was coming. The subject of the sentence was a word missing from his vocabulary, therefore making sense of it was impossible.

Up the road, he could see a trio of stake trucks advancing at a snail's pace with headlights blazing on high beams. Backlit pirates in full armor and weapons marched in formation in front of the lead truck. As the procession crept forward, the honking horns, music and amplified shouts grew louder and louder.

The parade eventually passed right in front of them.

"El otro gemelo," said the driver, pointing at a long-haired man with an eye patch standing in the back of the lead truck, glaring down at the crowd. He was surrounded by familiar faces.

At first, Tom couldn't believe his eyes. Ryan and the others had all survived the long voyage from Padre Island. They looked like they'd been through hell. Their faces were gaunt, as well as cut and bruised. They were in irons. But they were alive and he felt a wave of relief.

A hoarse voice assailed the crowd at the sides of the road through a megaphone loud-hailer. *"¡Mira, mira, mira!"*

Words Tom immediately recognized.

Lookee, lookee, lookee!

The announcer rode on the lead truck's running board: a Matachìn commander with dreads piled high on his head.

His heart pounding, Tom automatically reached under the poncho. His fingers closed on the pistol grip of his silenced submachine gun. He only held the weapon for a second, then he let its weight fall back onto the lanyard. Ryan and the companions were surrounded by pirates and armed men in red sashes. Under the circumstances a successful rescue attempt was impossible. To have any hope of saving them, and not dying himself in the effort, he had to pick a more favorable battleground than this. To do that he had to find out where they were being taken.

Because he had no other choice, Tom shouted a telegraphic question into the ear of his drunken friend, *"¿Adonde van?"*

"San Juan de Ulua, allá." The man waved the bottle of joy juice in the direction of the illuminated floating fortress.

That made sense. Put the surviving slaves, particularly the most dangerous ones, somewhere they couldn't escape.

It rankled Tom that there was nothing he could immediately do for Ryan or the others. It rankled him even more that maybe there was nothing he could do for them, ever. He knew it was possible they were going to be taken inside the ancient fort and there immediately chilled. A hard bit of business considering what they'd endured for the last three weeks, but Tom had a bigger score to settle for the Padre Islanders and that had to be seen to first, or it was never going to get done.

Whooping and hollering, his drunken amigos hopped off the tailgate of the pickup and joined the parade as the three trucks in the lead crept around a right turn toward the fort.

Without a word, Tom took his leave of them. He jumped down from the opposite side of the pickup. Nobody was looking in his direction as he cut between a pair of huge, rectangular concrete pads, the foundations of warehouses that had been swept clean by Skydark's tidal waves. Apparently his new friends had already forgotten him. He headed overland at a fast trot, making a beeline for the brightly lit power station compound

Tom's knowledge of predark power plants was extremely limited. He'd never seen a functional one before—when the sun went down in Deathlands, people lit fires or squatted in the dark. Years back, though, he'd come across an eighteen-page, full-color comic book published in 1999 by Mississippi Power and Light. Tom had no way of knowing it, but the pamphlet in question had originally been a company public relations gimmick, meant to be handed out to schoolchildren on field trips. Among other things, *Johnny Kilowatt and the Blackout Gang* made fun of environmentalists, and their concern over pollution and global warming—this while touting the enormous benefits of the industry to humankind. Solo sailing the hellscape's coast gave Tom plenty of time to read and study all the predark material he managed to collect in his travels. From the cartoon schematics in *Johnny Kilowatt,* he had soaked up the basic elements of large-scale, steam-generated electrical power.

On the other side of the wide swathe of hurricane fence, under the strings of lights that decorated the twelve-story cooling tower and boiler complex, were rows of cylindrical holding tanks for diesel. Tanks big enough to contain ninety thousand barrels of fuel each. According to the disintegrating comic book, diesel was burned to heat water to steam that was then used to turn the turbines and produce electricity.

The tank farm was an obvious target for some of the C-4, Tom thought. The heat and pressure from a plastique explosion would guarantee ignition. A raging, out-of-control oil fire would make a great distraction, and the dense smoke might help cover *Tempest*'s exit from the harbor, but after the blaze was either put out or allowed to burn itself out, the tanks could be fairly easily replaced. And so could the fuel if there was still an operational refinery on the coast.

He was looking to do some damage that would be much more long term, perhaps even permanent.

To the left of the main complex, and connected to it by drooping high-tension lines suspended on a series of tall towers, was the main transformer station, which converted the plant's raw energy into a form that was usable and that could be transmitted over long distances. It, too, was protected by a hurricane-fence perimeter. Even if he completely flattened the step-up station, Tom knew it could be rebuilt if enough spare parts were available.

He continued on to the ten-foot-high fence that surrounded the plant proper. The barrier was in a sad state of repair, rusting, with obvious makeshift entry and exit routes along its length—shortcuts the workers used to get to and from the job site, and for local folk who didn't want to walk around the huge complex to reach the other side. Tom lifted the edge of a flap cut in the mesh and slipped through.

As he approached the structure, he could see a few workers ten stories above him on the pipeframe catwalks that encased the boiler complex. If they noticed him crossing the compound, they didn't pay him any mind—which was more evidence that folks cut across the grounds all the time. The workers certainly couldn't have heard him coming. Up close, the plant's hum was a dull roar that masked even the sounds of the parade.

Tom located the generator room without difficulty; it was where the noise was the loudest. He tried an exterior door in the three-story, concrete block building and found it unlocked.

Inside the generator room it was so loud he couldn't hear himself think. It was broiling hot inside, too. Six-hundred- to one-thousand-degree heat blasted off the foot-diameter steam pipes that jutted from the far wall on his right. Banks of overhead lights reflected on the polished concrete floor and the pale green–painted housings of a row of immense machines. The floor vibrated steadily underfoot.

Tom took off his billcap and wiped the beads of sweat from his forehead. Comparing the layout to his memory of the comic book, it was easy to tell which end of the power train was which. Steam energy flowed from the towering boiler first to a high-pressure turbine, the machine on his far right, and from there it was forced back into the boiler through another set of pipes to be reheated. The steam was then pumped through two intermediate-pressure turbines—the second and third machines—and finally into a low-pressure turbine. All four of these units were supported by and connected to one another and to the even more massive generator at the end of the line by a single, 100-foot-long driveshaft. The four turbines turned a huge rotor inside the generator housing, which produced electricity.

A smile passed over Tom's face as another intriguing fact from the comic came back to him. The weight of the 100-foot driveshaft, of the four-turbine assembly, and of the rotor inside the generator was such that if the rotor ever stopped turning, even for a second, the entire system would become unbalanced, and an attempted restart would not only fail, but it would bring on complete destruction. The comic had made clear that in the event of a power loss, backup emergency power would immediately kick in to maintain a slow turning of the rotor to keep the system operational. Knocking out both power sources simultaneously would bring on the result Tom desired.

Lights out.

For eternity.

He walked down the row of machines, looking for the armored conduit that would indicate the power input lines. As he passed the generator, Tom saw a metal warning sign riveted to the housing above a capped valve that stopped him dead in his tracks. Though it was in Spanish, it used the universal symbol for explosion risk. From what he could make of the words, the system contained hydrogen gas under pressure. Essentially it read, Extreme Danger Of Explosion. Do Not Vent.

From his reading, Tom knew that hydrogen gas was highly flammable when mixed with air. Given the size of the machine and the fact that the gas was under pressure, there was probably a shitload of it inside. Fifteen pounds of properly placed C-4 could simultaneously breach the generator shell and the pressurized inner chamber, and ignite the gas, multiplying the explosive potential big-time.

The resulting fireball and shock wave would turn the generator, the turbines and the connecting driveshaft into so much junk. And they were the parts of the system that most likely could not be replaced. They all required precision engineering and metalwork, and large-scale, high-strength castings.

Tom relit the stub of cigar and managed to suck a final few satisfying puffs from it before he flicked away the soggy remains. If he'd thought to bring his harmonica along with him, at that moment he would have been playing and dancing a jig.

He exited the building and retraced his route to the tear in the perimeter fence. As he walked, heading in the direction of *Tempest,* he did the math in his head, adding up how much explosive it would take to ignite the tank farm, flatten the transformer station and blow up the generator.

Seventy pounds of C-4, give or take, he figured would bring the Dark Ages to this little corner of the world.

Chapter Ten

A lesser man than Ryan Cawdor, a man who feared eternal damnation, might have seen his last night on Earth as a preview of hell's coming attractions. The blistering, hammering heat. The pall of sulfurous yellow light thrown from widely spaced electric bulbs. The gut-wrenching melange of decomposition odors. The carpets of rats merrily scampering down the corridor. The sounds of human beings in agony, cursing, moaning, praying. The slow trickle of time passing.

Ryan watched his double sleep, as naked as a baby, on the damp stone floor. The rats gave their cell a wide berth. There were plenty of other, easier meals to be had. For his part, Ryan didn't sleep at all. He didn't even try.

The man of action was forced into inaction, into introspection. There was nothing he could do about his predicament, except to wait for it to play out. He fought down the urge to pace the bars like a wild animal, this to burn off pent-up energy. He wanted to reserve his strength right up to the end, even though he knew it was possible, if not likely, that he would die without being able to put up a fight. He never imagined it would come down to something like that. But then again, he never really thought about how he'd end up being chilled. His attitude had always been: why bother? His whole adult life he'd dealt with shit as it flew at him, without worrying about what might happen the next day, or even the next minute. He was into the brown up to his chin now. On his own, unarmed, vastly outnumbered, in chains, and imprisoned, the chances were damn good that this was the one nasty scrape he wasn't going to walk away from.

During the seemingly endless night, Ryan thought about his son Dean, stolen and lost now perhaps forever, never to be reunited with him. He thought about Krysty and the companions. The people he loved more than anything. He also thought about all the nameless, faceless others he'd chilled, and the legend of violence he was leaving behind. He knew that no matter his intent or the circumstances, he'd be remembered in the Deathlands only by the height of the pile of corpses he'd created.

After uncountable hours had passed, when Chucho finally stirred from sleep, Ryan said to him, "If there's no lock you can't pick, how about opening my cuffs and the cell door?"

"Wouldn't do you any good," Chucho replied as he stretched his arms over his head. "There's only one way in and out of here, and to get past it, you'd have to whip the twenty armed red sashes that guard this place. Before you could do that, they'd call for reinforcements from the fort. You'd never see daylight again. And right now that's my only goal. I've been locked away in this fuck hole for weeks now. I want to see the sun, to feel it on my face one more time before I die."

"You're not giving up?"

"Didn't say that. Our best chance is going to come after nightfall, when we're transported from here to the place of execution. They don't have enough red sashes to control the entire route. If we can break through their ranks and make it into the crowds, we've got a slim hope of getting out of this."

"Need our hands and feet free to do that," Ryan said. "Assuming you can pick the locks on my cuffs, what about yours? They're welded shut."

Chucho turned away for a few seconds. When he turned back, he held the empty cuffs by their connecting chain on a fingertip. "You mean these?" he said.

His wrists and the backs of his hands glistened in the electric light.

Effortlessly, Chucho popped the cuffs back on. "Rat fat," he explained. "The slipperiest *mierda* on the planet."

At once Ryan felt a great weight come off his shoulders. If they could both get out of this hell pit, if they could both get free, they could at least go down fighting instead of being butchered like hogs.

Ryan heard the sounds of distant boots scraping on the stone floor. The noises got louder; they were coming their way.

"They're bringing us a hot breakfast, right?" Ryan said.

Chucho laughed. "If you want *desayuno* in this place, you've got to catch and kill it yourself."

Twelve red sashes lined up in the corridor outside their cell. They stood an arm's length from the bars. They weren't carrying food, but they didn't come empty-handed, either. Four of them held nooses on poles.

A fifth man, who was apparently in charge, shoved a folded length of cloth through the bars to Chucho. After stepping back out of reach, he growled an order to Ryan's mirror image.

"The size of my *culebra* makes these pin-dick red sashes and priests nervous," Chucho said, flashing his white teeth as he wound the material around his waist, covering his nakedness almost to his knees.

The other seven red sashes raised their side-by-side scat-

terguns as the head guy unlocked the cell's iron door. After
the prisoners were made to kneel on the floor, the noose-
bearers entered and securely collared them, front and rear.

As they worked, Ryan sensed that the guards, despite
numbers and firepower, were not all that confident in their advantage. They seemed nervous, and he could smell the rank
fear in their sweat. Under the circumstances, Ryan had
expected the keepers to be more arrogant, more dismissive.
Perhaps contemptuous. But they were none of those things.
They were walking on eggshells.

He and Chucho were led slowly from the cell. A red sash
in front and one behind controlled each of them with the
poles and the airway-closing tension of their integral
garrotes. The rest of the escort didn't bracket the two prisoners. All ten red sashes walked on Ryan's left, which gave
them a clear firing lane and a stone wall for a pellet-and-
splatter backstop. As Ryan and Chucho advanced, hobbled
hand and foot, and collared, twenty shotgun barrels were
aimed at them.

A mobile firing squad.

Their excess of caution made Ryan crack a half smile. He
certainly didn't want to die, but if he had to take the last train
west, he'd be proud to check out beside a man who could
instill such unreasoning, pants-pissing terror in these assholes.

The entourage gradually spiraled up from the bowels of the
ravelin. There were no stairs to climb, just a slight, gradual
grade in the floor. The only sounds were the steady scrape of
boot soles and the rhythmic clanking of ankle chains.

Then a string of words growled in Spanish echoed down
the corridor. Quite loud and distinct, they seemed to come
from the rear of the firing squad escort.

The only phrase Ryan could understand and translate was *"Su mama..."*

Your mother...

Without a preamble of shoving or warning shouts, two of the red sashes immediately dropped their shotguns and started throwing punches at each other's heads.

The procession's advance faltered, then halted. The red sash leader looked around stunned as under a bare bulb full-power blows landed and straw hats went flying. Before anyone could intervene, the two combatants were rolling around on the puddled floor, hands around throats, trying to strangle the life from each other.

The leader bellowed a command and four of the red sashes slung their double-barrels and set to pulling the fighters apart.

Chucho laughed out loud at the show, thoroughly amused by it. He winked at Ryan with his one good eye and said, "Good trick, yes?"

Ryan had to admit it was that.

After a brief scuffle with the peacemakers, the two still-furious men were hauled to their feet. Their faces were bloodied, shirts torn, sashes askew and cowboy hats crumpled. The clearly aggravated red sash leader stationed one of them at the head of the line, the other at the end, then ordered the column to proceed.

Ryan and Chucho were marched through the ravelin's foyer, out the prison's only exit, into the heat and blazing light of the semitropics. From the height of the sun overhead, Ryan figured it had to be close to midmorning already. The red sashes lined up along the fort's ramparts sent up a round of raucous cheers when they appeared. Ryan heard music and drumming coming from that direction, as well.

The procession crossed the bridge over the deep canal that separated the ravelin and the fort. Looking in both directions down the sheltered waterway, Ryan glimpsed crowds of people gathered on the mainland, wildly waving colored pennants and juking giant heads on sticks up and down.

They entered the fort through the door of the cylindrical guardhouse, passed under the massive ramparts and stepped out into the broad compound-parade ground. To the left, on an elevated platform at the far end of the enclosure, the priests were indeed wearing their judge hats: tall, red cones with a matching, glittering fringe that hung down over their faces past their chins like curtains of perpetually spurting blood. They were also doing what Ryan assumed was their special judge dance—weaving serpentine, spiraling, shuffling, while beating on tambourines with what looked like polished human long bones. They were accompanied by an eight-piece band made up of accordion, fiddle, trumpet and congas.

Dressed in a gold-epauletted, white military tunic, the breast laden with rows of bright medals and matching white trousers, Fright Mask oversaw the festivities from a throne behind the judge dancers.

Ryan and Chucho were force-marched to the edge of the dais and there, thanks to the leverage provided by the noose poles, made to kneel in the sun in front of the judges and the governor-general of Veracruz.

Their submission proclaimed the final victory of the Lords of Death.

The red sash audience looking down from the battlements on three sides of the compound absolutely ate it up, yelling, whistling and hooting. Some even fired their shotguns in the air. Ryan could see the sun flashing off the bottles that were being passed around. The red sashes were getting drunk in the middle of the morning on this very special occasion.

After a few minutes the music and awkward dancing stopped, and the spider priest stepped to the edge of the platform, raised his arms to silence the crowd, then unleashed a lengthy preamble, his voice an odd singsong, like a ritual chant.

"What's he saying?" Ryan asked his twin.

Chucho didn't bother to translate the words verbatim. "It's just the usual bullshit," he said. "Itzamna, the head priest, is thanking the Lords of Death for the opportunity to serve them by publicly trying and executing their sworn, ancient enemies from the beginning of time. Namely, you and me."

After another short musical and dance interlude, the spider priest got down to business.

As the lesser priests took their seats on either side of Fright Mask, Itzamna read from a scroll. When he paused after a moment, the other judges beat on their tambourines with the stripped, polished leg bones. This was accompanied by cheers and hoots from the red sash mob. Then the head priest resumed reading. Every time he paused in the oration, the judges hit their tambourines, and the crowd went wild.

"He's listing the charges against us," Chucho informed Ryan. "And then the rest of the priests are voting guilty or not guilty. Beating on the drums means guilty."

"Figured that much," Ryan said. "I want to know what I'm dying for."

"We are accused of disemboweling priests and strangling them with their own guts," Chucho translated. "I only did that once, and I was sorely provoked. We are accused of burning churches to the ground after trapping priests and red sashes inside. Yeah, did that. Blowing up red sash garrisons. Poisoning wells in garrisons. Robbing treasure and payroll caravans. Destroying oil pipelines and a small refinery. Inciting mob violence and rebellion in that mining ville I told you about."

"You did all that, too?"

Chucho grinned.

"What about me?" Ryan said. "What are they accusing me of?"

"Well, since we're the Hero brothers it's sort of a two-for-one thing. You are the *dzul* twin. The white twin. I'm the *indio,* the dark one. Guilt by association, though we're perfect strangers."

"So everything you did to these bastards, I'm getting the blame for?"

"Pretty much. Sorry."

"Don't be. If I'd known about any of this, I'd have done the same as you. Mebbe a lot worse."

As the head priest prattled on, the listed crimes became more and more arcane, both philosophically and metaphysically. Even when translated by Chucho they were unintelligible to Ryan because he couldn't understand the terminology and complex mythological references: White Bone Snake, Black Transformer, Maize God…. It didn't matter what the hell they meant, according to Chucho, because every crime on the list was punishable by death.

The full charges against them took the better part of twenty minutes to read. No surprise, the verdicts were all guilties, punctuated by applause and volleys of shotgun blasts from the surrounding ramparts. Then the head priest recited a last bit from the very end of the scroll, which was further cause for celebration.

"How are we going to be punished?" Ryan said. "How are they going to execute us? Did the priest talk about that?"

"That's what all the noise is about," Chucho replied. "Are you sure you want to know?"

"I don't plan on being around when it's supposed to happen," Ryan said. "I'm just curious about what they have in mind."

"It'll be big fun for the priests, but not so much fun for us," his twin assured him. "First, they'll strip us naked in front of all the *Jarochos* down in the *Zócalo,* then they'll stick quills through our *culebras* to draw out the sacred blood for fire sacrifice. After burning our blood they'll hang us by the neck from the lighthouse parapet, and revive us. They'll do that a few dozen times, until they or the crowd gets bored, whichever comes first. After that, they'll chop off our arms and legs and cauterize the stumps so we don't bleed out. Then they'll cut off our male parts and fry them in hot lard right under our noses. When that's done, they'll open our bellies and yard out our guts."

"And that's how they chill us?"

"Nah, to chill us they'll burn us alive."

The spider priest lowered the scroll, stepped to the edge of the dais and addressed the kneeling prisoners. The crowd went suddenly silent.

Ryan looked over at Chucho expectantly.

"He's asking us if we have anything to say after the verdict and sentence," Chucho told him. "You know, any final words for the world to remember us by. Confessions to other crimes we weren't accused or convicted of. Pleas for mercy from the Lords of Death. Last-second conversions to their sickening, false religion. Itzamna's told us how we're going to die. Now he thinks we're going to grovel and tremble in fear, and thereby amuse the audience even more."

"When it gets dark I'll let my fists and feet do the talking," Ryan said.

"And guns, too, if we can grab some," Chucho said, "but first I've got a few things I want to get off my chest."

When Chucho tried to get up from his knees, his guards wouldn't let him. Displaying amazing strength in his thighs, he slowly rose against the power of the noose poles. Unable to lever him back down, they tried to choke him out. His face turned dark with suffused blood. His remaining eye bulging from the pressure, he stared up at the spider priest and pointed at his mouth.

The priest impatiently waved for the guards to loosen the nooses so he could speak his final words.

When he regained his breath, Chucho addressed the priest, Fright Mask, and the assembled crowd of traitors in a loud, clear voice. Ryan had no idea what he was saying. He might have been giving some kind of defense for his actions; he might have been promising to return as a ghost to haunt them. Everything was calm and peaceful until his very last line, which he directed at all and sundry.

When the red sash audience heard it, they went absolutely crazy. Not just booing and screaming, either. Joy juice bottles rained down on them from the battlements, shattering on the grass and the edge of the dais. Then came the stones, like hail.

Fearing his prisoners would be killed before the officially sanctioned event, the leader of the guards ordered a quick, strategic retreat. Ryan and Chucho were rushed to cover under the red brick colonnade.

"What did you say at the end that made them so nukin' mad?" Ryan said as they ducked into the shade.

Chucho shrugged. "I told them before the night's over I'd be in hell, fucking their grandmothers."

Chapter Eleven

Harmonica Tom Wolf threw back his head and cheered himself hoarse, waving his arms, stamping his boots—he and the thousand other men in straw cowboy hats, white shirts and crimson shoulder sashes. Tom wanted no part of what was being celebrated, but he couldn't risk calling attention to himself by standing sullen and silent while the crowd around him went wild. Not that anyone was looking in his direction at that moment. The militiamen who packed the edges of the fort's ramparts were all staring down at the quadrangle and the two prisoners kneeling there.

Ryan Cawdor was noosed, front and rear, and held down with long poles by two red sashes in front of a low stage at the eastern end of the compound. The prisoner beside him was similarly pinioned and pinned. From a distance, the second man might have been Ryan's twin brother. They had the same rangy, powerful build, the same long dark hair, the same noble bearing, the same black eye patch and scar—only the stranger's battle wound was on the opposite side of his face. After a moment or two it had dawned on Tom that the giant sculpted heads he'd seen the night before hadn't been meant to represent Ryan Cawdor after all; it was the other guy that they depicted, the guy with the missing right peeper. Ryan's running buddies—Krysty, Mildred, J.B., Doc and Jak—were nowhere in sight. There was no telling what had happened to them, or whether they had survived the night.

While the prisoners knelt, a dried-up little walnut of a man in red robes and a pointy red cone hat stood on the edge of the platform and read from a rolled-up piece of paper. His unamplified voice, though high-pitched and shrill, carried well; he was obviously accustomed to public speaking. Every time he paused in his singsong recitation, the seven other men in red hats and robes seated behind him on the stage beat on their tambourines with bone drumsticks, and the crowd cheered approval.

The excitement bordered on frenzy. It was fueled by a blazing sun that beat down on them and by the copious amounts of joy juice being passed from hand to hand. The man standing beside Tom suddenly thrust his shotgun in the air and touched off both barrels at once. The booming report echoed off the walls of the compound before it was lost amid the general clamor. The side of Tom's face went momentarily numb from the blast; he gingerly rubbed his ear, which felt like it had been rammed full of cotton with a barge pole. Scowling at the drunken shooter, Tom fought down the urge to unsling the 12-gauge he had commandeered, and force-feed the idiot its metal-shod butt.

All around him the red sashes began putting in their two cents, chanting a word in Spanish that he translated without any difficulty at all. "Death! Death! Death!"

Tom had no doubt what was going on. He was witnessing a show trial with a verdict that had already been decided. What, if anything, Ryan could have done to deserve this was a mystery to him. Had Cawdor committed some kind of crime against piracy while a prisoner on the Matachìn tug? Had he started a mutiny or a slave rebellion?

The seagoing trader accepted a half-full glass bottle that was shoved into his chest and pretended to take a deep swig from it—pretended because the backwash from a dozen strangers did not appeal to him in the least. Then he passed the joy juice on, wiping his mouth with the back of his hand. In the uniform and carrying the standard red sash firearm, he was invisible. No one even thought to question his right to be there.

Harmonica Tom had no shortage of balls.

But it was balls coupled with brains that had brought him, easy as you please, over the narrow bridge and right through the ancient gates of the island fortress. He had already sized up his red sash opponents as complacent, smug in their power, because just like their Matachìn masters they hadn't been challenged by their fellow citizens or any threat from outside for so long. Even for a homegrown militia, they seemed more than a little disorganized; that was another consequence of having faced no real adversaries in recent memory. Of course, it didn't take much in the way of organization to dominate unarmed shopkeepers and dirt farmers. One thing was for sure, if the red sashes had officers and noncoms, they weren't in charge here. There was no unit cohesion. It was every man for himself.

When the opportunity arose to do a little recce of the fort's interior, knowing that's where Cawdor and the others had been taken the previous night, Tom Wolf had seized it without a moment's hesitation.

Just after daybreak, while he was sawing up kilo-size blocks of C-4 into smaller chunks on his galley table with a predark treasure, his SOG Seal Knife 2000, he had heard heavy footsteps on the deck above. *Tempest* was being boarded. A second later someone pounded on the cockpit door so hard it rattled in its jamb, and the steel wire of the attached booby trap vibrated through its eye-screws all the way down to the PKM's pistol grip.

"*Sí, sí, momentito…*" he called out.

Putting the SOG's blade between his teeth, razor edge out, Tom quickly spread his poncho over the tripod-mounted machine gun at the foot of the cabin's aft stairs. The poncho didn't fully cover the weapon, and it did nothing to hide its obvious contours and upward aimpoint.

Boom-boom-boom! The pounding resumed.

Tom pulled a paper navigation chart over the primer-rigged chunks of plastique he had stacked on the table, then palmed the fixed blade knife.

"*¡La otra puerta!*" he yelled back. "*¡La proa!*"

Overhead, he heard what sounded like two sets of boots tramping hard up the deck for the cabin's forward entrance. Rushing past the staterooms amidship, he vaulted up the steep companionway and unlocked the door. Then he hopped back down to the deck, stepping back to block with his body the view down the corridor, the view of the shrouded machine gun.

The door above him swung outward, bright light spilled in, and a red sash charged down the steps without invitation.

No greeting.

No warning.

As the man descended, Tom noted the missing buttons on the front of his white shirt and a blubbery, hairless brown belly showing in the gap. The straw-hatted, red-sashed intruder held a double-barrel 12-gauge hard to his shoulder as he stepped onto the cabin's deck; his expression seemed inordinately pissed off. The whites of his brown eyes were pink, like he'd been caught out in a sandstorm. He brought with him the stink of joy juice, cheap perfume and recent sex.

The red sash braced his scattergun's butt on his hip, the barrels pointed at Tom's midsection.

As second pair of boots started down the stairs, Tom moved a little to the side to further block the first guy's view into the aft cabin. But the man was looking around much closer to hand. Looking for something small and valuable to steal? Tom thought. For something worth killing him over?

The trader's mind raced, putting together the pieces of his predicament. If there were more red sashes outside, he reasoned, they'd have come aboard, too. They wouldn't be waiting around on the other boats or on the dock. Not while these guys pocketed all the good stuff. If there were others they'd at least be poking around on *Tempest*'s deck. This, Tom decided, was a two-man team.

Almost immediately, the first guy zeroed in on his big stainless-steel Model 625 Smith hanging in its holster from a wall hook.

Shiny.

A leer twisted the red sash's mouth as he reached out to touch the grips. From his expression it was evident that he'd already picked out his prize. And from his body language, he figured Tom, like everyone else hereabouts, was going to be too cowed to try to stop him from taking it.

The second man was already a third of the way down the companionway, which was so steep he could see hardly anything of the cabin below him, just the foot of the stairs and the deck.

Tom darted past the first guy as the other man's boot began to come down on the next tread; just before it touched, he hooked it with the heel with his hand, sweeping the leg outward. The second red sash fell over backward and dropped; as he fell, the back of his head bounced hard off the edges of the steps behind him.

Thud, thud, thud, thud.

Tom let the SOG's no-slip Zytel grip drop into his palm, and driving with his legs as he pivoted, he sent a savage, sixty-degree upward thrust into the base of the other man's skull. Bone yielded like so much cardboard, crunching as the knife's razor point penetrated his brain pan. It was the kind of full-power strike that demanded a hand guard—without it Tom's fingers would have slid down the blade's edge, themselves cut to the bone.

For a moment Tom held the man by the left shoulder and by the steel rammed into the back of his head, then he shifted his weight onto the balls of his feet and rammed the guy face-first into the bulkhead, using his full body weight from behind to further drive in the blade. With a second, sickening crunch, it slipped in all the way to the hilt.

As the red sash's bowels released, one more nasty fragrance was added to the man's stench.

The elapsed time was no more than five seconds.

Tom let the man slip to the deck and turned toward the other guy, who was lying on his back at the foot of the stairs. Despite his own head injury, red sash Number Two was trying to pull it together. His eyes were only half focused, and his fingers fumbled weakly next to his hip as he tried to get hold of the pistol grip of his double barrel which had fallen to one side.

Perhaps he was a nice guy when he was off red sash duty.

Perhaps he had a wife and ten kids.

Perhaps he liked dogs.

It didn't matter.

Tom knee-dropped all 185 pounds of himself onto the front of the man's exposed throat, one blow that crushed the larynx like an eggshell.

The body under him jolted at the impact. After a momentary pause, there was a shrill whistling sound. With all his strength the red sash was trying to breathe, but despite the effort was only managing to suck a tiny, utterly insufficient wisp of air through the squashed passage and into his lungs.

As Tom stood, the guy clawed at his own ruined throat. His face rapidly went purple, then black, his eyes bulged, his mouth agape, tongue protruding, heels drumming frantically on the deck. After a minute or so he stopped moving. The extreme tension in his body just slipped away.

Tom ran up the steps, pulled the companionway door shut and locked it. He descended to the bottom stair and sat on it, gasping for breath.

Then he saw the first guy was bleeding around the hilt of the knife, and it was dripping onto the deck mat.

"Shit!" he said. He jumped up and grabbed the man by the back of his shirt collar and dragged him to the main stateroom's head. He opened the shower stall door and shoved the man in, positioning his wound so it dripped into the floor drain.

Getting the seven inches of SOG out was a lot harder than sticking it in. Tom had to stand on the back of man's neck and work the handle back and forth to widen the entry wound and dislodge the blade. When he pulled the knife free, blood spurted out in a gusher.

And continued to spurt.

The red sash's heart was still beating.

Tom wiped off his knife on the tails of the white shirt. The coppery odor of blood mixed with all the other smells in the enclosed space made him want to puke. Holding his breath, he turned on the shower bilge pump to send the gore over the side and into the bay. He knew he couldn't risk dragging the bodies up on deck in broad daylight. He was going to have to wait until after dark to get rid of them. And there was room in the shower stall for two, if he piled the dead men on top of each other.

Back in the corridor, as he prepared to haul the second corpse out of sight, he heard sounds of activity outside. Not on his boat, not on the boats it was rafted to, but on the dock and street beyond. There were loud voices. There was laughing. Car horns honked.

It sounded like another parade.

When Tom popped up on deck for a quick look, he saw scads of red sashes trooping toward the fort. Hundreds and hundreds of them. They weren't marching in orderly ranks; they were a raucous mob.

That's when it had occurred to him that he could join the party with minimal risk to his central goal: payback for Padre Island. Based on his recce of the night before, blowing up the power plant looked like it was going to be a piece of cake. He figured if Ryan and his companions were still alive this morning and he could pinpoint the location where they were being held, there was a chance he could rescue them in the chaos that was sure to come after he turned off the lights.

At least he could try to rescue them. Considering who they were and what they had endured, considering he had been in-strumental in getting them into this mess in the first place, he owed them that much.

Tom stripped off the dead man's white shirt and red sash

before depositing his body in the shower. The other guy had bled out from his head wound by that time, so he shut off the bilge pump.

After putting on the shirt and sash, he uncovered the PKM and double-checked the selector switch to make sure he was leaving the booby trap set, the weapon ready to fire. With the dead man's straw hat pulled low on his forehead, he gathered up the dropped scattergun and climbed the forward companionway onto the bow deck. He locked the door behind him, then joined the happy throng that was headed to the fort.

That had been almost two hours ago.

Two hours in the broiling sun, pretending to be jubilant.

On the platform below him now, the priest read from the tail end of the scroll. Tom's ear for Spanish was improving slightly, enough at least to gather that Ryan and his look-alike were both going to be executed after nightfall.

Something that pleased the crowd no end.

Their attitude changed when Ryan's double rose up from his knees, overpowering the two men that held him tethered. The moment of triumph instantly deflated. The red sashes around Tom groaned, grumbled and shook their heads in dismay. They didn't want an exhibition of strength and courage in the face of death, they wanted the prisoner to stay on his knees.

Ryan's twin began to speak, rapidly and without a hint of fear in his voice. Because of the speed of the speech, and the way the man ran his phrases together, Tom could only pick out scattered words here and there. There was a delay while his brain recovered the meaning of the ones he recognized, but by then the double was fifty words ahead.

Instead of racking his brain trying to figure out what the

guy was saying, Tom concentrated on the way he was saying it. The look-alike didn't act like a prisoner, despite the chains. He held himself proudly erect and he turned from side to side, addressing the enemies that packed both sides of the battlements. He was defiant, unbroken, unrepentant even though he was helpless and, it would seem, doomed. Tom found the reaction of the militiamen milling around him very strange. It was obvious that they considered the condemned man a threat, larger than life, even under these circumstances.

The double's last sentence was spoken very slowly and very painstakingly enunciated, word by word. So slowly and so plainly that even Tom could understand it.

A shudder of shock passed through the throng, as if they had been bitch-slapped in unison, this while Tom had to bite his lip to keep from laughing out loud.

Talk about big balls! The look-alike had them.

Meanwhile, Tom's fellow red sashes went berserk. Screaming in outrage, they unleashed a wild fusillade of joy juice bottles. The rain of breaking glass came from the battlements on both sides of the central compound. The prisoners and their red sash guards immediately covered their heads with their arms. One of the guards was struck in the back of the neck. The bottle burst on impact, his straw hat went flying, and he dropped as though he'd been head-shot.

The red sashes around Tom who found themselves without bottles to throw scrambled to pick up rocks from the ground. They fought over the pebbles.

It was clear to Tom that the men guarding the prisoners were unprepared for this eventuality; for a full minute they stood frozen in place. It was lucky for them and for the prisoners that there weren't that many loose stones lying around on the walkways. But Tom figured it was only matter of time before it was shotgun pellets instead of rocks and bottles flying down.

Finally the guards got themselves organized and hurried the prisoners through the red brick colonnade that Tom stood atop. All the red sashes, Tom included, rushed to the opposite side of the battlements. Ryan and his mirror image reappeared almost directly below them, collared, noosed, and hustled as fast as their ankle chains would allow onto the footbridge and toward a windowless, gray, stone block building that squatted on a shaved-flat atoll of coral.

The crowd yelled curses and taunts at the running men. Bottles shattered on the bridge's stone rails and splashed into the water on either side. When shotguns started booming along the battlements Tom winced, but the discharges were aimed at the canal, not the condemned.

After the entourage disappeared safely through the arched portal of the prison, the crowd continued to yell and jump up and down, this in celebration of their sending helpless prisoners running for cover, running for their lives. The militiamen actually believed they had just won a victory for their side.

For his part, Harmonica Tom stifled the urge to yawn. At least now he knew where Ryan was being held, and he had a rough idea how many hours he had left to figure out a way to free him.

After fifteen minutes of celebration, the red sashes started filing out of the fort. Tom went with the flow, accepting countless back-slap congratulations, pretending to cheer with the others.

As he retraced his route over the narrow footbridge to the mainland, he had a momentary unflattering thought. He could

just keep going. He could back *Tempest* from its mooring in
broad daylight, sail out of the bay and dump the corpses at
sea. He could let the legend of Ryan Cawdor die here.

Tom considered the idea for about three seconds, then dis-
carded it. Aside from the responsibility he felt for Cawdor and
the companions, aside from his hatred for the Matachìn and
their minions, it occurred to him how much larger his own
legend would grow if he swooped in and saved the one-eyed
warrior from execution.

Being legendary was bad for the health, but good for
business.

It made folks think twice about back-stabbing and double-
dealing. Besides, Tom liked the idea of giving a man like
Ryan his life back. And his twin, too. Another bred-in-the-
bone ass-kicker. If he could, he would free them both, along
with the other companions.

After he crossed the bridge, he stepped out of the flow of
the mob, which was headed back toward Veracruz to prepare
for the execution, and walked around the edge of the stone
quay. The channel between the fort and the prison looked deep
enough for *Tempest*'s keel, but because of the connecting
footbridge and the height of his ship's masts, it had to be a
motor-in, back-out situation. And the necessary left turn was
very tight for a forty-foot sloop. In the dark and in a hurry,
there was a big risk, if not a likelihood, of grounding the ship
in the attempt.

Tom completely circled the ravelin on the peninsula side,
confirming the fact that there was just one way in and one way
out: through the arched portal on the far side of the footbridge.

A tough nut to crack.

Particularly if he wanted to get away with a whole skin.

When Tom returned to *Tempest,* he saw he had more visitors. Very short ones. Half a dozen children were sitting on the port deck with their legs hanging over the side. Ages about seven to ten, four boys and two girls, they were laughing, pushing at one another, and throwing rocks at something in the water below.

First thing Tom thought was the red sash he'd weighted down with concrete blocks had popped to the surface. A floater.

Not a good thing.

Tom boarded *Tempest* and walked up behind the kids, looking down over their heads into the water.

There was no floating corpse. Just three big-ass sharks swimming around in tight circles less than a yard from the bilge pump's exit pipe. The twelve-foot-long hammerheads had been attracted by the blood he'd put in the water.

"¡Bastante!" he told the little rock chuckers. The kids looked surprised and very disappointed that their fun was at an end. They were even more disappointed when he gently but firmly shooed them off his boat.

Tom looked down at the hammerheads. He wondered if they'd already located the other guy's body. If not yet, they would soon. And when they did, how long would it take for sharks of that size to tear his legs off? A minute? Two minutes? Or to chew through the leather shoulder-sling tether that kept him connected to the concrete blocks? Ten seconds? Would the corpse then stay trapped under the keels of the rafted boats? Or would it slip out into the bay? Like a drifting log, a place for seagulls to rest and preen. It was too late to do anything about it now. He certainly wasn't going to go over the side to make sure the body was where he left it.

Looking over his shoulder, he saw the kids had wandered off down the road. Tom climbed across the rafted boats to the dock. He walked over to the ruined warehouse and picked up a pair of scavenged concrete blocks from a palette.

When it got dark enough to dump the other bodies over the side, he would use chain to fasten the ankle weights. Something sharks couldn't bite through.

Chapter Twelve

Krysty's body was simultaneously pressed into the bunk bed mattress and jolted by a muffled impact. The latter awakened her from her stupor for a half second; as she slipped back into a black pit of exhausted sleep, it happened again. The yawning lurch. The crushing weight of g-force. Punctuated by a bone-jarring thud.

In the back of her mind she knew something important had changed; something was wrong. Then she realized the constant rumble of the black ship's diesel had disappeared; it had been replaced by the loud hiss of the hull knifing through the sea and the whistle of the wind gusting through the stays.

They were under sail.

As the schooner plowed through oncoming seas, Krysty forced her eyelids open, then with an effort, focused on her surroundings. There were no windows in the cabin she shared with Mildred. The walls were featureless sheet steel. The only light came from a caged bulb in the center of the ceiling.

Rising groggily to her feet, Krysty tried to rouse Mildred who was out cold on the upper bunk. The doctor didn't wake at the sound of her name. There was a stripe of a white crystalline substance, like sugar grains, across her brown cheek. Mildred had been drooling in her sleep.

Putting a hand on her shoulder, Krysty gave a gentle shake.

Nothing.

Then a harder shake.

Mildred moaned and slowly opened her eyes.

As the ship climbed the back of a wave, Krysty's legs suddenly went weak in the knees and her head started to spin. Very much alarmed, she steadied herself by gripping the edge of Mildred's bunk.

What she was feeling made no sense. Krysty had been stuck on board ship for many weeks, and had been exposed to the elements in a variety of unpleasant sea and wind states. She was accustomed to the rolling motion and the violent wave impacts. She knew whatever it was, it wasn't seasickness. This sensation was entirely different. She wasn't sick to her stomach. Her mind and her coordination were what was impaired: her thinking muddled, her limbs tangle-footed. It was all she could do *not* to creep back into her bunk and pull the covers over her head.

Clinging to the bed frame, Krysty realized with a shock that she had no idea how much time had passed since she and Mildred had crawled into their respective bunks. Time was the vital element; Ryan's life depended on it.

The last thing she remembered was breakfast, although she couldn't recall how long ago that had been. She and Mildred had been served tall, hot stacks of golden-brown pancakes, drizzled with melted butter and some kind of sweet brown syrup, with separate bowls heaped with crisp strips of bacon.

She remembered how good the food had smelled and tasted. She had been so hungry. Barely awake, she had gobbled it down, hand over fist. Mildred had attacked her food with the same enthusiasm. They had eaten like starving animals.

Now Krysty was hungry again. Her stomach's rumbling and gurgling was her only gauge of the elapsed time.

Three hours to digest?

Mebbe four?

Could it be past noon already? she thought in growing despair.

Mildred pushed up to a wobbly sitting position on her bunk, bracing herself against the impacts with a hand pressed to the cabin wall. "The diesel has stopped," she said thickly, her eyes still closed.

"Sounds and feels like we've picked up some real speed," Krysty said. "They must have all the sheets up."

Mildred opened her eyes. "How long have we been running with the wind?" she asked. "How long have we been asleep?"

Krysty read her thoughts. They were the same desperate, anguished thoughts that she had.

That they might already be too late to save Ryan.

"I don't know," she replied. "I just woke up."

"Oh, God," Mildred groaned. She let her face fall into her manacled hands.

"What is it?"

"The wind's hard behind us now," Mildred told her. "Don't you see? No matter how far south we've come, to retrace our route and return to Veracruz we're going to have to beat back against it. We're going to have to zigzag, tacking back and forth the whole way. It'll take us twice as long to cover the same ground, maybe longer."

Krysty felt her knees go soft again; her head was spinning. She had to clutch the bed frame harder to keep from falling. Had she and the companions been kidding themselves all along? Thinking that they actually had the power to do something to save Ryan? Had they chosen to ignore the real extent of their predicament and his because it was too horrible for them to deal with? Had they clung to a comfortable lie because it had gotten them through the night?

The awful truth was now staring Krysty full in the face.

No predark whitecoat technical wonder, no mat-trans system, no airship, not even a high-speed, gasoline-powered watercraft was going to pull this rabbit out of a hat. There was no way to reverse the impending course of events. Time and circumstance had finally conspired to defeat them.

If Ryan's survival depended on the companions' help, he was doomed.

Krysty sagged against the bunk frame. The love of her life was gone forever. Her prehensile hair drew up into curls around her neck, ears and temples, withdrawing to seek safety and comfort from the gnawing pain.

"This is the end of everything," she told Mildred, her voice catching and breaking on the last word. Tears rolled from the corners of her emerald-green eyes; her lower lip and chin began to quiver uncontrollably. She was losing it and she didn't care. "This is the end of us."

Mildred put a hand on Krysty's shoulder and squeezed. "We've got to go back after him," she said. "No matter how long it takes to get there. We've got to take over this ship and go back for him."

Krysty just stared at her, the tears still falling freely.

"We can't grieve over a death that hasn't happened yet," Mildred said. "And may never happen. You're letting your exhaustion get the better of you. You've got to keep fighting it. We all have to. Until we go back and see for ourselves, we won't know whether they really killed him or not. Anything is possible. We can't count Ryan out. Not ever. No matter the odds."

"I know that."

"He wasn't counting on our help to get away."

"I know that, too." Krysty backhanded the wetness on her cheeks and with an effort took hold of herself.

"We have to focus all our attention on turning the ship around," Mildred said. "That's our goal. And to reach it, first we've got to get out of these shackles."

"You're right, of course, you're right," Krysty said, nodding. Then another wave of weakness struck, this time even more severe. She shut her eyes and hung on for dear life until it passed. "Damn it, Mildred," she said, "why am I feeling so dizzy? And why am I so hungry?"

"I don't feel so great, either," the doctor admitted. "And I could eat my own boot sole right now if I had something to cut it up with. It's probably just a side effect of the starvation. We've been without full rations for weeks while rowing our butts off. All of a sudden we're eating our fill and doing nothing. Our bodies don't know how to react to the change. That plus the accumulated exhaustion and stress, mixed in with the roll of a strange ship. I think whatever it is, it'll pass quickly."

"It better happen soon."

Krysty didn't bring up the possibility of using her Gaia power to break the shackles. Nor did Mildred. They both knew it was an absolute, last gasp resort. Krysty was drained as it was. Tapping into that vast energy source would incapacitate her completely, making her a burden instead of an asset in the takeover of the ship.

A wave impact slammed Krysty's hipbones against the

edge of the bunk so hard it made her moan in pain. Since she had gotten out of bed, there had been a distinct change in the ship's movement. The yaw and pitch of the deck had become more extreme, the vibrations of the hull as it slammed into wave troughs much stronger. The sound of the wind outside had grown louder; it shrieked through the lines. The seas were getting bigger, steeper, more jumbled. The weather was definitely worsening.

Then the cabin's door bolts clacked back. The door swung open, revealing the two female whitecoats. They stood in the corridor, their short legs braced against the roll of the deck, swaying back and forth as they bore trays of food. They were grinning to beat the band. White teeth. Sparkling black eyes.

So happy.

They stepped into the cabin and uncovered the plates they carried, releasing trapped spicy and oh-so-enticing aromas. The meal consisted of some kind of shredded meat—beef or pork—rolled up in corn tortillas and smothered in a deep red sauce and melted gobs of white cheese. On the side of the plate was a big dollop of squashed-up beans, again topped with melted cheese.

Mildred thanked the little women in Spanish as she accepted the plate and fork they handed up to her bunk.

The smell of the food close up made Krysty's mouth water. She couldn't hold herself back. She held the plate up to her chin and shoveled it down, groaning with pleasure, hardly pausing for breath. She and Mildred scraped the metal plates with the edges of their forks to get the last drops of sauce and melty cheese.

The whitecoats poured them cups of water to wash it down with.

As Krysty finished a second cup, Mildred tried to engage the women in conversation. She spoke at length in their language, asking questions, but they didn't say a word in return. They just smiled and nodded at her, and smiled at each other.

Mebbe they were under orders not to speak to us, Krysty thought. Then her mind turned to other, more important things. She and Mildred needed to open their wrist and ankle cuffs; that was the first order of business. To do that, they needed a tool, something to pick the lock with.

Something metal.

As Krysty stacked the licked-clean plates on top of each other, while Mildred held the whitecoats' attention with rapid-fire Spanish, she managed to sneak out her fork and slip it up her sleeve.

The merry little whitecoats didn't seem to notice the missing utensil when they took away the plates and cups.

Krysty waited until they had closed and locked the door from the outside before showing Mildred the prize.

"That just might do it," the physician said.

"Needs a bit of a minor adjustment first," Krysty said. She used the face of the steel bed frame to carefully bend three of the tines over and out of the way, forming a makeshift lock pick with the fourth. "Try to hold your feet still."

Krysty inserted the fork tine into the ankle manacle's keyhole and Mildred dangled her legs off the edge of the top bunk. The way the boat was sloshing around, it wasn't easy to hit the target.

After a few moments of fumbling around in the keyhole to no effect, Krysty had to stop and straighten. Lowering her head combined with the motion of the ship had made the dizziness return.

"Did you ask the whitecoats what time it is?" Krysty said.

"I asked them several times. They wouldn't answer. They just giggled. Strangest whitecoats I've ever seen."

"You need to hold your feet still."

Mildred pressed her hands against her shins, pinning her heels to the bed frame.

Krysty got the tine back inside the keyhole and began digging around, trying to trip the mechanism.

After a minute or two she was forced to stop again. "This isn't working," she told Mildred. "We're bouncing around too much. I can't get pressure on the latch with the point of the pick. It keeps slipping off."

"Let me jump down off here, then," Mildred said. "If I sit on your bunk, it'll give you a better angle and I can hold my feet flat on the bed. It should make it easier for you to work."

Mildred climbed down and hopped onto the lower bunk. Krysty sat on the edge of the bed and resumed poking around inside the keyhole. The change in position offered only a slight improvement. Every time the ship bottomed out in a wave trough, Krysty had to start over.

Mildred's eyes slowly closed, her breathing deepened, and her head dropped to her chest. When her chin hit her breastbone, she woke up with a start. "Oops, conked out there for a minute."

"Are you okay?"

Mildred adjusted a pillow behind her back. "Yeah, I just need to get a little more comfortable."

In seconds, Mildred was sound asleep and snoring.

Krysty kept working on the lock, but to no avail. It got harder and harder to find the pressure point inside the mechanism. She worked until she was too sleepy to concentrate. Then she had to stop.

And when she did, she, too, almost immediately fell asleep. She came to with a jerk when the ship did another resounding bellyflop. Krysty realized she was on the verge of passing out. She had the presence of mind to hide the fork inside the top of her boot before that happened.

She looked up at the top bunk. It might as well have been Mount Everest. No way could she make it up there. Krysty crawled in beside Mildred on the narrow mattress and the moment she closed her eyes she was dead to the world.

Chapter Thirteen

From the depths of the sweltering dungeon came the chant "Chu-cho, Chu-cho, Chu-cho." On the eve of the execution of Ryan's double, the other prisoners were saluting him. There were no red sash guards wandering the corridors to make them shut up. Nobody cared what they said or what they did inside the squalor of their cavelike cells. They were already ghosts.

But they were passionate ghosts.

And their standard-bearer was about to take the last train west.

Then the chanting turned to spirited singing and clapping. Ragged, off-key, out-of-time, the rousing, oompah-pah ballad echoed through the half darkness. Ryan could pick out his cell mate's name in the refrain, over and over again.

"What's all that about?" Ryan asked.

"It's the story of my very first revenge against the priests and red sashes put to music," Chucho replied.

"Touching."

Chucho shrugged. "They are my people and they love me, but they don't really know me. They only know my legend, the myth I created. They are in love with a man I fashioned out of smoke."

"Sounds like you did a hell of a job."

"No, it wasn't me who made it happen," Chucho said. "My people gave it substance because they needed so badly for it to be true. We have endured far too much, for far too long at the hands of the Atapul dynasty. I supplied the hope, they put the flesh on it and pumped it full of blood."

Gradually the strains of the song lost steam and faded away. Though the dungeon's background noises returned to scattered moans and screams for help, and pleas for a merciful death, there were occasional shouts of Chucho's name and "Viva!"

Ryan figured they'd been back in the cell five or six hours, which meant it had to be getting on to evening outside. His thoughts returned to Krysty, J.B., Doc, Mildred and Jak, dragged off to who knew where, for who knew what. He and the companions had been separated before, and by even greater distances and obstacles. But never as prisoners. Always one or the other had had their freedom and room to operate.

Under the circumstances how lost, how vulnerable would they be without him? Could they pull it together aboard ship to escape and save themselves? Ryan felt an uncomfortable twinge of doubt. The Matachìn were not only accustomed to handling slaves, they had made a science out of it, using restraints, starvation and physical and mental exhaustion, and a minimum number of enforcers to get the job done. Their method left no wiggle room whatsoever. In the three weeks the companions had been captives at sea, there hadn't been a single moment when the tables could have been turned. Ryan flat out didn't know if his friends could survive, let alone find a way to free themselves. And the not-knowing sat like a ten-pound cannonball in the pit of his stomach.

Chucho nudged him with an elbow and broke his unhappy train of thought.

Ryan's double produced a sliver of bone about two inches long. "Let me see to your shackles," he said.

"If you take them off me now, the red sashes are bound to notice."

"Don't worry, I'll show you."

With deft flicks of the pick, Chucho unlocked Ryan's wrist and ankle cuffs. The manacles dropped with a clank to the damp stone floor. For the first time in weeks Ryan was able to take a stride longer than two feet. He paced the width of the cell, stretching his legs.

"Now we have to put them back on."

Chucho lifted the hem of the cloth wrapped around his waist and teased out a bunch of the four-foot-long threads. He closed the cuffs back around Ryan's ankles and secured them in that position with winds of thread that in the dim light were almost invisible. Outside, at night, they would be invisible. Chucho did the same with the wrist cuffs. "When you want the shackles to come off," he told Ryan, "just pull the chains between them tight and the threads will break. Be careful, though, don't stretch the chains too much when they're walking us out of here. We don't want them to fall away before we're ready to make our move."

Ryan heard distant boots scraping on the stone floor, headed their way. Then the prisoners started yelling, stamping their feet and rattling their bars. It sounded like feeding—or breeding—time at a mutie zoo.

"Are they coming for us now?" Ryan said.

Chucho smiled and shook his head. "No, the red sashes are bringing the condemned their last meal. Our fellow prisoners can smell the goodies. That's why they are making such a fuss."

"Must smell pretty damn good, then."

"Compared to raw rat butt hole, anything smells good."

Four red sashes approached the outside of the cell. One held a pair of big ceramic bowls; one held a pair of glass bottles; two carried scatterguns. The gunners poked their shouldered weapons through the bars, giving the food-bearers cover as they opened the door and set the meal on the floor.

Ryan did a visual inventory from the far side of the cell: whole roasted chickens, potatoes, maybe tomatoes, some other vegetables, and beakers of something red to drink, probably wine.

After leaving the food within reach, the red sashes backed out of the cell and relocked the door. They didn't stick around to watch the condemned eat. They left without uttering a word.

Ryan could smell the food from ten feet away, and it smelled wonderful. He wasn't the only one who caught wind of it. As soon as the food-bearers took their leave, rats came hipping and hopping down the corridor. First in ones and twos, then in dozens. They milled anxiously just beyond the bars, wanting to rush in and have it, but they were afraid of the light and the prisoners inside.

Ryan hadn't eaten for a very long time. He hadn't eaten well for even longer. He made a beeline for the food before the rats summoned up the necessary courage. With his bare hands he ripped a leg and thigh from one of the chicken carcasses and with the juices running down his forearm was about to stuff most of it into his mouth when Chucho stopped him with a hand.

"Don't eat it," he said.

"Because they spit in it?" Ryan countered. "Who gives a damn?"

"Not spit."

"Piss? Who cares?" Ryan tried to raise the chicken to his mouth, but Chucho stopped him again.

"No," Chucho insisted.

"Come on, you're not telling me they shit in it!"

"No, they added *las opiatas. Morfina.* Drugs to make us weak as kittens. So we don't try to escape and so we don't fight so hard when they torture us."

"I figured they'd want us screaming in pain," Ryan said, tossing the untouched chicken back into the bowl in disgust. "Screaming is always a big crowd pleaser."

"Oh, we would still scream," Chucho assured him. "We'd scream our heads off. The drugs don't stop a person from feeling pain. You still feel everything they do to you. You just can't do anything about it. It makes the victims easier for the executioners to deal with, to move around. Like meat puppets with lungs."

Chucho used a foot to nudge the bowls even closer to the bars, until they were actually touching them. Then he backed away. He motioned for Ryan to move with him to the rear of the cell.

Sensing their opportunity, the bravest of the rats moved in. At first they stuck their heads between the bars, nibbling furtively over the rims of the bowls. Those who were edged out grew bolder and entered the cell to get an open spot at the troughs. In a minute or two, they were eating in a competitive frenzy and their fellows, in droves, were scampering down the corridor to join them.

Chucho signaled Ryan to wait, to have patience.

It didn't take long. All of a sudden one of the feeding rats did a two-foot back flip, landed belly up with its legs and tail twitching feebly.

It was ignored by the others, and a new rat quickly moved in to take the empty place.

Ryan watched as rats started falling over, one by one. The growing mass of the fallen didn't stop those behind from sampling the food. Soon the bowls and a surrounding section of stone floor were covered by a pile of furry unconscious bodies.

Laughing, Chucho approached ground zero, which sent the still hungry survivors scurrying out of the cell and down the hall. He started gathering up the rats, two by two. Using threads from his garment he securely tied their tails together, and then flipped them back out in the corridor. He worked quickly, giving the impression this was not the first time he had pulled the trick.

"When they wake up, won't they be surprised?" he said to Ryan as he cinched his knots tight, making a critter with eight legs and two heads, legs and heads pointing in the opposite direction. "They won't be able to bite their tails off to escape. To get away they'll try to kill one another. If one of them succeeds, it will have to drag the corpse of the other behind it."

Ryan didn't say anything. It seemed like a lot of effort for a childish joke. Mebbe it was a cultural thing. Mebbe Chucho really hated rats.

Once again other prisoners started calling to their hero from the darkness down the hallway.

Ryan couldn't understand what they were saying and his double didn't translate. Ignoring the unintelligible back and forth, he asked Chucho, "So, when is our execution going to happen?"

"Who knows? Things never happened on time here even before the Matachìn showed up. The red sash traitors are very disorganized. There is much to be done in preparation, and they are probably still busy drinking to get up their courage to watch us die. They have to set up security along the parade route."

"What if they take us to the city in separate trucks?" Ryan said. "That will make escape much more difficult."

"They won't do that. Two trucks would be harder to protect. More work."

Then Ryan caught the scrape of more bootsteps, again coming their way. "Are they coming back for the plates?" he asked Chucho.

"I don't think so. Listen…"

Ryan heard a different kind of rhythmic chanting. This was joyless, monotonal grunting; it sounded like a funeral dirge. Then came the unmistakable metallic rattle of tambourines, the same musical instrument he'd seen in the hands of the priests.

"I think it's time," Chucho said. "They are coming for us. We have to pretend we're drugged. Keep your head down and don't make any fast movements. Keep to the shadows as much as you can. Do whatever they tell you, but do it slowly."

With that, Ryan's double picked up the remaining food and dumped most of it into the cell's toilet, a rusting, galvanized bucket. He poured the wine into the bucket, too, then put the empty bowls and bottles back in plain sight.

Ryan stood gripping the cell's bars, looking down the low-ceilinged hall. He could see the execution detail approaching. The priests were in the lead, all eight of them, swaying in unison as they chanted and shuffled along under the weak electric light. Some of them swung incense burners beside their ankles. Behind them was Fright Mask, and behind him was a contingent of red sash guards. They came to a halt outside the cell.

The governor-general of Veracruz stepped forward, stopping at the other side of the bars. Despite Chucho's warning to stay back, Ryan stood his ground; he did half close his eye and pretended to be using the bars to hold himself upright.

As he had earlier in the day, Generalissimo al Modo wore the white uniform, the high pile of dreads in their golden cage. He was also carrying a gold-scabbarded, pearl-handled saber with pommel tassel. The corridor's stark lighting made the deformations of his face seem all the more exaggerated, and horrifying. Ryan assumed the oral surgery had done something untoward to his salivary glands—Fright Mask was drooling between his golden fangs. Long strands of clear slime swayed off his chin.

Up close the general's eyes radiated something that struck Ryan as very strange. He didn't get the sense that there was a person trapped and peeking out from behind that hideously sculpted, permanent grin. It was like some other kind of creature was looking out at him. Something alien, perhaps not of this earth. Something that had traveled to places where human beings were never supposed to go. And done things there that human beings were never supposed to do.

At Fright Mask's signal, the priests advanced. Keeping well back from the bars, the men in the pointed hats and bleeding veils began their ritual, which consisted of mumbling punctuated by the occasional shout, a shuffling line dance, and the fanning of incense into the doomed men's cell.

To Ryan it smelled like burning hair.

He stepped back from the pall of noxious smoke, moving

slowly as Chucho had suggested. He moved to the rear wall, beside his cell mate. In a whisper, out of the corner of his mouth, Ryan asked Chucho what was going on.

"They are preparing us for sacrifice to the Atapuls," the look-alike hissed back. "This is the priests' purifying ritual."

"How about giving us a purifying bath?"

"It's a spiritual cleansing," Chucho said. "It doesn't require soap and water. We don't smell too bad compared to the Matachìn."

"Yeah, they work hard at it."

Amid the clouds of burning hair smoke, the spider priest, Itzamna, whipped out a clutch of pale tubular objects.

Ryan nudged Chucho.

"They're bird quills," his double informed him, "plucked from sea eagles' wings."

Ryan estimated they were ten inches long and a quarter inch in diameter.

Itzamna leaned down, stuck his head next to the nearest censer, sucked in a mouthful of hair smoke, then puckered up and blew it through one of the quills. The smoke didn't just come out the far end; it also seeped out through a series of holes drilled along the top of its length.

Chucho continued the hushed explanation. "He's blessing the pointed instruments they're shortly going to push cross-wise through our limp dicks. The holes they've drilled allow the blood to drip into the hollow tube and out the lower end."

"Then what?" Ryan said, grimacing.

"They'll smear the collected blood on parchment and burn it in a sacred pot for the Lords of Death. Since they are far away in Xibalba, they won't be present in spirit or flesh at our executions, so the priests are sending them an offering—

and an announcement of the proceedings—they can smell and taste."

"A smoke signal."

"That will reach all the way to the Underworld."

When the priests finished, Fright Mask addressed the prisoners.

In hushed tones, Chucho translated. "It's pre-execution boilerplate. He says he represents the civil authority of Veracruz. His power is granted directly from the god of gods, the Great One, himself, Atapul X, who has ordained a proper punishment for the numerous crimes of which we've been convicted. Atapul X who controls the great city-states. Who controls the navies. Who controls the seeds of plague. Who is responsible for all human suffering. Who takes that suffering as his due. Who considers human beings to be his personal playthings."

Ryan noticed that during the delivery of the speech the governor-general's drooling had taken on epic proportions. The threads of slobber trailed more than two feet from his chin, their globular ends swinging back and forth like pendulums. The glistening strands were absolutely mesmerizing. The more Fright Mask talked, the longer they grew.

Ryan caught himself wondering how long the damned things could get. Could they drip all the way to the floor without breaking?

The governor-general looked like a ravening beast. Had the Lords of Death made him so? Had he begged them to be horribly altered, or was it a requirement of the office he held? Or had his Masters done it on a whim? And how exactly had they managed to make the changes without killing him in the process? Some arcane, predark whitecoat sleight of hand no doubt. Ryan imagined more man-beasts just like him, sitting atop each of the thrones of the other subject city-states. Moving a jaw and face so distorted had to involve constant, perhaps excruciating discomfort. The upper and lower jaws couldn't be closed because of the size and position of the artificial fangs.

Some price to pay for power.

Fright Mask directed a stream of vitriol at Ryan's cell mate.

"He says I've been a thorn in the side of order and civilization for too long," Chucho told him. "How the world is going to be a better place without me. Justice for all the red sashes and priests I've killed."

From somewhere deep in the prison, the Chucho song started up again. Very faint at first, then louder and louder as other prisoners joined in.

Fright Mask recognized the words and melody, because he instantly stiffened. He turned and shouted something down the corridor.

Ryan guessed it was shut up or die.

Despite the threat, or because they understood the limits of their oppressors' power under the circumstances, the prisoners kept singing.

Some of the red sashes hurried off to try to enforce their commander's order for silence. A futile gesture, as the singers in one corridor might stop while others elsewhere in the dungeon picked up the refrain.

Meanwhile, Fright Mask addressed more drooling diatribe at the central subject of the popular folk song. The remaining red sashes found gratifying whatever it was their leader said. They smiled and nodded. However, the tirade didn't have any noticeable effect on Chucho.

Ryan was surprised at that. He half expected an angry outburst from his double. Scathing words in return. Dire threats of revenge. A lunge at the bars. Or some obscene ventriloquism. But Chucho held both his tongue and his temper. He winked at Ryan.

At Fright Mask's command, a red sash pulled out a ring of keys and unlocked the cell door. This while five other traitors held Ryan and Chucho at blasterpoint. The noose-bearers stood at the ready as the door creaked back.

The governor-general howled at the prisoners, his copious spittle spraying across the bars.

"He wants us on our knees," Chucho said.

"Sure, why not."

Ryan and his look-alike dropped meekly to the stone floor.

The noose-bearers advanced into their cell with extreme caution. Holding the poles like lances out in front of them, they approached the chained and kneeling men.

As the nooses were extended above their heads, Fright Mask sputtered something else in their direction.

"What did he say?" Ryan asked Chucho.

"Time to start the dying."

Chapter Fourteen

Harmonica Tom squeezed back through the slit in the power plant's rusting hurricane fence, careful not to catch his bill cap, poncho or backpack on the ragged edges of the mesh. It was much easier slipping out than it had been slipping in, because over the course of half an hour he had considerably lightened his load. Behind him, in separate parcels scattered through the plant's generator room, the tank farm and the step-up station he had left close to seventy pounds of prepped, primed and ready-to-rip plastic explosive. Only about twenty pounds of the stuff remained in the pack on his back.

As he'd anticipated, the job had been a cinch. Case in point: he'd actually run into a plant worker between the rows of ninety-thousand-gallon fuel tanks. The guy in the hardhat was walking one way as he was walking the other; this shortly after he'd mined the base of an oil reservoir with five pounds of C-4. He and the worker had passed each other with a nod and a wave. The worker hadn't even looked back.

Spread out ahead of him, Tom could see the parade route leading from the illuminated fort to the glowing city. It was marked by pools of light thrown by the peninsula's mercury vapor lamps. The vibrant radiance of Veracruz reflected off the solid, low overcast of the sky. The night was moonless and starless.

Made-to-order for what he had in mind.

Tom heard amplified music in the distance, coming from the direction of the main square. Along the waterfront, the city's lighthouse was ablaze with red-colored spotlights. Because he'd done a quick recce before sunset, he knew it was going to be the venue for the executions. Grandstands had been set up in the middle of the road for high-ranking spectators. From what he'd gathered on the backstreets and in the alleys, the mood of the common people of Veracruz was nothing short of dread. Away from the scrutiny of red sashes and priests, their jubilation transformed into anger and sorrow. Expressing displeasure or alarm over the upcoming festivities was dangerous. While loitering on the street, Tom had overhead a mother warning her quartet of wide-eyed, knee-high children not to cry over the fact that their beloved Chucho was scheduled to die that night.

And when a red sash appeared around the corner and saw the tear-streaked little faces, he pushed past the other pedestrians, caught hold of the mother's arm and twisted it behind her back. Then he threatened her with an immediate beating if she didn't put an end to her children's sobbing.

At that point Tom had reached under his poncho for the grips of his MP-5 SD-1. Before things got out of hand though, the woman squirmed from her tormentor's grasp and hurried her children away.

The red sash had called something at her back. Something nasty, no doubt.

As soon as the bastard left, strutting off like a rooster, the people still standing around on the sidewalk spit on the pavement and cursed him. And then they muttered prayers for Chucho. Not Ryan, just Chucho. As Tom had guessed, they didn't know the Deathlands warrior from shit.

Back on *Tempest* he had looked up the word *gemelo* in his predark Spanish textbook. Whatever the "twin" business was about, the folks of Veracruz weren't buying it, at least not in private, when there were no red sashes or priests around.

The daylight recce gave Tom his first real understanding of the plight of these people and their relationship to the Matachìn. They were victims, as much as his fellow Deathlanders on Padre Island. They had been terrified into passivity. Even though they outnumbered the red sashes a thousand to one, they allowed themselves to be dominated and exploited by them. For reasons that were not obvious to Tom, they had convinced themselves that they couldn't fight this enemy and win.

The damage he was about to do to the local infrastructure would cause them all to suffer—man, woman and child. There was no doubt about that. Mebbe it would give them a chance to break free? Sometimes good things came in ugly packages. But whether that was the ultimate outcome of the demolition job was not his particular concern. After all, they were foreigners, strangers to him. His countrymen and women were locked up in that stone shithole of a prison. His people were dead and left unburied on Padre Island, food for the flies, rats and gulls.

To pay back an unspeakable evil, a lesser evil had to be committed. Hey, shit happened, Tom told himself. And it almost always happened to the people who deserved it the least.

It took him fifteen minutes of fast walking to reach *Tempest*. Tom entered through the forward companionway and retrieved a loaded ballistic nylon duffel from the main cabin. Back on the foredeck, before he set the bag down inside the ship's dinghy, he opened the zipper and took out a Petzl headlamp, which he slipped over the crown of his bill cap. He then swung out the dinghy on its davit, lowered it into the water and climbed in.

Sitting on the thwart seat with his back to the bow, Tom dipped his oars and began rowing slowly along the shore, past the ruined piers, toward the ancient fortress. The rafted-up rows of small commercial vessels were deserted. The only people he saw on the streets beyond were hurrying away for the parade or the big show in the city.

When he glanced over his shoulder to check his progress, he could see the fort was lit up. The towering battlements looked as white as bone in the hard glare of the spotlights. He rowed close to the stone quay east and opposite the main complex. Other boats were moored there, tied up to the end of the surviving pier and to each other. They, too, were deserted. As he eased around the last of the boats, into the protected water in the lee of the fort, there were no challenges from the ramparts even though he was in plain view and he could see the heads and shoulders of men moving around up there. He figured the fort's sentries were too occupied with other duties—or too drunk in celebration—to notice or care about one guy in a dinky little rowboat.

Tom knew that most of the red sashes were three miles away in the city, manning the security detail for the executions. Plenty far enough away so they couldn't interfere with his plans. That's where most of the civilians were, too, where in a few minutes it would be pitch-black.

What would happen there in the dark, when the red sashes were surrounded by the people they had been abusing? he asked himself. When there was no one taking down names? The possibilities made him crack a smile.

Come daybreak it wouldn't just be paper heads on poles lining the streets.

And the new heads would be wearing straw hats.

Looking over his shoulder, Tom steered the dinghy deeper into the little embayment, toward the edge of the channels that formed saltwater moats around the three-story main fort and the story-smaller prison block. Down the narrow, central canal, which was bracketed on either side by stone battlements, he could see the footbridge that led to the dungeon. It was two hundred feet away.

Close enough.

Tom stopped rowing, shipped his oars, unzipped the duffel and took out the remote detonator. While the dinghy drifted, he carefully stood and pointed the device in the direction of the power plant. He could see its lights on the horizon, above and between the roofs of the peninsula's warehouses.

At that moment someone yelled down at him from the top of the fort's eastern tower. A challenge? A warning?

Either way, it was a little late.

He flipped off the safety and hit the red "fire" button.

There was a half-second delay. The radio signal had to cross the intervening ground before it triggered the blasting caps. When the explosions came, they were virtually simultaneous.

A very, very big bang.

The blinding flash underlit the belly of the cloud cover, sandwiched between earth and sky, spreading faster than an eyeblink in a wider and wider circle, its brilliance overwhelming and obliterating the glow of Veracruz.

For an instant it was almost as bright as day.

In that instant a series of images burned into Tom's retinas.

The exploding main transformer sent a barrage of phosphorus-white comets the size of wag wheels hurtling skyward.

The power plant's walls blew out sideways and the entire complex collapsed in on itself, vanishing in a ball of flame. Even wider fireballs erupted within and engulfed the tank farm.

A half second later the sound wave struck. As it boomed over Tom, and then out over the bay, he could feel the rumble shaking his bowels. With his upright body acting as a sail, the concussion gust actually pushed the dinghy backward.

When the flash faded, it was lights out.

Plug pulled.

The only light that survived was from scattered wag head- and taillights, or combustion. Flames hundreds of feet high raged in the tank farm, but they didn't illuminate anything past the plant's perimeter fence. The glorious city had vanished into a field of impenetrable, velvety black.

Tom sat in the dinghy. Having taken his bearings just before the lights went out, he began rowing down the center canal for the footbridge.

In the pitch-darkness above him on the left, he heard the red sashes in the fort yelling and cursing. Out there somewhere, a male voice screamed in terror and the cry was cut short by a loud splash.

As he made for the fort end of the bridge, Tom smelled the oil smoke that was pouring from the tank farm, driven by a slight breeze across the peninsula. Overhead he felt a looming presence. He reached up with the tip of an oar and tapped something solid. He was directly under the footbridge, and therefore out of view of both the fort and the prison—even if they had portable spotlights close to hand. When the bow of the dinghy scraped against the stone pillar, he shipped his oars and turned on his headlamp for a second. Long enough to unzip the duffel and take out a hunk of C-4 and the detonator rigging. He slapped the charge on the bridge's support and primed it. Then he shut off the headlamp and rowed under the bridge, along its length to the opposite end. It took only five pulls on the oars to reach the other side.

As he hopped out of the boat and onto the prison island's quay, he heard the flat whack of muffled blasterfire. It sounded like a volley of 12-gauges. It could have come from Veracruz, or from inside the prison; he couldn't tell which.

No one had crossed the bridge above him. Not from the fort or the prison. The sudden blackout appeared to have paralyzed his opposition. At least momentarily.

After securing the dinghy, with the H&K machine pistol in his right fist, duffel slung over his left shoulder, Tom felt his way along the front of the prison to the arched portal of the entrance. He flicked on his headlamp again to locate the door latch, then quickly shut it off. When he tried to open the door, he found it was bolted from the inside. It took him another ninety seconds to pull another chunk of plastique from the duffel, to pack it into the doorjamb and to insert the trigger and blasting cap.

Across the canal, along the fort's ramparts, a few lights were appearing here and there. They were weak, and for sure they weren't battery-powered flashlights. They were lanterns, and kerosene burners, Tom guessed. Accordingly, there was no focus or penetration of the light they cast, just a ring of illumination around the lantern-bearers. The thickening smoke coming from the tank farm didn't help the situation, either. There was a lot of yelling back and forth.

But not at him, this time.

The red sashes were shouting at one another.

In the distance, he heard the steady bleating of car horns, a chorus of horns of different pitches, followed by another flurry of shotgun blasts and some sustained autofire—definitely from Veracruz this time.

Panic was setting in.

Panic was Tom's main ally.

He retreated back along the prison's front wall, to a little alcove he had noted earlier in the day. He crouched, facing away from the blasts, ducked his head and once again hit the remote detonator's boom button.

This time the flash and shock wave were inseparable, and he felt the heat of the double explosion through the back of his poncho. The five-hundred-year-old bridge let out a groan and half of it dropped into the canal with a tremendous splash. The massive prison door blew off its hinges and slammed into the bridge's decorative columns. Loose bits of both went sailing off into the dark, slapping into the water and the stone facades.

Tom waited a full minute for the debris to stop falling, then, his ears still ringing, he turned on his headlamp and ran for the prison entrance. A torrent of dust and smoke poured from the gaping hole where the doorway had once been.

Without pause, he rushed through the entrance, the silenced H&K up and ready to rip. As he stepped across the threshold, even he was taken aback at how rad-blasted dark it was inside.

Well-digger's-ass dark.

Pit-of-hell dark.

Can't-see-your-hand-in-front-of-your-face dark.

The Petzl headlamp's powerful beam couldn't pierce the

swirling smoke and dust, which was so thick it was hard for him to breathe.

It occurred to him that maybe he had used a little too much plastique.

Then he stepped on something that yielded to his weight. He stepped off quickly and kicked at it. Whatever it was, it was loose; it skidded away from the kick. Leaning down, fanning the smoke away from the floor, he saw it was a severed arm. Blown clean out of its socket.

As Tom moved deeper, the dense clouds began to thin and dissipate. There was no way of telling how many red sashes were inside the anteroom before he blew the door. But looking around, he could tell no one was alive. Red sashes were in large pieces on the floor or their still bodies were covered with blood. Or they had been buried alive. The explosion had caused huge sections of the limestone block ceiling to spawl off, crushing whoever was unlucky enough to be standing beneath.

The headlamp lit up the floor-to-ceiling iron wall and gate that divided the anteroom from the cell blocks. It lay in a twisted hulk, torn from its mounts in the stone, and wrenched off to one side.

It was eerily quiet as Tom walked on.

As though everyone inside had been struck dumb.

The concentrated stink that rose from the floor, walls and oppressively low ceiling was unreal. He had to stifle the urge to cover his nose.

The dimpled, sweating limestone wall on his left reflected greasily in the light of the headlamp. The rock had been polished and oiled by thousands upon thousands of palms sliding over it. Then he caught the sound of footsteps and whimpering, both of which were coming his way.

Out of the darkness beyond the forty-foot penetration of the Petzl's beam, four red sashes staggered forward. As they stepped into the light, he saw their faces were covered in white dust. They held their arms outstretched like blind men, then shielded their eyes to block the painful glare.

They were all armed with double-barreled 12 gauges, even if the weapons were shoulder slung, even if they weren't looking for a fight.

Sometimes fights just happened, ready or not.

Tom didn't slow down. At point-blank range he shot them down like dogs, stitching 9 mm lead across their chests, sending them sprawling. The stutter of the silenced machine pistol was drowned out by the whine of through-and-throughs ricocheting off the walls and floor.

He walked past the twitching bodies, straining his eyes and his ears for some sign of Ryan and the others.

Huddled at the foot of the left-hand wall, he came across a pair of priests in red robes and tall, conical hats. They cowered there, kneeling in a shallow pool of some unidentifiable liquid; they appeared to be unarmed. They, too, were coated in rock dust. When the priests saw his light coming toward them, they started clapping their hands and mumbling something Tom couldn't quite make out. But it sounded like they were thanking their godawful gods for rescuing them from the darkness.

Moving closer, he recognized the one thanking the loudest as the spider-bellied bastard who'd read the execution order for Ryan and his double.

If they weren't part of the solution, they were part of the problem.

As he walked past, Tom shot them both once in the back of the head. Thwack. Thwack.

Priests in a puddle.

Problems solved.

A little farther on Tom came to a fork off the main corridor, a left-branching hallway. His headlamp beam swept over and into the first of a long bank of cramped cells. On the other side of the floor-to-ceiling bars, he saw a filthy, nearly naked human figure. The whites of the man's eyes shone for an instant, radiating terror, before they squinted shut.

Two eyes shining back told him it wasn't Ryan.

Tom looked into the next cell. There was a heap of rags on the floor. A bare foot with a grime-encrusted sole stuck out from under it.

"Ryan?" Tom said softly.

No answer.

No movement.

Farther down the dank hallway, beyond the range of the headlamp, and from deeper in the dungeon around him, the survivors were starting to stir, they were slowly coming to life. Tom had no idea how many prisoners were caged in the pitch-dark, but the noise they made was getting louder and louder. Shouts. Moans. Screams. Cries for help. Very soon, he realized, the din and the echoes of the din down the cavelike halls would make it impossible to hear himself think. He had to locate his targets and get them the hell out before things deteriorated even more.

Tom didn't have time to go up and down the labyrinthine passages, searching for Ryan and the others cell by cell. He didn't have a map of the interior. Getting lost was not an option.

Rather than shout Ryan's name down the cell blocks as he walked the main passage, something that he knew would certainly draw dozens if not hundreds of affirmative replies from the other prisoners hoping for rescue, he had a better idea.

A signal only Ryan would recognize.

Tom reached into his hip pocket and took out his harmonica. After wetting his lips, he began to play a loud and lively tune with his left hand while he held the H&K up and ready in his right. The bright, rhythmic notes echoed and reechoed, bouncing down the winding corridors.

Chapter Fifteen

"Time to start the dying…"

Fright Mask's saliva-spraying declaration turned out to be prophetic, but not at all in the way he'd intended.

The noose hung suspended two feet above Ryan's head as he knelt on the floor beside Chucho. The one-eyed warrior strained to hold himself in check as the red sash pole-bearer began to lower the garrote-on-a-stick. He knew that when the loop was snugged up around his neck, the ability to free himself from the ankle and wrist cuffs would become irrelevant. Ryan hated all forms of restraint with a newfound passion—he had been locked up in them night and day for more than three weeks. And he hated this particular brand of restraint the most of all. There was no doubt in his mind that the noose pole was another of the Matachìns' inventions: it smacked of their brutal ingenuity. Strangulation at a distance of five feet was the perfect way to control prisoners who had nothing left to lose. Unconsciousness was just a cord-pull away.

As luck would have it in this case, a very distant cord-pull.

Before the red sash could drop the loop, the entire structure, from the bedrock-coral foundation up, was rocked by a tremendous explosion. The floor shuddered violently underfoot, limestone dust from the ceiling rained down on Ryan's head. The noose-bearers froze, poles extended, looking wide-eyed at each other instead of their quarry.

Then the lights went out.

Suddenly it was darker than dark. And the darkness was like a blow to the head. Like having the eyes plucked from their sockets, and the sockets then stuffed with wads of cotton wool. Perspective, proportion, proximity, all were gone, as was all sense of up and down.

It was so dark no one dared move.

No one except Ryan Cawdor.

Perhaps he had an advantage already being half-blinded. Perhaps his life in Deathlands had trained him to react by instinct, to seize opportunities at a moment's notice. Eight feet away in the pitch-black, the cell door stood ajar. His enemies were caught flatfooted.

"Now," he said softly to his look-alike.

Further explanation was unnecessary.

Ryan and Chucho snapped the threads that held their heavy wrist and ankle cuffs in place, but neither man tossed the manacles aside. Instead, they gripped them by the middle of their connecting chains—turning the restraints instantly into wicked, close range, offensive weapons.

In effect, battle axes or nunchakus.

Great minds thought alike.

Shifting his brace of chain link and heavy steel bands to his left hand, Ryan found and grabbed hold of his double's wrist. Again, no explanation was necessary; it was a necessity that had instantly occurred to them both. Chucho in turn locked his fingers around Ryan's wrist. Not just twins anymore, but conjoined twins. Thus connected, they couldn't lose each other in the dark, and they wouldn't hit each other by accident.

As one, the two men rose from their knees, windmilling their manacles as they rushed forward, toward the open cell door. Ryan's cuffs immediately thunked into something.

The something squealed like a stuck pig as it fell back.

He laid a second blow on top of the first, putting his entire body behind it, as though he was trying to drive in a spike with a sledgehammer. On his right, Chucho was doing the same to his own noose-bearer, only with a much more spectacular effect. Hot blood, presumably from a head wound, sprayed over the side of Ryan's face and neck as the other pole-man collapsed under a rain of whistling blows.

In his mind, Ryan had locked in the last-known position of Fright Mask relative to the cell's exit. In two quick strides his left shoulder was brushing against the edge of the iron doorjamb. He pulled Chucho through the doorway and out into the corridor.

"*¡Fuego! ¡Fuego!*" the governor-general howled.

His red sash scattergunners didn't pause to consider that there were friendlies in the line of fire. That's how afraid of Chucho they were. They cut loose blindly into the blackness, shooting their weapons from the hip. Double muzzle-flashes lit up the inside of the cell. In the narrow, cavelike, enclosed space the flurry of 12-gauge reports was deafening.

It was spitting-distance target practice without a target.

Stray buckshot ricocheted off the back wall and whined down the hallway.

Ears ringing, the acrid smell and taste of burned gunpowder filling his nose and mouth, Ryan turned in Fright Mask's direction. As he did so, he ran headlong into a red sash on his left. Rocking back on his heels, Ryan swung the manacle nunchakus, clobbering the man out of the way. The red sash's shotgun clattered as it hit the floor.

"*¡Otra vez! ¡Otra vez! ¡Fuego!*"

Ryan caught something new in the governor-general's voice: it was the shrill edge of panic.

But al Modo hadn't taken into account the trouble his red sashes would have reloading their weapons in absolute darkness, this while retreating under toe-to-toe attack. As they fumbled to break open the actions of their double barrels, as they fumbled in their pockets for more shells, they lost their bearings. And in the suffocating, all-encompassing blackness, once lost, bearings could never be found. The corridor echoed with their whimpers and frantic curses.

Meanwhile, with Chucho in tow, Ryan had zeroed in on the sound of the governor-general's voice. Fright Mask was very close. Shifting the brace of chains to his right hand, Ryan lunged forward with his left, fingers outstretched, searching for a grip on a soft, vulnerable throat. Instead, they closed on a handful of piled dreadlocks. Before he could jerk down and drive the general to his knees, the matted coils of hair slipped out of his grasp like so much greased rope.

As al Modo backed away into the nothingness, he yelled for help.

The governor-general was in no mood to stand and fight, but he had no choice. Help was not coming soon enough.

Ryan heard the sound of steel on steel: al Modo had drawn his ceremonial saber. Then came the hiss as it sliced back and forth in the pitch-black. The breeze it made brushed his face.

Forehand.

Backhand.

He felt Chucho squeeze his wrist hard, a warning. As the next backhand slashed, Ryan's look-alike struck with his nunchaku, catching the stroke at its weakest point, its terminus. Cuffs and chain screeched across the long blade.

Fright Mask growled as he tried to free his saber from the temporary trap.

But by then Ryan had gathered himself a handful of golden epaulette. He drove his shoulder into the center of the general's chest, firing upward through his legs from the balls of his feet, throwing his entire weight into the strike. It caught Fright Mask off balance and lifted him clear of the ground.

To Ryan's surprise, their dual trajectory ended abruptly, and much, much sooner than he'd expected. They both slammed into something solid. The impact with the corridor wall sandwiched the breath out of al Modo and he dropped. Ryan felt a stab of pain in his neck, and momentarily saw stars as he, too, slumped to the floor.

"Let go of my wrist," Ryan told Chucho, who had been dragged to his knees behind them.

Reaching around the front of Fright Mask's neck, Ryan grabbed the free end of the manacle chain he held, then he pulled it up past the exposed throat, over the hideous face. He couldn't see what he was doing, but he could hear and feel the chain links scraping against the golden fangs. Ryan jerked back hard, yanking the manacles into the corners of the governor-general's mouth like a horse's bridle. Jamming a knee in the middle of the man's spine, he leaned back, applying pressure to the jaw hinges.

"Nuh! Nuh!" al Modo whined, shaking his head, twisting his torso, trying to claw backward to reach Ryan's surviving eye.

"Are you choking him to death?" Chucho asked with obvious delight. "I wish I could see…"

"Choking is too good for him," Ryan answered. At that

moment he was thinking about revenge. He was thinking about the Padre Islander boy, Garwood Reed, about how he had died. "This is for the boy he had butchered on the church steps," Ryan said. "Tell the piece of shit that."

Chucho translated.

And as his double spoke the words, as the words sank in, Fright Mask went wild in Ryan's grasp, flailing his arms and kicking out with his legs in a last-ditch attempt to free himself.

Ryan twisted the chain into a knot behind the governor-general's head. With the links holding down his tongue, Fright Mask couldn't cry out. They didn't stop him from slobbering, though. When Ryan felt that cold, stinking slime smear across the back of his hand, it was his turn to go crazy. He started ramming the man's face into the limestone wall. The sculpted nose broke on the first impact, then the golden fangs, then the rest of his front teeth, then both his jaws.

But it wasn't enough.

As Doc Tanner had said, there was hell to pay.

"For Garwood," Ryan snarled. "For Garwood Reed..." Grunting from the effort, the one-eyed man slammed the governor-general's disfigured head against unyielding rock again and again, until the skull finally shattered and flew to pieces. Blood and brains splattered across Ryan's face and forearms.

In disgust, Ryan hurled down the rag-doll corpse. As he pushed back from it, his hand brushed the saber al Modo had dropped.

"Here, Chucho, take his blade," he said, rising to his feet. He groped a hand in the dark, trying to find the shoulder of his look-alike.

Before he made contact, a second explosion shook the

darkness, this one much closer, much more devastating. The initial shock wave dropped Ryan hard to his knees. In the same instant it wrung an agonized groan from the corridor's stone ceiling; with a resounding crack it started to cave in.

A blast of rock dust swept over him. He heard terrible screams. Then something hit him in the head and he passed out.

Gasping for air, he came to. For a moment he was disoriented. It was black as the pit of hell. He knew he'd hadn't been unconscious long because the air was still thick with dust. He tried to move his legs and couldn't; something heavy had fallen across them just above the knees. He reached down and felt the slab of limestone that held him pinned. He tried to move the rock, but it wouldn't budge. The saber had fallen somewhere in the dark, so he couldn't use it to get leverage.

"Chucho?" he called, choking on the dust when he drew breath. "Chucho, are you okay?"

There was no answer.

"Chucho!"

No answer.

Ryan felt a slight breeze across his cheek. A steady breeze. Which could only mean an exit to the outside had been opened—either the main door, or a breach in the perimeter wall caused by the explosion. He wasn't the only one who felt the wind and understood what it meant. He could hear red sash and priest survivors stumbling around, turning face-first into the breeze, following it to find the way out. The sounds of their bootsteps grew fainter and fainter.

A couple of minutes later a flurry of bullets whined down the corridor. There were no gunshot reports. Just bullet flights, zinging and skipping off the stone walls. Someone was firing a silenced automatic weapon. What that meant Ryan had no clue. But he guessed it probably wasn't good.

As he tried to free himself again, and again failed, he heard strains of music coming toward him out of the dark. He recognized the instrument and the tune at once; and from the instrument and the tune, the musician. A wide smile spread across his face. He cupped a hand to his mouth and shouted as loud as he could, "Tom! Tom! This way!"

A tiny glow appeared in the center of the all-encompassing blackness; it seemed to be a long ways off, but Ryan knew the distance could have been an illusion in the absence of landmarks. The dim light approached, bobbing up and down. It was so faint it didn't illuminate the sides or ceiling of the corridor. That was because of all the dust in the air. As it got closer, a tightly focused beam grew brighter. It speared through the dark, spotlighting a half-naked man sitting on the rock-and-body littered floor about thirty feet away from where Ryan lay trapped.

"Ryan?" said a familiar voice.

"Wrong twin, Tom," Ryan said. "That's Chucho. I'm over here. Can't move my legs out from under this rock."

The light turned and pinpointed him. He shielded his good eye from the glare with a hand. The light turned back to Chucho.

On the other side of the hallway, the double quickly rose to his feet, his manacle nunchakus cocked back. "You know this man?" he asked Ryan.

"Hell, yes, he knows me," Tom said, playing the spotlight's circle over the unmoving human forms half hidden by limestone cave-ins. "I've come to break both of you out of this shit pit. Help me get the rock off him so I can finish the job."

Together the three of them shifted the slab. As Ryan tested his legs for injuries, Tom set his duffel bag on the floor. From it he took two headlamps, which he gave to Ryan and Chucho. As they adjusted the straps, he dug out a pair of beat-up, Argentine knock-off .45-caliber blasters.

In the light of his headlamp, Ryan checked his pistol's mag and then eased back the slide until he saw brass to make sure a live round was chambered.

"Now let's go surprise the others," Tom said to Ryan. "Can't wait to see the looks on their faces when I waltz up, big as life."

Hammer locked back, his index finger resting against the .45's trigger guard, Ryan said, "Krysty, Mildred, Doc, J.B. and Jak were taken away last night, right after the parade. They were separated from the rest of the galley slaves and marched onto a black ship that was docked at the fort. It sailed off, don't know where to, but they've been gone almost twenty-four hours now. We're wasting precious time, let's get out of here."

"I have to do something first," Chucho told him.

Ryan and Tom watched as he returned to the cell, took a set of keys from the belt of a dead red sash, then walked down the hallway. He unlocked the next cell in the row, freeing the man inside. He spoke softly to the prisoner in Spanish, first handing him the ring of keys, then giving him his headlamp. The man nodded enthusiastically, pulled on the light and hurried off into the dark.

Chucho cupped hands to mouth and shouted down the corridor after him. Whatever he said, it set the rest of the prisoners cheering and chanting his name.

When the look-alike returned to Ryan's side he explained, "I told our neighbor it was his duty to let all our brothers go free. I told our brothers it was their duty not to live their restored lives in vain, but to take back what has been stolen."

In a matter of seconds the hallway started echoing with the sounds of cell doors clanking back.

Then the familiar anthem started up again, this time with a new ferocity.

"Catchy little tune," Tom said. He hummed along with the refrain as they headed toward the exit, three abreast, blasters at the ready.

Ryan's spotlight picked up crumpled human forms at the foot of the wall, forms in red robes. The ring of illumination played over what was left of Itzamna, the spider priest. His cone hat and blood veil had gone missing, and half of the top of the right side of his head was blown off, from midcrown to temple. Above the corpse, a black splotch of pulverized bone and brains glistened on the wall. Ryan was satisfied with the outcome, even if he didn't get to do the honors himself, face-to-face.

The farther they advanced toward the exit, the less dust there was. By the time they reached the anteroom, the air had cleared. As they headed for the doorless portal, Ryan said, "What about red sash reinforcements coming across the bridge?"

"The Bridge of the Last Sigh," Chucho said.

"It's gone," Tom told them. "I dropped the far end of the bridge in the water when I blew off the door. The men in the fort will have to swim across the channel to help out. And they won't do that because they don't have a clue what's going on. I made sure none of the prison guards got out alive."

"But they can still shoot at us across the gap," Ryan said.

"Shut off your headlamp," Tom said as he turned off his

own. "I've got the dinghy tied up and waiting outside. Don't make any noise. We need to scoot out of here without attracting attention to ourselves."

With that, the trader led the way, slipping out the front entrance.

Ryan followed close on his heels and felt the fresh salt air hit his face. He sucked it deep into his lungs. The combustion lanterns scattered here and there along the fort's ramparts glowed pale yellow. They didn't throw a strong enough light to expose the channel or the prison island's quay.

No more than five minutes had passed since the explosions at the bridge and prison portal. Ryan knew the red sashes were thinking the fort was under a concerted attack. Something they didn't seem prepared for. He could sense the chaos on the battlements. Officers were yelling orders. Lanterns were hurried back and forth. All to no apparent avail. The militiamen were afraid of more demolition on the perimeter. They wanted to keep out of the line of fire. This made defending the walls a challenge.

Chucho and Ryan hustled into the dinghy. Tom pushed off the bow, then hopped in. The little boat drifted in the dark while the trader picked up the oars. Soundlessly, he turned the dinghy and then began to stroke for the end of the channel.

As they glided along, Ryan watched the battlements above, blaster in hand. He knew that firing from the dinghy was a desperation measure. It came right before jumping over the side. Shooting would give away their position. Caught in the channel with no cover, they would be turned into bullet sponges.

The bellowed commands from the red sash officers and the shouted-back answers from the militia covered the soft splashes of the oar strokes.

As the tiny boat slid out of the channel and into the protected finger of the bay, Tom rowed harder, really putting his back into it. He only eased off after they had reached the quay and the tied-up vessels on the opposite side. Rounding the corner, putting the pier and the boats between them and the fort's line of sight, Tom spoke, slightly out of breath from the exertion.

"Turn on your headlamp for a second," he told Ryan. "Keep me on course. Don't want to run into anything."

Ryan flicked on his lamp, lighting up a narrow strip of black water off the bow. He suggested Tom veer to port a bit, then shut off the lamp. Every few minutes he repeated the procedure, keeping them away from tethered boats and the shoreline, until he saw the familiar masts of *Tempest*. She sat moored broadside to them, dead ahead. Ryan shut off the light and left it off.

When they got close, Tom shipped his oars and let the dinghy glide up alongside the hull. He paused, listening for any unusual sound from above, as did Ryan and Chucho. There was nothing, just the creak of the rafted boats rubbing against their fenders and the edge of the dock. They hooked the dinghy to the davit cables and one by one climbed aboard *Tempest* amidships.

Only when all three were on deck was the trap sprung. A gruff voice growled an order at them in Spanish.

"Hold it," Tom told Ryan and Chucho.

The warning was unnecessary as they couldn't see anybody to shoot at.

More Spanish came at them, from the stern it seemed.

A lantern suddenly appeared at their feet, its light-proof cover pulled off, apparently by a hidden cord. The weak glow illuminated the three boarders, but little else.

"He says we're outnumbered," Chucho translated. "He says to put our guns on the deck and our hands on top of our heads."

"He could be bluffing," Ryan said, his trigger finger itching. "We don't even know if he's armed."

Chucho rattled off a terse reply. "I asked him why we should do what he says."

A verbal command from the stern caused four other shielded lanterns to be revealed. In the additional light, Ryan could see that there were three red sashes hunkered down in the cockpit, and three others crouched on the far side of the cabin. All of them held blasters braced and leveled.

The red sashes whispered to one another, repeating a phrase Ryan knew well. *Los gemelos heroicos.*

"It's all right," Tom said. "Let's do as he says. Don't worry, I've got this deal covered."

Ryan couldn't see how that was possible, but the trader had gotten them this far, against worse odds. Besides, the only other options were bad and worse: a one-sided gun battle or a late-night swim leaking blood from a dozen buckshot holes. When Harmonica Tom put down his submachine gun and revolver, Ryan did the same. Chucho reluctantly followed suit.

The leader of the red sash boarding party stood in the cockpit; the others remained behind cover with their weapons trained. The lanky, hatchet-faced man ordered Ryan, Tom and Chucho to come aft; this they did with their hands on top of their heads. The red sash stopped them short of the cockpit, then reached down to the deck and uncovered a shape hidden by a canvas tarp. To make sure they could see what lay there, he picked up the lantern from the companionway roof and held it close.

Ryan recognized the remains of a human corpse. It had been savagely mauled, gutted from gullet to goobers, arms chewed down to the bare bones, leg bones gnawed off in ragged stumps at the knees. The still-wet crimson sash over its shoulder looked almost black in the lantern light.

"Goddamn hammerheads," Tom muttered. "It's Bob."

"Who?" Ryan said.

"Bob Tothesurface, the red sash I chilled and sank with a couple of concrete blocks yesterday. Before the lights went out, he must've popped up. Somebody found what was left of him, mebbe even these triple stupes."

The leader snarled something at the captives, jabbing his double barrel at them for emphasis.

"He says he's taking us back to the prison," Chucho said. "He says there will be a big reward for our capture and promotions all around."

"You tell him something from me," Tom said. "Tell him this word for word. There's an even bigger reward waiting for him and his pals belowdecks, in the cabin. They probably don't want to have to share it with the priests. Tell him they can have it all to themselves if they let us go."

"They can have it, anyway," Ryan said. "We can't stop them."

"That's the point I want to get across. It's theirs for the taking. Just tell him what I said. Tell him I'll unlock the companionway door for him."

Upon hearing the offer, the leader stepped back and waved Tom forward, down into the cockpit with him. As the trader lifted the padlock on its hasp, he spoke in a flat, emotionless voice.

"All hell's about to break loose," he told Ryan and Chucho. "Get ready to make your move."

Tom lifted off the lock and put it in his pocket. He took hold of the door and opened it halfway, then paused. Impatient to get on with it, the leader grabbed him by the shoulder and shoved him out of the cockpit, back beside Ryan and Chucho. Eager to see what the big prize was, the other red sashes rose from cover and moved aft.

The leader ordered two men to keep the prisoners in their sights, while the other three packed in behind him, very excited, indeed. Picking up the lantern from the deck, the leader threw back the door all the way.

Heavy automatic fire thundered from belowdecks, howling, up-angled hell that Ryan could feel right through his boot soles.

It blew through the edge of the top step, through-and-throughing the four red sashes, ripping them to shreds. In the strobe-light flashes of sustained autofire, the disintegrating bodies cakewalked in reverse, puppet-jerking out of the cockpit, tumbling backward over the stern rail. The sounds of their splashes were lost in the ravening din.

The PKM continued burning rounds until it came up empty. That took less than ten seconds.

In the meantime, Ryan, Chucho and Tom jumped the remaining two very surprised red sashes. Their shotguns seized by the barrels, a head butt and an elbow strike, respectively, freed the weapons from their grasp. Then Tom and Ryan turned the scatterguns on their former owners, firing point-blank into their guts. They, too, toppled backward over the side.

Trapped blaster smoke boiled out of the companionway door. The roar of autofire echoed across the bay.

"Cast off! Cast off!" Tom told Ryan and Chucho. "There's no way we're going to sneak out of here now."

Ryan made for the bow; Chucho untied the stern. As the

one-eyed man coiled the line on the foredeck, *Tempest*'s engine rumbled to life.

"Ryan, I need you back here!" Tom shouted as he backed the sloop away from the pier, spinning the helm hard over.

To Chucho he said, "Throw those goddamned lanterns over the side. Do it quick!"

When Ryan jumped down into the cockpit, Tom hit the cabin's light switch. "Go below," he said. "Disconnect the trip wire from the PKM. Then reload it. There's a couple of 100-round magazines on the galley table. Bring the weapon and extra mag up here. We need to put the sting back in *Tempest*'s tail."

Ryan ducked down the steep steps. The footing on the cabin deck was treacherous: spent hulls had rolled every which way. The sloop did a K-turn and accelerated forward; Tom was heading for the harbor entrance as fast as he could go. After unwinding the wire from around the pistol grip and trigger, Ryan dumped the empty magazine and slapped in one of the full ones. Then he released the PKM's pivot mount from the tripod. Snatching up the extra mag, he lifted the thirty pounds of gun and ammo to his shoulder and carried it up the stairs.

Tom shut off the cabin lights the moment he appeared on deck. "Use your headlamp to mount the blaster," he told Ryan. "Then shut it off."

Outside, *Tempest* was sliding through inky blackness. Behind them, as Ryan fitted the PKM into its swivel rail mount, he could see the dim lights along the fort's ramparts, and brighter wag head- and taillights moving between the fort and Veracruz, but the going directly ahead was almost as pitch-dark as it had been in the prison. The overcast skies had reduced visibility to practically nothing. The green beacon light that marked the entrance had been extinguished. Tom was sailing by the seat of his pants. After he'd locked the heavy blaster in place on the stern rail, Ryan turned off the headlamp.

Almost immediately loud cracks and piercing whistles rolled over the water from the direction of the fort. High over the harbor, a quartet of red signal flares burst, one after another. As they slowly descended, they cast enough light for Ryan to see one hundred yards or more ahead.

They cast enough light for the fort's gunners to see the sloop making for the end of the peninsula and the open sea.

"Fuck!" Tom said, looking up at the bright pink lights.

The fort's cannons punctuated his comment, with more booms than cracks this time. The volley of shells plowed into the sea well ahead and behind them, detonating with stunning force and sending plumes of smoke and water and red-hot shrap skyward.

"They're bracketing us, trying to lock in the range. Give them a taste of that MG, Ryan!"

If the flares' light exposed *Tempest* to the fort's fire, it also exposed the fort to Ryan. He shouldered the PKM and strafed the ancient battlements with steel-jacketed rounds. Every tenth round in the mag was a tracer, which made it easy for him to track his bullet fall. It wasn't precision work, though. Not without a telescope. Not without a fully illuminated target. He walked autofire up the walls to zero in on the gun emplacements.

When the cannons' muzzles flashed, Ryan rained a hail of slugs down on the afterimages.

Which slowed the barrage, but didn't end it.

Before the first batch of flares splashed down, a second volley was launched to keep the target in view.

Cannon rounds landed close on either side of the ship, blowing foaming divots in the black water, so close that Ryan felt the hell gust of their explosions and heard the scream of hot shrap flying between the masts.

As he reloaded the PKM, Tom took evasive action. "Keep your heads down!" the trader cried, cutting the helm hard to starboard. He wasn't giving the red sash gunners an easy broadside to hit. Although he ran a zigzag, evasive course, he kept the smallest possible target—the stern—facing their muzzles.

Ryan racked the PKM's actuator, chambering the first round in the box mag. He noted there were no ships in pursuit. At least not yet. He put the lack of response down to the general disarray and confusion from the blackout and the dispersal of red sashes and Matachìn forces along the execution parade route.

Between the booms of the cannon, he heard sporadic small-arms fire coming from downtown Veracruz. It sounded like the good citizens were rising up, and the red sashes were burning ammo to fight them off.

Another reason they weren't being chased.

When the second round of flares winked out in the sea, darkness closed in, but Harmonica Tom already had his compass heading. As they cleared the bay entrance, they met a breeze hard from the north, gusting steadily, and a three-foot, running chop.

A third volley of flares lit up the bay.

"Take the helm, Ryan," Tom said. "Put the wind behind us, while I get the sails raised."

As he spoke, there was another distant boom far off the stern, from the direction of the fort. One final, desperate cannon shot, lobbed extrahigh, came whistling down. One lonely miss, exploding some two hundred yards short.

Tempest scooted away into the blackness.

Chapter Sixteen

Tempest sliced through the wind chop with hardly a shudder. Though Ryan couldn't see it, he sensed the expanse of empty black sea and sky ahead. He only had a rough sense of their direction, but he knew Harmonica Tom was putting as much distance between them and the harbor as quickly as he could.

The strong crosswind that drove the ship did nothing to cut the humidity, and the air was much warmer than his body temperature. It was like breathing in steam. Riding on the breeze was the raw stench of the raging petroleum fires they'd left behind, a stench straight from the bowels of hell.

Ryan looked off the stern and saw only darkness behind them, sky and land made indivisible. He remembered what Veracruz had looked like the night before. The brilliant glow of its electrics, so full of promise, of hope for the resurrection of human civilization. It turned out that the hope was tainted by the usual suspects, the murderous and the avaricious; not that that mattered in the long view. It was all gone now.

A nest of busy ants crushed under a boot heel.

The outcome gave him no satisfaction; just the opposite. Too many innocent people had been harmed. And would be harmed for years, perhaps decades to come. Was there an upside? Could the people of Veracruz seize the opportunity and throw off their oppressors? Or would they buckle under once more? It was out of his hands—as if it had ever been in his hands in the first place. Before the end was in sight he had no doubt that more innocents would suffer and die. The revenge for what had been done to Garwood Reed and his fellow Padre Islanders had just begun.

Ryan was free of chains for the first time in nearly a month, but instead of elation and relief he felt anxious, keyed up. He wanted to run until his lungs and legs gave out, but he couldn't even pace the ship's deck. It was so dark on the water he couldn't see his hand in front of his face. The only light was the faint reddish glow of the helm's control panel and compass. Although Ryan was free of physical restraints he hadn't escaped yet, not really. He would never be free while his companions were missing and in chains. He couldn't go back to Deathlands without them, without finding out what had happened to them.

Black sea. Black sky. Black ship.

And the entire world to get lost in.

The monumental scale of the task made him feel something he didn't expect, something he didn't like one bit, something he wasn't used to: it made him feel inadequate.

After they had run with the wind for the better part of an hour, Tom switched on the deck and cabin lights. The yellow glow barely penetrated the surrounding gloom, but at least they could see the limits of the ship.

"No one's coming after us?" Chucho said, glancing aft.

Ryan looked behind them, as well.

Nothing but sea back there.

And darkness.

"Even if they are," Tom replied, "by now we're way past their line of sight, over the curvature of the earth. No way are they going to see the deck lights. I'll leave the mast lights off. No need to tempt fate."

"Couldn't a ship come up on us from behind? Overtake us?" Chucho said.

"There wasn't a ship in that harbor that could catch us, not while we're being pushed by wind like this. Not even the Matachìn tugs. And that's assuming they guessed right on which direction we took."

Tom looked down at his feet. A fan of blood and guts lay spread across the cockpit's deck, narrow at the companion-way end, much wider at the stern rail. They were standing in the splatter the PKM had blown out of the red sash boarding party. Their boot soles had smeared pink streaks on the no-slip textured fiberglass.

"How about you two cleaning up the mess?" Tom said. "Or we'll be tracking it belowdecks."

"I don't mind," Ryan said.

Chucho shrugged.

The Hero Twins set to work in the cockpit, and along the coaming and port rail. With hand brushes they scrubbed down the fiberglass and the stainless-steel fittings, and then sluiced everything out the scuppers with the wash-down hose. When they were done, they rinsed off the soles of their boots, as well.

After they had finished Tom wrinkled up his nose and said, "You two could really use a wash, too. Use the shower in the main cabin. There's extra clothes in the drawers under the bed. And while you're at it, open the front companionway door, get some air flow going, blow the cordite stink out."

Ryan's stomach rumbled ominously, like distant thunder. "We haven't eaten in a while, either," he said.

"There's a pot of beans on the side of the stove," the trader said. "Some tortillas, too. Cooked bacon. Hardboiled eggs. Fruit on the table. Help yourselves."

Ryan followed Chucho down the stairs.

There was spent brass everywhere.

"Go on, you get washed first," Ryan said. "I'll pick up the shells so we don't trip and break our necks."

"Don't worry," Chucho said, "I won't use all the hot water."

After gathering up one hundred or so empty casings, Ryan helped himself to food: a bowl of cold beans with crumbled bacon and chopped egg sprinkled on top. He used the corn tortillas to scoop it up and shovel it in. From the aroma of garlic and onion, he thought it would taste better. It was like shoveling ashes, and it was nukin' hard to swallow. He wasn't used to having his mouth so full.

As he finished up, Chucho returned to the galley in shorts and a T-shirt, his long hair dripping wet. He immediately dished himself some grub. He was still eating when Tom joined them belowdecks. Once the skipper had the sails trimmed out the way he wanted them, he had lashed ropes to the wheel—his version of an autopilot. Ryan had seen him do this many times before.

"I set a rough course, east southeast," Tom said. "Gonna let this wind put more distance between us and the Matachìn."

"How are we going to find the others?" Ryan asked him. "Where do we even start looking?"

Harmonica Tom grimaced and shook his head, stroking the ends of his long, sandy mustache.

"You said something about a black ship?" Chucho said. "Sailboat?"

Ryan nodded. "Three-masted schooner."

"I know that boat. It is the property of the Lords of Death.

A special-purpose ship. If your friends are on it, I know where they are being taken."

He turned to Tom and said, "Do you have a chart of the land and sea to the south?"

Tom pulled a map from his bookcase. He unrolled it and spread it out on the galley table. "We are here," he said, indicating the waters off Veracruz.

Ryan's double planted a brown fingertip on the paper.

Not on the Lantic side, but the Cific, at a dot of an island near the coast.

And a long way from where they were.

"Xibalba," he said. "They are being taken to Xibalba. The island was called Coiba before Armageddon. Or Devil's Island. It was a government prison, for the most dangerous criminals."

"That's Panama," Tom said. "Or at least it was." He did a quick handspan calculation of the distance. "It's at least fifteen hundred miles from here."

The trader indicated the narrowest part of the landmass with his finger. "This here is a ship canal, dug from east to west across the isthmus way before Armageddon, connecting the two oceans." He looked at Chucho and said, "Are you telling me the canal is still there? It wasn't hit by a nuke strike?"

"It's not there, but it wasn't hit by a missile," Chucho answered. "Nukeday brought terrible earthquakes to Panama, to all of Central America. The quakes broke the canal's locks. When that happened, water came pouring out of the artificial lakes. Water from the lakes is what filled the canals and floated the ships. More water dammed up than you can even imagine. When the locks broke there was an incredible flood in both directions, east and west from the high point of the canal. It washed out most of the city at the Atlantic end and badly damaged the city at the Pacific end. Now, the only time there is water in the canal is when it rains. And the only way to cross Panama is to go overland."

Ryan tapped at Coiba island on the map. "Why are they being taken to this place?" he said.

Chucho shook his head.

"Come on, what is it?" Ryan said.

"I won't lie to you, it is very bad, my friend," the look-alike said. "I don't understand the whitecoat science behind it. I don't know anybody who does. I know the outcome because I have seen it myself. The Lords of Death take ordinary people to Xibalba and turn them into monsters by poisoning their blood. They do this to create more *enanos,* their plague carriers. After the transformation they send these soulless devils out into the world to do their bidding, to spread disease, destruction and fear. The *enanos* want to live so badly, they will do anything the Lords tell them. Even unthinkable things. They can't help it. The Lords of Death delight in exploiting the weaknesses of animals and men. They have conscripted the animal that transfers blood, the mosquito, and the human being who makes it, to their cause. The mosquito can't help drinking blood. The human being can't help hoping things will get better, and in that hope, finds a reason to survive.

"There is no way to tell the devils from regular people. They don't look sick. They don't act sick. That makes everyone a suspect, until the dying is done and only the *enanos* are left standing. The Lords of Death have fielded an army that is more powerful and deadly than the Matachìn. An army that can't be seen and can't be stopped. They'll make your friends soldiers in that army, if they live through the poisoning of their blood."

"Whitecoat shit," Tom swore.

"How long does it take to turn somebody into one of these things?" Ryan said.

"A few weeks. But it is very painful, and as I said, many more die than live through it."

"How do you know all this?" Tom said.

"I've captured some of these *enanos,* and I've tortured them, holding out the promise of merciful death until they told me all they knew. And I have traveled…"

"You've been there?" Tom said. "To this Xibalba?"

"After I escaped prison the second time," Chucho said, "or maybe it was the third. I needed to cool off, to make myself scarce for a while. I came to Panama with a comrade in arms, a fellow former prisoner who hated the red sashes and priests as much as I did. We crossed the fifty miles of jungle to the Pacific side of the canal. We wanted to see if the Lords of Death were really gods. And if they weren't, to kill them in their beds. We stole a rowboat from the mainland."

"What happened?" Tom said.

"Never got close enough. The Lords live in and around the old prison compound—an island in the middle of an island. We landed on the beach at Coiba but we never found the gates of Xibalba."

"Why not?" the skipper prompted.

"There are many bad things there."

"You mean, Matachìn?" Ryan asked.

"No," Chucho said. "We didn't see any pirates. The island is covered with jungle so thick you can't even hack through it. Under that canopy it is very dark, very hot, and there is no air to breathe—a green hell. The only way to advance is to follow the creeks up and down the steep ravines the water has cut in the mountainsides. It is very slow going, the footing is treacherous—a deep, ankle-grabbing litter of palm fronds and leaves, and hiding in the litter there are snakes. Suspended in the branches and strangler vines overhead, there are vampire bats. In the creeks, themselves, hiding under the log jams are crocodiles. But worst of all are the dogs."

"Dogs?" Tom said, a puzzled look on his face.

"They're the offspring of the animals who were on the island back when it was a prison. They've been running loose in the jungle in wild packs, breeding, killing, eating anything they can catch for over a hundred years. They're not afraid of anything or anyone. And you can't outrun them, either."

"You made it out," Ryan said.

"Barely. We were deep in the jungle when they picked up our scent. We could hear them baying off in the distance. We couldn't see them, but from the sounds of the howler monkeys we knew they were circling and closing in on us. We turned back for the boat at once. They were on our heels as we broke through to the beach. Big, powerful dogs. Eighty, ninety pounders. Huge heads and jaws. Wet to the skin from crashing through the brush. Snarling and snapping, crazy for the kill.

"My friend was pulled down from behind as we ran. He was still screaming when I hit the water. There was no time to try for the boat. I had to swim away for my life. A few of the dogs followed me in, but they quickly gave up. They smelled the fresh meat on the beach, and knew they were losing out on an easy meal. I treaded water off the island for a long time. I was lucky the sharks didn't find me. When I swam back for the boat, there was nothing left of my friend but the bloody rags of his clothes scattered over the sand. The dogs had torn up his body and dragged the parts into the jungle to eat. I rowed back to the mainland by myself."

"So no one knows what's in this Xibalba?" Tom said.

"Or if this Atapul X or any of the Lords of the Dead are real?" Ryan added.

"The *enanos* know what's there. The ones I questioned thought Atapul X was real. They claimed to have seen him sitting on his golden throne. They described a palace hidden in a wide clearing, deep in the heart of the jungle. Sumptuous, spacious apartments for each of the twelve Lords. Many slaves, many minor devils to provide them companionship and amusement. Hanging gardens, broad avenues and displays of stolen treasure.

"The *enanos* all told me that the approach to the gates of the underworld is lined with many terrible trials, many deadly traps. These are designed to protect the Lords of Death from intruders. We never got close enough to encounter any of them."

"What are the Lords of Death so afraid of?" Ryan asked.

"Afraid?" Chucho said. "No, they're like the Xibalban dogs. They're not afraid of anything. They've perfected their domain and their dominance, they are content with pulling the strings that make the wider world jerk. They want nothing to disturb their pleasure."

"How did criminals get to be self-appointed gods?" Tom said.

"The story the *enanos* told me is this," Chucho said. "Nukeday broke open the prison and freed the island's convicts who were being used for weapon testing by whitecoats from the north. Coiba was and is remote and dangerous, the perfect place to develop secret and illegal weapons of disease. If the diseases accidentally got loose, their spread could be controlled, and no one cared if the prisoners lived or died. After all, they were the scum of the Earth. When the predark die-off rate was unexpectedly high, the whitecoats had to import nonconvicts for the tests.

"After Armageddon, the prisoners used the island as a base for their piracy. In the early days, Matachìn recruited crews from the ruined port towns on the Atlantic side, and they conscripted sailors from captured ships on the high seas. The choice they offered was to join them or die. They tried to move their operations north to the cities of Cancun, Veracruz and Tampico, where the real booty was, but even with expanded navies they didn't have enough fighters to do the job. They were driven back, time and again. That's when they forced the few surviving whitecoats to start thawing out the disease weapons, bringing the freezies back to life."

"And the god business?" Tom said.

"That plays on ancient fears and superstitions to keep the populations under control, using minimum manpower and without resorting to more plague. Too much plague would kill too many people, and without workers to rob and enslave, the Lords would have nothing. The only way to end their reign of evil is to find them and kill them all."

"How long will it take to get there?" Ryan asked Tom.

The trader pointed at a dot on the map that read Colón, a city at the Atlantic end of the canal. "A week, mebbe ten days, depending on the wind. If it dies on us, it'll die for the black sloop, too. We shouldn't lose any ground on them."

"They have a full day's start on us now," Ryan said. "How are we going to make it up?"

"Don't know if we can," Tom said. "Depends on how much of a hurry they're in to off-load their cargo, how much sail they put up."

"Even if we can't catch them at sea, maybe we can get to them before they reach the other coast," Ryan said.

"The trail across the isthmus to the far side is fifty miles long," Chucho said. "It's hard going through jungle and there are many, many places for ambush."

"Then we'd better catch them before they leave Colón," Ryan said.

Chapter Seventeen

J. B. Dix stood near the bow of the black ship as it porpoised through white-capped, milky-azure seas. As the ship lurched, he leaned this way and that, swaying on the balls of his feet, eyes half shut. He felt like he was floating a foot or two above the deck's rough planking.

Defeat.

It tasted like chicken.

In a spicy red sauce.

Lassitude had set in on the second day out of Veracruz, a combination of the stultifying heat of the tropics, which he was not used to, and the realization that Ryan was by then most likely chilled, and that he had been unable to do anything to prevent it.

A hand pressed the middle of his back and gave him a hard shove toward the port rail. Then came a familiar gobbledy-gook command from behind.

J.B. didn't understand Dr. Montejo's words, but by now he knew what they meant. Get moving. Every day, once a day, the head whitecoat took the captives up on the top deck for limited exercise and a dose of fresh air. They were brought up individually, in chains and at blasterpoint. J.B. and the whitecoat were trailed by a very bored Matachìn holding a 9 mm submachine gun by its pistol grip.

J.B. lurched onward, face into the wind, forced to take baby steps by his manacles. How many days had they been sailing south nonstop? It was hard to keep count. At least a week, perhaps more.

The idea that he and the others could overcome their captors had turned out to be a pipedream, a bitter pill to swallow. As on the slave galley, the Matachìn had given them no window of opportunity for revolt. They'd foreseen and plugged every possible crack.

J.B. hadn't laid eyes on Mildred or Krysty since they'd left Veracruz. The separated companions had yelled back and forth to one another through their cabin-cell doors, but they could hardly make out the words for the intervening walls, the wind in the sails and the loud, constant hiss of the hull sliding through the sea. As of a few minutes ago, the women were still alive.

On the morning of the third day Doc had deduced that they were being drugged at every meal. It appeared their only choice was not to eat, but if they didn't eat, they'd be too weak to stage a successful escape. It was another cruel irony, something the pirates excelled at.

As J.B. headed for the stern, he visualized the round, brown faces of the female whitecoats as they brought in the tainted food. So bright, so happy, so bubbly. Not smug or superior or dismissive. They were simply glad to be of use. As twisted as their work was, it was clear they loved it.

Once a day the companions were taken out of their cabin, individually weighed, measured with calipers and examined, this while Dr. Montejo took careful notes. Then he escorted them on their slow circuits around the top deck, keeping track of the number of turns they did and the elapsed time.

The head whitecoat seemed very pleased by the course of events, as well. There was always a hint of glee in his dark eyes, infuriating glee. J.B. had noted that he never perspired, either, no matter how hot the sun got.

Since they'd left Veracruz, J.B. hadn't seen High Pile, the Matachìn commander, either. But there were always dread-locked sailors on deck when he took his forced constitutional. They made comments as he baby-stepped past them. Un-pleasant things from their tone of voice. And their laughter.

If he could have gotten hold of one of their gut-hook machetes, he would have given them something to laugh at. He would have split their filthy heads from crown to chin, and washed his hands in the jetting blood.

Five baby steps later, the gory fantasy had vanished. J.B. couldn't hold it in his mind to further flesh it out. Two steps more and he couldn't even remember it. As he staggered on, a brand-new thought popped into his head. How many miles had the black sloop covered so far?

The Armorer's grasp of geographical detail outside Death-lands was skimpy at best. Traveling around the clock, he guessed they could have made somewhere between 150 and 200 miles a day. If he could have recalled the number of days they'd been at sea, he might have been able to frame a coherent answer—assuming, of course, he didn't forget the question while he was struggling with the butt-simple multiplication.

Another few shuffling steps and he had indeed forgotten it.

A flurry of new questions occurred to him. How far south were they going? Were they headed to the ends of the Earth? Was there even such a place? Why would the pirates take them there?

There were no answers to those, either.

In a minute or so, the questions themselves disappeared.

J.B. found it strange and deeply unsettling that he couldn't manage to be sad over Ryan's presumed death. Not a single tear had he shed. It felt as though all his emotions had been ripped out, or buried under the paralyzing weight that filled his limbs and muddled his mind. He couldn't grieve for the fates of the other companions, he couldn't even grieve for himself. Only one thing kept him from being a complete zombie—he still had his fury, his outrage. Deep down, the heat of it, like embers of a fire that had burned out, remained. He clung to its familiar but fading warmth.

Doc and Jak had experienced the same, inexorable withdrawal from reality.

"I get the distinct impression that we are being fattened up, like cattle in a feed lot," Doc had said in a brief, lucid moment between opiate-laced meals.

"We stop eating?" Jak had asked.

"We haven't regained our full strength, yet," the Victorian said. "We may have to wait until the ship reaches its destination to make our move."

"What if this is our best and only shot at getting away?" J.B. had countered. "What if it only gets harder from here on?"

Doc had had no answer for that.

They couldn't get any information out of the whitecoats. Their keepers wouldn't respond to questions. Not even when Doc put them in Spanish. All they ever got back were toothy smiles.

The captives were being humored.

Nothing mattered, as long as the procedures went smoothly, as long as they ate their dinners and submitted to the daily examination. And the longer the voyage stretched on, the less anything mattered. Death would have almost been preferable to this limbo, this half existence. But J.B. didn't want to buy the ranch so far from home. And he didn't want to check out with chains around his wrists and ankles. He wanted to die with a blaster in his hand, having fired every round in the mag into his enemies' guts.

Although J.B. and Doc had tried to pump the Fire Talker in the cabin next door for information, Daniel had never let slip anything of use, either. It was hard for J.B. to believe he didn't know any more than they did about where they were going and why. Over the days and nights of confinement, the freezie's through-the-wall ramblings had become more and more disjointed. He kept confusing the science fiction series he'd worked on before skydark with events in the current reality. He had begun to mix up the predark pulp publisher and staff with the Lords of Death.

Was he raving because of the opiates in his food?

Or because his mind had cracked under the strain like a raw egg?

Over and over, Daniel recapped the tedious plots of his novels. Even worse, he dramatized the pivotal scenes in the 250-title story arc using an array of irritatingly unconvincing voices.

Apparently this was something he could do while drugged.

He never tired of the activity.

And he seemed to delight in how crazy it made Jak.

There were dents in the sheet steel wall where the albino had pounded with his fists to try to end the monologues. At one point, Jak had tried to articulate to Doc and J.B. the reasons for his violent loathing. In his halting speech, he'd said, "Stink hole never shot blaster, never chilled face-to-face, piece of shit liar never shuts up."

Which just about covered it, as far as J.B. was concerned.

As J.B. and his whitecoat escort rounded the black ship's bow, he saw the tiniest dark sliver of coastline on the starboard horizon. It hadn't been there before. One of the sailors let out a holler and pointed in that direction. Soon, all the pirates were yelling and pointing. A few moments later the deck banked sharply as the sloop heeled over, steering for the strip of land.

J.B. turned back to look at the helm and saw that High Pile was behind the wheel. The commander had decked himself out in full battle gear, his body armor oiled and gleaming, glittering masses of looted trinkets in his rat's nest coiffure and wrapped in coils around the ankles of his boots. He had applied a fresh coat of mascara to his eyes, his long beard was braided into a half-dozen jutting pigtails, and he held a stub of a cigar clenched between his teeth.

Mebbe this is it, Dix thought. Finally, the end of the line.

Under a hammering sun, a knob end of land gradually slid into view, and upon it sat what appeared to be a large city, its extensive skyline backlit in hard silhouette. The low-lying panorama was dominated by a pair of enormous predark buildings, fifteen or sixteen stories high. They were bigger than anything he'd seen in Veracruz. Structures half as tall clustered around their flanks.

J.B. had to shield his eyes from the painful glare off the water, glare that was magnified by the lenses of his spectacles. When he glanced over at Dr. Montejo, he saw delight in the whitecoat's face.

The closer they got to the shore, the less appealing the place looked to J.B. It wasn't just the backlighting that made the buildings appear so dark.

Everything was green.

Dark, dark green.

Even the twin towers were shrouded with vegetation.

The jungle had reclaimed its turf.

MILDRED LET HERSELF be half dragged up the companionway by a dreadlocked pirate. If it was unbearably hot below the black sloop's decks, it was even hotter above. As she and her odiferous escort stepped out into the air, the tropical sun's rays scorched her bare arms and shoulders like a flame.

Pretending to be drugged was easy. To convince her captors, all she had to do was half close her eyes, hang her head, go semilimp, and shuffle her feet as she was towed along. Behind her, Krysty was pulling the same stupefied act. After the first twenty-four hours aboard ship, after eating three of the wonderful meals, Mildred had figured their food was being tampered with. Krysty's stolen fork was confiscated that same night while they were unconscious. After that they'd been left to eat with their fingers. What they were experiencing wasn't just exhaustion or the effects of long-term starvation: it was opiates.

Mildred decided that the whitecoats had to be sprinkling the drug in the delectable sauces instead of injecting it into the meat. It was the only way to assure the captives got a full dose. To test this hypothesis, she waited until the little brown women left the cabin to bring meals to the others, then she carefully washed off all the meat in the sink. She and Krysty ate it, and ditched the rest of the food down the drain. Her guess was right. The chicken, pork and beef didn't soak up the drug from the sauce. In an hour or so, the feeling of stupor and dizziness completely vanished. Unfortunately, there was no way to communicate this discovery to the men.

J.B., Doc and Jak were already lined up on deck when she got there. They didn't look well. And from the dilated state of their pupils, they weren't faking it.

She and Krysty had tried to warn them about the food, but they couldn't tell if their shouts had been heard.

As it turned out, the menfolk had figured it out for themselves.

"Grub is poisoned," was the first thing J.B. said to her. His speech was badly slurred and he was having trouble standing. The second thing he said was "Ryan's probably dead by now."

That was likely true, as well.

Mildred felt a catch in her throat, an agonizing ache that spread down to her breastbone. Under the circumstances, grief was a luxury. It was also another form of shackle, an even more debilitating one when survival depended on a clear mind. She refused to give in to it. That's what Ryan would have done. That's the way he would have wanted it.

Doc and Jak were in no better shape than J.B. They had known the food was tainted and they'd eaten it anyway. Probably because they'd figured out they had to have it to regain their strength. Mildred was amazed that they hadn't realized they could just wash it off and be safe. Maybe they discovered the problem too late, or maybe by then they were too drugged to reason it out. Maybe the whitecoats had kept better watch on them, making sure they ate it all. At least she and Krysty were drug-free.

Mildred scanned the green vista across the water ahead. She had a fair idea of how far they'd come. Because they weren't doped up, she and Krysty had been able to keep track of the number of days they'd traveled and to estimate the average speed. Because the pirates thought she was drugged to the gills, or because they didn't give a damn, they had been less careful about what they'd said in Mildred's presence. She had overheard them mention a name that she knew. A possible, even a likely destination.

Colón.

Panama.

In her former life, before she had been cryogenically frozen, Mildred had never visited Colón City, but she knew a little about it, having closely followed the news coverage of the U. S. invasion and fall of the Panamanian military dictator, Manuel Noriega, in 1989. She knew Colón was situated at the Atlantic entrance to the Panama canal.

If the city had been taken back by the jungle, the world-famous canal was nowhere to be seen.

As the black sloop neared the entrance to the bay, High Pile ordered his crew to drop sail and he started up the ship's engines. It appeared the route to landfall was too tricky for wind power. Though broad, the bay had filled in on either side with dense stands of mangrove scrub, leaving a deep but narrow central channel. Cloudy, turquoise water lapped against a dark, impenetrable tangle of tree roots. The thin, overcast skies and the reflections off the jungle gave the air an oppressive, yellowish tinge.

A sickly place, Mildred reckoned, cooking at a slow simmer in the ninety-plus heat of midday. The atmosphere was sulfurous, thick with the smell of biological decay. Of swamp muck. Ahead, between the bow of the black ship and the overgrown ruin of a city, the beach was not sand, it was a flat of beige-colored, pestilential mud.

The city's buildings, covered with greenery, reminded her of the Mayan temples in Guatemala she had vacation-toured before skydark. Enormous complexes, buried under mounds of earth and vegetation; every distant hilltop the tip of yet another lost temple. How many people had lived in Colón, the gateway to the Pacific, before the end of the world? She guessed a couple of hundred thousand.

Something truly catastrophic had happened here.

Something different than the tidal wave damage Veracruz had suffered.

In Veracruz, the surviving population had been large enough to keep the jungle beaten back, to maintain a semblance of the predark status quo. Whatever had happened in Colón, its impact had been much more devastating to infrastructure and to the human population. Mildred had to figure the canal was a likely target for a Soviet MIRV on hellday, but this disaster hadn't been the *direct* result of a nuke strike. If it had, there would have been the remains of a crater, a dead zone filled in with seawater. No buildings would have been left standing. Perhaps the all-out exchange of 2001 was over and done with before the Soviet ICBM aimed at the canal left its launch pad.

As she looked for the canal entrance, the first of the series of locks that raised and lowered ship traffic, and saw nothing but mangrove swamp, it dawned on her. The canal was gone. The locks were gone. Maybe the dams that held back the fresh water used to lift the ships over the isthmus were gone, too.

Somewhere in the back of her mind she recalled a number: fifty-two million. That was how many gallons of fresh water it had taken to move a ship from one end of the canal to the other. To supply the enormous quantity of water, great rivers had been dammed, vast man-made lakes had been created.

Mildred shivered, despite the heat, as she imagined the towering wall of water, water brown with a century's worth of backed-up silt, rushing down the canal's channel, scouring away everything in its path. A tightly focused laser beam of a disaster.

Just because this end of the canal hadn't suffered a direct hit by a nuke, it didn't mean the destruction wasn't nuke-spawned. Chances were, the all-out exchange and the breaking of the dams were connected; chances were, they happened on the same day, at roughly the same time. The backbone of Central America was volcanic, Mildred knew, and it had a long history of violent earthquakes. The Soviet earth-shaker warheads launched against North America were designed to induce far-reaching geologic cataclysm.

Central America was a hair-trigger waiting for just the right tight-and-curly.

She looked around and saw no beached container ships rusting among the mangroves, and farther off the stern there was no breakwater to protect and mark the bay's entrance. A lineup of cargo ships would have been anchored in the bay, off the canal entrance on the fateful day, waiting for their turn to cross the isthmus. As big as the tankers and freighters were, they would have been no match for the wave that came crashing down on them. To drain the hundreds of trillions of gallons of backed-up water would have taken a very long time. The torrent would have continued unabated for many hours, driving the wrecked ships far offshore to sink, disassembling the breakwater, boulder by boulder.

The poor people of Colón had had no chance. There was nowhere to run, but up. A few of the lucky ones might have made it to safety in the top floors of the tallest buildings. The rest, caught unaware at street level, unable to understand what was happening, unable to react in time, would have been washed out to sea with everything else that wasn't nailed down—and most of what was.

Ahead, the narrow ship channel was marked at intervals with tied-together clusters of floating, oil-stained, white plastic jugs fixed to the bottom with nylon rope. Closer to shore, two sailing ships were moored on the edge of the channel, anchored fore and aft to keep from drifting onto the flats. Their crews were nowhere to be seen. Farther on, in much shallower water, a half dozen small, open, fishing boats were tied to another claptrap buoy. There were no power vessels of any size, which made Mildred wonder if the Matachìn kept all their engine-powered ships farther north, closer to the primary sources of fuel. That made sense if fuel supplies were limited, and transport was difficult.

Beyond the fishing boats, she could see the uneven stumps of immense, concrete pier pilings, the pier decks having been ripped away.

Framing the nasty bay on three sides were low, heavily jungled hills. Had all this vegetation, had this complex ecosystem really survived a "nuclear winter"? she asked herself. A global deep-freeze that had supposedly lasted ten years?

Mildred had always had serious doubts on that subject—after all, who supposedly had been keeping track of the time and temperature, postnukeday? Was it some anonymous ass-scratcher living in a cave? Where were the readings taken? How? Over what span of years? As a scientist, Mildred knew precise definitions as well as precise measurements were vital to understanding natural phenomena. What was the ass-scratcher's definition of "nuclear winter"? Did he-she even have one? Or was this just one more in a long line of Deathlands myths, contrived by idiots for idiots to pass the time while they cracked and ate each other's nits?

If the presumed "nuclear winter" had been a globe-encompassing event, it couldn't have begun and completely dissipated as quickly as a generation. That kind of rapid freezing and warming on a planetary scale simply wasn't possible, short of a change in earth's orbit. If a "nuclear winter" scenario had happened after Armageddon, it was most likely localized to the Northern Hemisphere, where the missile strikes and counterstrikes had landed, where the atmospheric dust clouds would have been the thickest; and if there had been increased glaciation, it hadn't been of any consequence.

And that didn't address the point that ten years of unusually cold, localized weather didn't even qualify as a mini–ice age, let alone "nuclear winter."

A short distance from the shoreline, half in, half out of the water, was the twisted base of an enormous, latticework steel tower. It jutted like the bloody skeleton of some prehistoric reptile. The other end of the ruined tower was submerged, buried under the pale mud. In between, Mildred could see the rusting framework, some two hundred feet of it, just under the murky surface.

The waterfront of Colón had been rebuilt after the disaster, albeit on a much less ambitious scale. The modern city had become a shantyville on stilts over the stinking tidal mud flats, a maze of whitewashed, single-story buildings connected to one another and to the solid ground inland by elevated wooden walkways on flimsy-looking, pecker-pole pilings. Beyond the peaks of the sheet metal roofs, on the other side of a narrow road cut, was a twenty-foot-high, solid wall of green leaves and branches.

At High Pile's bellowed command, the pirate crew hopped to it, anchoring the black sloop securely fore and aft, within one hundred of the nearest shanty-on-stilts.

There were no fortifications in evidence. No gun emplacements, either. It seemed strange to Mildred that the Matachìn port sat undefended. Maybe it wasn't a stronghold, after all. Or were all the potential threats so far away that defense wasn't an issue?

Krysty shuffled up alongside Mildred, her red hair hanging lank around her shoulders. They didn't look at each other; they certainly didn't speak. They had decided not to talk in front of their captors. They didn't want give away the fact that they were lucid. And perhaps get themselves forcibly injected with drugs. The whitecoats could have done that anyway, used hypodermics to dose them, but they seemed to want everything to be nice and friendly, all happy-face smiles, even when they were doing someone an injury.

The pirates lowered three large rowboats over the side. The companions were forced into one of them, then joined by a trio of Matachìn guards. High Pile, the whitecoats and more pirates got into the other boats, leaving the black ship with a skeleton crew.

At least the companions weren't doing the rowing this time.

While they sat packed shoulder to shoulder on the stern thwarts, the pirates facing them amidships hauled back on the oars. The pirate lounging in the bow held a submachine gun balanced on his lap.

The sun flashed on the golden trinkets wound around their boot tops. When Mildred glanced down she saw a name etched on a dangling locket: Lupe. A delicate, heart pendant on a thin gold chain. There were other names, too, and different styles of bracelet and necklace. Trophies of pillage, of rape and murder, worn like badges of honor, like combat medals.

One of the rower-Matachìn caught her looking at his trinket collection. A lewd gleam in his eye, he puckered up and blew her an obscene kiss.

Animals, she thought.

Stinking animals.

Mildred wondered what had kept them in check on the journey south. After all, they had had access to the cabin she and Krysty shared. Drugged women in chains. That sounded made-to-order for these creeps. Their lust, she reasoned, had to have been controlled by fear. If not fear of the wrath of their commander, then fear of the wrath of the Lords of Death. Which, upon reflection, didn't bode all that well for any of the captives. It probably meant some greater purpose—or far nastier end—awaited them.

The Matachìn beached the bows of the boats on the mud flats. Then Mildred and the others were hoisted out by the armpits by pirates on either side. The seas were warm as bathwater. And this was as close to a bath as the Matachìn got. There was no way the captives could have navigated the oozing muck with their ankles in chains. The pirates sank in up to their knees as they struggled to lug them to the lip of a slimy concrete ramp that led up to the walkway.

At High Pile's signal, two of the Matachìn waded back out to the boats, pushed one off the mud, jumped in and started rowing for the ship.

A welcoming committee awaited the others on the platform

above the ramp. If the five men were Matachìn, they had gone paramilitary. They wore jungle camouflage T-shirts and BDU pants. On shoulder slings they carried the same stubby little 9 mm submachine guns as the pirates. As the prisoners slowly ascended the ramp, little brown-faced kids peeked out at them through the glassless windows and doorless doorways of the shanties, then ducked back.

High Pile and Dr. Montejo approached one of the camou-flage greeters, the one with the most radically sculpted face. He was wearing a broad-brimmed straw hat. To Mildred's surprise, the commander and the whitecoat didn't salute, or offer to shake hands or simply nod, they immediately pros-trated themselves on the walkway, raising their butts in the air, pressing their noses into the rough boards.

Subservience in spades.

The man they genuflected to grunted something and the two rose.

When High Pile spoke to his superior, Mildred thought she caught a proper name, or maybe it was a title or rank: Nibor. Something like that. High Pile repeated it every six or seven words.

The sun, filtered through the mesh of the straw, cast a tiny checkerboard of light and dark across Nibor's face. His head and eyebrows were shaved. The tops of his ears had been shaved, as well, cut into points, and the lobes excised entirely. Narrow seams of scar tissue marked his brown cheeks, running from under the centers of his lower eyelids to his jawline, dividing his face into three unequal sections. Golden artificial fangs on his lower jaw curled out in front of his upper lip, the philtrum of which had been split like a dog's, the fleshy drapes pulled back, so the sharpened points of his natural teeth could show. He wore a necklace of ivory-colored, human finger bones, separated from each other by strung, gold-filled human teeth.

Mildred knew extensive plastic surgery when she saw it. She had seen it on the governor-general of Veracruz, as well. Whoever had wielded the #15 scalpel was a highly skilled surgeon, with the artistic vision of a raving psychopath.

Was Nibor a priest or a warrior? Mildred wondered. Or perhaps he was a combination of both.? The uniform he and the others in the welcoming committee sported was suitable for action, not empty, mumbo-jumbo ceremony. The others all had shaved heads, but less extreme facial alterations. It occurred to her that the scarifications, like the height of the piled dreadlocks, might be symbols of rank—only permanent, until death. Was the quintet a military wing of the Lords of Death priesthood, or perhaps some specially tasked, elite guard unit?

A conversation ensued between High Pile, Montejo and Nibor. As it progressed, Mildred managed to get the general drift. The Matachìn commander first bragged to his superior about what his men had done in Tierra de la Muerte, how they had laid waste to Padre Island, and brought back these five most suitable subjects, which he was turning over to Nibor with the greatest respect. High Pile announced that he and his crew would remain in Colón to await the return of the prisoners. Whereupon he and they would ship back to their real job: pillaging and chilling.

Nibor nodded. His reply was difficult to understand because of the oral modifications, which tended to muffle and distort his speech, but to Mildred it sounded like he said, "In a month they will be back here."

Dr. Montejo was proud of his work, too, and he butted in, pointing out his success in restoring the captives to full and robust health.

Instead of a pat on the back, he got a disinterested grunt from Nibor.

High Pile turned and gestured at his crew, then told the dog-faced man that he and his sailors had grown tired of banging the little *brujas*. And that he hoped the local whorehouse would give them some better variety.

Brujas? Mildred asked herself. Witches? Was High Pile talking about the little brown whitecoats?

The two women in white giggled and tittered behind their upraised hands, happy as clams that they rated a mention to the Big Man, even if it was in the form of a complaint about their job performance.

Leaving Mildred to wonder where in hell all three of them had been trained, how they'd been trained, and by whom. It appeared that in these climes the status symbol of the white lab coat had lost much of its objective, professional luster.

At least she knew that wherever they were being taken by Nibor the plan was for them to eventually be brought back to Colón, and then taken north again. Which meant they weren't going to be chilled in the immediate future—not on purpose, anyway.

"*¿Su enano, dondè esta?*" Nibor said.

"*Allà,*" High Pile replied, pointing back at the water.

Out on the mud flat, the rowboat had returned from the ship bearing another passenger on the stern, this one swaddled, bagged head to foot in black mosquito netting. Though the passenger's ankles weren't manacled, the pirates carried him—or her—over the mud to the ramp.

It wasn't until the shrouded one reached the top of the ramp that Mildred recognized who it was: the Fire Talker, Desipio. The mosquito netting was like a beekeeper's suit, with sewn-in arms and legs. The reason for the protection was a puzzle she couldn't immediately solve, or bring herself to care about. Obviously, the piece of shit had been transferred from the hold of the tug to the black sloop.

The pirates kept him at a distance from the other captives, and their bodies as a barrier between them. An extra precaution.

Doc, J.B. and Jak weren't in any condition to do him serious harm, as much as they might have wanted to. As for Mildred, she held her own fury in check with the thought that at some point soon she would get her chance to pay back the bastard who'd betrayed them and gotten Ryan Cawdor chilled.

The dog-faced man waved for the Matachìn and their entourage to follow. Mildred and the companions were ushered along the walkways to dry land. Except for the curious children, the inhabitants of the little ville-on-stilts had apparently all taken cover, waiting for the potential Lords of Death storm to pass. The column walked along a deeply eroded dirt lane on the edge of old Colón. Most of the standing structures were rubblized, home to small, darting lizards. Much larger, striped iguanas slithered from sunning spots on concrete pads into the safety of the bush.

The modern city above the treetops had been eaten alive by jungle. The empty window frames of the high-rises had been invaded by clusters of green creepers, like scavenger worms boring through the eye sockets of skulls. The farther they moved from the water, the hotter it got, and bug song sawed from every branch and leaf. The rilled road soon gave way to a narrower, tree-shaded lane. The shacks on either side of the path had to be of more recent construction. No way could those ramshackle affairs have withstood the force of the flood, although some were thrown up on the ruins of the predark structures. Strangler vines wrapped around trunks and branches, their trumpetlike, bright yellow flowers gave off a dizzingly sweet perfume. Some of the tree branches were laden with fruit, as well. Papayas and guanabanas lay rotting on the ground. Black-and-white pigs too drained by the heat to gorge themselves lay panting on their sides in the shade at the sides of the road.

The land of plenty.

Mildred wondered what the population of Colón was now. A few hundred souls, maybe? A thousand at most? It was hard to say because there could have been dwellings off the lane, in clearings deeper in the jungle.

Ahead, peeking up over the treetops on the right, was a much bigger structure that had obviously ridden out, or more likely been missed by the wall of flood water. Two stories high, and easily 250 feet long, one side of its facade bordered the lane. It looked like an enormous Spanish hacienda from colonial times: white plaster perimeter, red-tiled roof, black wood trim.

As they got closer, where the concrete and plaster had fallen away, Mildred could see hugely thick brick walls underneath. At one time, shaded balconies along the second floor had overlooked the lane. They were long gone. All that remained were the jagged black remnants of their support posts. Steel shutters covered the second-story windows and balcony doors to keep out the heat—and presumably incoming bullets. There were holes in the roof where tiles had slipped away. The ground-floor windows facing the lane were massively barred.

Mildred noticed a pair of recent, rather crude additions to the corners of the roof: machine-gun posts, with their own palm-frond sunshades. Across the lane from the hacienda, the jungle branches had been reduced to white-tipped stubs.

Gut-hook machetes at work.

Mildred guessed she was looking at the Matachìn HQ.

They were led through the story-and-a-half-tall double wooden gate. Mildred immediately smelled fresh horseshit. Sure enough, in the far corner of the yard was a stable. The enclosed compound was bordered on four sides by the wings of the hacienda. To their right, in front of a palm-frond roofed patio, four horses were tied to a hitching post and two horse-drawn carts stood waiting. There were no gasoline or diesel-powered wags in sight.

The Matachìn, High Pile included, directed their attention to the shaded tables under the palm fronds, and the dozen or so brown women who lounged on the chairs and couches there. The pirates unleashed a predictable chorus of whistles and kissing sounds. The gaudy sluts grinned and waved for the men to join them, pointing at the full bottles of joy juice on the tabletops. A couple of them jerked down the necklines of their peasant blouses to expose black-tipped breasts.

This made the pirates very happy.

While High Pile and his crew hurried over to introduce themselves, the paramilitaries hustled Mildred and the companions into the back of one of the horse carts. Their chains were looped through iron rings in the cart's low rear and side walls. When they were secured, Nibor and one of his lackeys helped Daniel into the cart, as well. They put him forward, chaining his cuffs to the front wall, well out of the reach of his fellow passengers.

Daniel didn't say anything.

Nor did any of the companions speak to him.

Over on the patio, the sluts were getting comfortable on the pirates' laps, holding the bottles up so their new friends could drink their fill.

One of the paramilitaries climbed onto the driver's seat of the companions' cart. Wherever they were headed, the 9 mill subguns were not enough firepower. Nibor handed the cart driver a well-worn Soviet RPD—a 7.62 mm, 100-round, drum-fed, light machine gun. Mildred saw there was a mount for a bipod on the barrel right behind the front sight, but the bipod's legs were missing—it looked as if the weapon had been customized with a hacksaw. The driver set the machine gun on the seat beside him, close to hand. Dog-face and the three others slung identical weapons across their backs, then mounted the saddled horses. Montejo and the little women climbed into a second, supply-loaded cart, and the doctor took the reins.

With a lurch, the two-cart, six-horse convoy set off across the courtyard and through the open gates. The slow movement caused air to flow over Mildred's sweating body and face, but it did nothing to cool her off.

Mildred soon realized why they weren't riding in wags, why there were no wags in evidence inside the compound. Wags never could have made it over the shambles of a road, which deteriorated even further as they put the hacienda behind them: broad, slick patches of exposed bedrock, potholes deep enough to bury a man. The jarring reality of a no-tech world was something she'd learned to expect from the hellscape. The fabled survival of progress in these latitudes was nothing but a charade.

This was no better than Deathlands.

As they jolted off the walls and bounced on the floor of the narrow-wheel-based cart, Mildred turned her attention to the Fire Talker. Through the netting, she could see he still wore his ridiculous camouflage do-rag, a survivalist affectation that virtually shouted "Poseur!" She could also see how pale his skin had become. That was understandable: he hadn't seen the light of day for more than three weeks.

The puzzle of the mosquito netting vexed her.

"Why are they keeping you under wraps?" Mildred asked him.

"I had a bad reaction to bug bites," Daniel said matter of factly. From the dopey smile on his face, he was feeling no pain at present, thanks to the residual effect of his breakfast.

"That's why they locked you in the hold on the tug?" Mildred said.

"Uh-huh."

"You looked pretty goddamned lively to me on Padre Island," Krysty said. "Not sick at all when you set the pirates on us."

That wasn't the only thing that made no sense to Mildred. "And you didn't catch whatever it was that chilled the islanders," she said.

"Lucky, I guess."

Mosquito bites. Virus. Viral transfer. Daniel's isolation outside the target zone. Netting to protect those around him when he was out of doors. Suddenly it all fell into place for Mildred, and it didn't make her a happy camper. Fists tightly clenched at her sides she said, "Either you were lucky, or you brought the plague to Padre Island with you. You brought it there in your blood."

"What are you saying, Mildred?" Doc asked as he tried and failed to follow the thread of logic.

"I think our shitweasel here is a carrier," she said. "I think he's the source of the infection that slaughtered all those people on Padre. His blood is loaded with the disease virus. He's a walking biological weapon. Skeeters bite him, pick up the virus in his blood, then bite someone else and give it to them. On and on, until just about everyone in the surrounding area is infected. The disease would spread through an isolated population in a big hurry."

"You bastard!" J.B. growled, lunging for the Fire Talker only to be brought up a yard short by his chains.

Daniel jerked back, instinctively raising his netted hands to protect his face. When it was clear he was in no danger, he lowered his hands.

"It is true?" Krysty demanded of him.

Daniel didn't try to deny what Mildred surmised. He just shrugged it off. The cat was out of the bag. No big deal.

"What kind of a creature are you?" Krysty said.

"I believe the technical term for him is mass murderer," Doc said.

"It's in my blood," Daniel admitted. "I can't help it. I didn't put it there. I didn't ask for it. They did it to me."

"Who did it to you?" Mildred said.

The Fire Talker didn't answer.

"He told us he was part of a whitecoat experiment before nukeday," J.B. said. "Said it went wrong."

"You may not have asked for it," Krysty said, "but you can control how it's used."

"She is referring to your moral fiber," Doc added. "Or lack thereof."

"That isn't my fault, either," Daniel countered. "It was my parents. They rejected me when I was little because I was different. I wasn't like them, or anyone else in the family. They couldn't understand my need to read adventure books and to try to write them. They were always yelling at me about it. I had to hide my short stories or they'd burn them in the fireplace. They thought I was lazy and a daydreamer, maybe even somewhat mentally defective, and they were sure that I'd never amount to anything. They wanted me to do something worthwhile with my life, something that made good, steady money like my cousins who owned a fast-food franchise and a strip-mall copy-and-mail service center. I could never live up to their expectations, and they never lived up to mine. That's haunted me ever since I was seven years old. My parents have been dead more than a century and I still think about their rejection every day."

All the buck-passing and boo-hooing set Mildred's teeth on edge. "You're a monster," she informed him. "A self-made fucking monster."

"It isn't like I chilled those people with my own two hands," Daniel countered.

"Yeah, you don't have the stones for that," J.B. said.

"They call you *enano,* that means dwarf," Mildred said.

"I am not treated well, if that's what you're getting at. I am regarded as a necessary evil."

"You're pure scum, so why should anyone treat you otherwise?" Krysty said.

"Because what I've got inside me has done a lot for them," Daniel replied. "It's served their cause."

"What do they intend to do to us?" Mildred asked.

Daniel shrugged again, this time in apparent disinterest.

"Where are they taking us?" Mildred pressed.

"They call it Xibalba," he answered after a pause. "Someplace even warmer."

"To hell, you mean?"

"Pretty much."

It was Jak's turn to make a grab for the Fire Talker, and he moved in a white blur. The morning's drugs seemed to be wearing off more quickly than usual, perhaps because they were all perspiring so heavily, sweating the dope right out of their systems. Despite a valiant effort, the albino youth came up well short at the end of his chains. This time the freezie bastard didn't even flinch. He just sat there as calm as could be, his arms folded over his chest, grinning from ear to ear.

The companions rode on in stony silence. They had learned the hard way that they had to watch what they said in front of the net-draped backstabber.

Ahead, Mildred saw that brown water covered a long section of the lane. Dog-face and the other horsemen slowed down before they entered it. As the companions' cart rolled onto the swampy section of roadway, the wheels began to shudder and the cart box shook so violently it felt like it was going to fly apart. When Mildred looked over the side, the bow wave created by the front wheels revealed the cause of the rough ride. The road metal was made of foot-wide tree trunk sections, no doubt tropical hardwoods impervious to rot. They had been pounded straight down into the mud, edge to edge. This to keep the horse carts from sinking in over the tops of their wheels.

They left the tree trunks and began climbing up a shallow grade. The sides of the road rose much faster than they did. Soon it was clear they were traveling in a man-made ditch. It was more than fifty feet deep. A shallow ooze of water meandered down the middle of it. In rainy season, Mildred knew the flow along this route would have been a torrent. In places the side walls had caved in, top to bottom, from erosion, forcing the lane to wind back and forth around the mounds of toppled earth and rock.

"Where the fuck are we?" J.B. asked.

"We're in what's left of the old ship channel," Mildred told him. "Believe it or not, this is the Atlantic entrance to the Panama Canal."

"What canal?" J.B. said. "It's practically nukin' dry."

"Remarkable!" Doc exclaimed as he took it in. "This project was under way when I was time-trawled, but the French were a far cry from finishing it."

"They never did finish it," Mildred told him. "They turned it over to the U.S. around 1900. Took another fifteen years to get it done."

"When completed," Doc said, "it was supposed to be one of the wonders of the modern world."

"Not so wonderful," Jak said. "Looks like nukin' big shithole."

After they'd gone farther, Doc said, "But where are the locks? There have to be locks."

"My guess is they broke open, probably from earthquakes on nukeday," Mildred said. "One after another, like dominoes falling. Then the force of the water released from the dammed-up lakes tore the gates right out of the bedrock, tore out all the shoring, too. Thirty years of sweat and sacrifice, gone in the blink of an eye."

After what Mildred estimated was a three-mile journey, they exited the far end of the narrow channel. In front of them the vista broadened, exposing a plain of destruction all the way to the western horizon. It was the former artificial lake bed.

This was a different sort of devastation, a vast table of low, scrub vegetation and bare rock, broken here and there by densely forested humps and hills—the high points in elevation that had been turned into islands when the river valley was flooded to form the lake. When the trillions of gallons of water had flowed out to sea, it had scraped the landscape clean, right down to the bedrock. The road in front of them was much wider and well traveled. It ran string-straight for a good mile, then it disappeared around a forested mound.

They descended onto the sweltering plain. Skeletons of one-hundred-foot-tall trees, two centuries dead, drowned when the land was inundated, were smothered in drooping tangles of strangler vines. The second growth scrub was no more than eight feet high, and packed into dense patches, presumably where some topsoil remained. Clouds of black flies buzzed over potholes filled with stagnant water. Wide swatches of wet mud, possibly quicksand, lay just off the rutted path. The convoy made slow but steady progress, heading toward the flanks of the low islands-hills.

When Mildred looked behind them, off to the right, she saw a vast wedge of smooth concrete embedded in the lake's rim. The dam hadn't burst, after all. That explained the extent of the damage to Colón. The full force of the flood had gone out the ship channel, through the city, into the bay, not the natural river channel well to the west.

Under the blazing sun, in the still air, the blistering heat and humidity, it was hard to breathe.

"It must be close to fifty miles to the Pacific side of this ditch," Mildred said to the Fire Talker, pointing over his shoulder to the west. "Are we going that far? Is it all going to be like this?"

The poseur didn't answer her. He was pretending, and not very convincingly, that he was asleep.

Over and over, Mildred kept asking herself, What do these fuckers want with us? Why us? Why were we pulled out of the line in the fort? And the other survivors of Padre and the three weeks of rowing dragged off to ritual slaughter? It was High Pile who'd done it, she recalled. It had been his decision to spare their lives—for something. The bits of the puzzle were there, she could feel it, but she couldn't quite piece them together.

Not yet, anyway.

If they were going to get out of this mess, Mildred knew they were all going to have to stop eating. She also knew it was possible that J.B., Doc and Jak would experience withdrawal symptoms—fever, itching, sweating, nervousness. Symptoms that would be difficult to hide. On the trail there would be no way to rinse off the drugs. They would have to ditch their food, somehow. And do it in front of Daniel without his catching on. That wasn't going to be easy.

Looking at the sniveling bastard feigning sleep to avoid confrontation, she wished she'd had another yard of slack in her chain. Kicking in his head, even if it didn't save their lives, would ultimately save the lives of innumerable others.

As they approached the first of the islands-hills, coming within perhaps two hundred yards of it, Nibor called a halt to advance. He and the other horsemen dismounted. Their cart driver locked the brake, then picked up the RPD.

For a split second, when he stood and turned the weapon toward them, Mildred's heart sank. She thought, This is it.

They've taken us out to this waste ground to finish us off. That's what the others thought, too; she could see it in their eyes.

Then her whitecoat's logical brain kicked in. Driving all the way out here just to execute them seemed like a whole lot of trouble for nothing.

Her analysis proved correct.

The cart driver held the light machine gun braced against his hip, aimed not at the passengers, but at the scraggly line of scrub trees off to their left. Dog-face and the other three horsemen aimed their weapons toward the forested hill and points on either side.

Then they all cut loose at once, unleashing a thundering roar of overlapping autofire that echoed out over the flatland.

In the distance Mildred could see leaves and branches clipped off and dropped by the sprays of bullets, and puffs of dust where they struck and skipped off the bare ground; this in a broad half circle in front of them.

Five hundred rounds fired in forty-five seconds.

If there were hostiles out there lurking, if there were savage critters out there lying in wait, they either turned tail or fell flat on their bellies.

The warrior priests were sending a message. A don't-fuck-with-us, we have ammo to burn.

Nibor and his men reloaded their RPDs with fresh drum magazines before the convoy moved on.

Chapter Eighteen

Commander Guillermo Casacampo lay in a stinking, moaning heap. The hiss of the Coleman lamp on the floor beside the mattress played counterpoint to the erratic slurp and slap of sweaty flesh as three of the hacienda's sluts rendered intimate service.

The woman astride him had a determined, screwed-up, go-for-broke expression on her face as she merrily humped away. The other faces were busy, hidden behind the curves of her flipping hips, busy making lollypops of his testicles.

Casacampo was in hog heaven, lying back, smoking a fat, black cigar while getting seriously laid. Similar exertions earlier in the evening had caused his high-piled hair to fall loose and tumble around his shoulders. The sluts were wearing borrowed golden trinkets, from his coiff's treasure trove, on their brown wrists and around their slender necks. All three were shaved bare as babies between the legs; not like the whitecoat witches, he thought, who were woolly mammoths down there.

These sluts really knew how to screw. They performed half twists of the hips at just the right phase of the upstroke.

And their enthusiasm for the work was appreciated.

He puffed away on his stogie, head cradled on a forearm, watching his *verga* slippery slick, dipping in and out of suctioning, superheated heaven. He clenched the cigar between his teeth. Oh, that half twist! It had nailed him, again. The pirate's hips jerked up from the mattress in a flurry of rapid, savage thrusts. The slut squealed and hung on to his chest for dear life, her legs flapping to the sides, her arms flapping to the sides, titties flapping every which way.

Glorious.

When his release faded, Casacampo sank back onto the sweaty sheets, taking the cigar out of his mouth so he could more easily gasp for breath. The slut disengaged herself and rolled onto her back beside him.

A chorus of rhythmic moans was coming from rooms down the hall. Moans punctuated by shrill cries that almost sounded like pain. But these Colón sluts weren't hurting; just the opposite. His crew was hammering it, doing credit to the Matachìn name.

Then his head began to spin. It spun so fast he had to close his eyes and hang on to the edge of the bed. How much had he drunk, how much looney-weed had he smoked? How many times had these sweaty little bitches brought him to climax? For the life of him, he couldn't remember.

A month of this kind of excess was the kind of R&R the doctor ordered, a just compensation for the dangers he'd faced, the valor he'd shown, for the victories he'd laid at the feet of the Lords of Death.

One of the other sluts picked up a jar from the floor, dipped a finger it to its contents, then started smearing the semiliquid stuff on his rapidly diminishing *verga*. The jungle concoction was cool at first, then warm, then warmer still. He felt a tickle deep in his pelvis as his manhood slowly but surely became hard yet again.

Music drifted in from down the hall. A happy, rhythmic tune. One of the sluts was playing a harmonica. No doubt about it, he thought, these Colón ladies were multitalented mistresses of the fuck. Not so much to look at from the neck up, as most of their teeth had cracked edges, like they'd been used to open beer bottles. But they didn't giggle like idiots the whole time they were being banged, like some he could name.

Casacampo took a long pull on his cigar as the anointing slut hurriedly straddled his hips. As she leaned back, impaling herself on him, he gave her a resounding smack on the behind.

Giddyap.

Then the room's door opened and slammed back.

Everyone on the mattress looked as a naked pirate staggered in, his eyes bugging out of his head.

At first Casacampo thought the sailor was just wild-ass drunk, then he saw that his throat had been cut from ear to ear. Blood sheeted over his bare chest and dripped down his legs onto the floor.

The wounded Matachìn fell to his knees, unable to speak, begging for help with those bulging eyes and bloody outstretched hands. A shadowy figure appeared in the doorway right behind him. A savage boot between the shoulder blades drove the dying man face-first into the floor.

Casacampo blinked in shock and the cigar dropped from his gaping mouth. In the glow of the lantern, he saw the straps of a headlamp, then the black eye patch. He saw the silencer-equipped submachine gun and the machete stained crimson from gut hook to hand guard.

Then a second man stepped alongside the first.

Another eye patch, only the opposite eye socket was covered.

Both of them were alive. Both of them had escaped execution.

The commander prayed that he was merely asleep, that it was a dream brought on by all the joy juice and the marijuana he'd consumed. But it was not. It was all too real. He threw the slut off him, threw her so hard she flew from the mattress and thudded in a heap to the floor.

"You're not going to be needing that," Chucho said with a smirk, pointing the fat shroud of a submachine gun silencer at his *verga*.

"*¡Whuh puta!*" Casacampo snarled, groping alongside the mattress for his other weapon.

Not a chance.

The blue-eyed Hero Twin put a boot sole on the barrel of the 9 mm subgun, pinning it to the floor as he raised the machete to strike. The sluts ducked their heads and scattered for the far corners of the room.

A stinging kick in the backside wrung a groan from the pirate commander.

"Get up, asshole," Chucho ordered. "You're coming with us."

Surely there would be rescue, Casacampo thought. Surely his crew would mount a counterattack.

Chucho tied his wrists behind his back with a plastic cable tie, cinched it up so tight it nearly made him whimper.

The blue-eyed Twin then asked Chucho a question. Casacampo didn't understand.

Chucho answered in kind, then he translated his reply into Spanish, "Fuck the bastard, let him go naked."

"Come, my brown beauties," Chucho said as he waved the

women to their feet, then ushered them out of the room like a mother hen. "These stinking murderers will never molest you again."

Casacampo couldn't help but bristle at that characterization. The "beauties" in question hadn't objected in the least to being molested; in fact, they had insisted on repeated such impositions.

Barefoot, bare-assed, his tower of dreads—the symbol of his rank—deconstructed, the commander was unceremoniously booted through the doorway and into the second-story hall.

Someone will nip this effrontery in the bud, he assured himself. Two one-eyed men couldn't have killed all my crew.

Chucho shoved him onward, toward the main staircase. He stumbled past the open doors of rooms lit by white gas lanterns. The other sluts had all fled. In every room his men lay naked, butchered like hogs on the mattresses or the floor, sprawled in spreading pools of their own blood. No one had gotten off a shot. No one had gotten off a shout.

It then occurred to him that the piercing cries he'd heard from down the corridor hadn't been from sluts in climax, and weren't cries of pleasure, but of surprise, pain and sudden death. The Hero Twins had made their way down the hall, room by room, to take him last of all. Drunk on joy juice, high on marijuana, in the midst of a marathon screw session, his pirates were not expecting that kind of trouble. Still, how could two men overcome ten times of their number and not raise an alarm?

It turned out that there was a third member of the team. Another gringo waited for them at the top of the stairs. He had long flowing mustaches and a big, stainless-steel revolver on his hip. Like the others, he carried a silenced submachine gun and wore a headlamp, this over the crown of his billcap.

Casacampo offered up no empty threats as he was urged down the staircase by the Hero Twins' boots. These scum could go fuck themselves before he'd say a word to them, he told himself as he was kicked off the bottom step. He was a Matachìn commander, after all. Born to fight and die. There would be hell to pay for this indignity.

To his right, the quarry tile floor was wet with blood. More pirates lay dead with their throats cut, their dreads soaking up the spilled gore like sponges. He could see the yawning second mouths under their chins, their necks had been sliced all the way to their spinal columns.

In his mind, Casacampo tried to keep track of the crew he'd lost so far, and those still left to put up a fight. By his count there were still at least eight at large, more than enough to chop down these running dogs.

Chucho and the blue eye hustled him out the double doors onto the covered patio. By the light of the guttering candelabrum, he saw more dead men, these killed by wire garrotes, their eyeballs bloodred, their faces black and bloated. Their tongues protruded as if they were giving final, obscene, black raspberries to the world.

Out in the courtyard there was yet another corpse, this one facedown, the back of its skull split open.

The intruders turned on their headlamps and the beams cut through the humid darkness. Obviously, they were confident that they had killed everyone inside the hacienda. The machine gunners on the rooftop were dead, too, Casacampo reasoned, or they would have opened fire by now. The commander realized that Chucho and his two friends had to have recced the grounds before the assault; they knew how many Matachìn there were and where to find them.

Sixteen dead. He was down to three on his side.

Even odds.

When he was marched through the open stable doors, his hope evaporated. In the light of a lantern sitting on a hay bale, he saw three bodies hanging by their necks from the rafters. They dangled dead still, spines snapped, necks stretched to the splitting point.

If the Twins and the gringo had fired a single shot to bring any of them down, there was no evidence of it. The commander, despite his resolve to stay strong to the end, was taken aback. They had killed nineteen trained, battle-seasoned pirates and none of the victims had made a sound, or apparently put up a fight.

It was hard to shout a warning when your throat was cut so deep that your vocal cords were severed, or when a wire noose was squeezing off your air and the blood flow to your brain.

Casacampo had always considered Chucho's reputation to be overblown, fabricated out of whole cloth to make the priests and red sashes seem less incompetent. For one man to do so much damage to them, and get away with it again and again, he had to be bigger than life, right? The commander was having second thoughts about that assessment now. What if all of it was true? True, and then some?

They made him stand in front of his hanged men, then the gringo with the mustache told him what they wanted.

"¿Cinco gringos, dondè esta?"

Bad accent, worse Spanish

Casacampo hawked and spit on the man's boots.

Looking down at the splotch of nasty on his toe, the gringo

shook his head and clicked his tongue in disapproval. In more bad Spanish he informed the commander, "We're going to give you to Chucho then."

The renowned bandit and murderer had picked up a hand scythe from a hook on the stable wall. He slashed the crescent of pitted steel back and forth, testing its balance and reach.

Casacampo's heart thudded up under his chin. He had faced death many times before, but never naked, never with his hands tied behind his back.

To make things much worse, Chucho was staring fixedly at his flaccid manhood as he whipped the scythe back and forth.

Defiance, pride, honor melted away—they were just words, after all. They were replaced by ungodly fear.

Casacampo felt a warm wetness in the straw under his bare feet, looked down and saw to his horror that he was pissing himself.

Chapter Nineteen

Mildred watched the Panamanian coastline glide by: staggered ranks of round-top mountains dark with jungle, and closer in, the brilliant flash of white surf breaking along miles of deserted beaches. Once again the vibration of twin diesels was putting her buttocks to sleep. As much as she could, given the minimal slack in her restraints, she shifted her sitting position on the ship's deck.

Her four companions, the shitweasel Fire Talker, the three whitecoats and their warrior-priest captors were running north from Panama City, and had been for almost eight hours straight. Their transportation had been upgraded considerably, from horse carts to a thirty-six-foot Bertram sportfisher. Its twin, fuel-injected Caterpillar diesels really put out the power: Mildred estimated their cruising speed at 25 knots or better. It was plenty fast enough to cool off the sweltering air and evaporate the sweat dripping down her face and running under her arms.

The going was actually quite pleasant for a change; this was the easiest part of journey so far. Of course it would've been even better if she and the others hadn't been chained to the rails of the Bertram's stern deck bait well. There hadn't been enough room around the well to hook Daniel up alongside them and still guarantee his safety, so he was fastened about six feet away, to the base of the port outrigger. That was nothing to cry over, either.

The overland crossing of the Panamanian isthmus had been a three-day, two-night ordeal. The two nights were spent in outposts along the old canal route, in secure bunkers built into hillside caves. They were big enough to house a mule train, and they had their own freshwater cisterns. It was still unclear what their captors were afraid of, but their tension escalated as the sun began to set. They pushed the horses hard to reach shelter before nightfall.

Whatever it was the warrior-priests were scared of, it didn't have the brains or the dexterity to open the bunker doors from the outside between occupations, and thereby lie in wait for the next convoy.

Although Mildred never saw anything moving, the forest on all sides came alive with breaking brush and shrill screams as evening descended. She had to wonder if there were muties in the Panamanian jungle, the same sort of brutal chillers that infested Deathlands. Or were there brand-new ones? Or was the mutie plague limited to the hellscape and the ground plowed and planted by the all-out nuclear exchange? Or had the stickies and scalies of the hellscape just not migrated this far south yet? Lot of questions, no answers.

By unspoken agreement, the companions had begun ditching their food at every meal. The Fire Talker caught them at it on the first day on the trail, but instead of turning them in to the whitecoats, he demanded they give him what they weren't going to eat themselves. He wasn't really that desperate for extra rations, but he wanted more drugs, he wanted more oblivion. And the companions gladly accommodated him. It not only got rid of most of the evidence; it shut him up.

On the afternoon of the third day, they had reached the shore of the Pacific. As it turned out, the rupture of the canal's Pacific-end locks and the outflowing of Miraflores Lake, which was a teacup compared to the artificial reservoir on the Atlantic side, hadn't devastated Panama City at all. Though its infrastructure had survived the canal's destruction on skydark more or less intact, Panama City's population had entirely vanished; as with Colón, the jungle had taken it back.

For different reasons.

Along the fractured, eroding highway on the edge of the city they had seen crude, hand-painted signs. Warning signs that looked weathered, many decades old.

Plaga.

Plague.

Was it the same one that had devastated Padre Island? Mildred wondered. What were the odds of a second, incredibly deadly, unheard-of bioweapon popping up in this neck of the woods?

Slim and none.

The simplest answer was usually the right answer: Occam's Razor.

The little convoy had continued on, past the warning signs, toward a jagged skyline of towering buildings that framed a placid bay. There was no way of telling whether the disease was still in evidence, but there were definitely dangers of other kinds. As the horse carts rolled along, down a broad, creeper-covered side street Mildred saw a pair of sleek, black jaguars loping along, hunting for dinner. High above them, flocks of noisy scarlet macaw glided between the broken-out windows of high-rise towers.

The companions had spent their third night out of Colón

with a warrior-priest garrison bivouacked in the old Panama City yacht harbor. The yacht basin was either a safe distance from the plague zone of the central city, or the plague had in fact burned itself out. The harbor had been turned into a transit point for small craft shipping, both commercial and passenger. There were a dozen converted pleasure craft moored there, sail and power boats from thirty to sixty-five feet long.

The Matachìn evidently had access to the intact fuel stores of Panama City, and probably enough diesel to last them another hundred years.

Mildred couldn't be sure whether the introduction of the plague to Panama City had come before or after the bioweapon had been used in Mexico on the Atlantic side. The destruction and loss of life in Panama City had definitely gotten out of control, though. There was no strategic advantage to completely wiping out a population of what had to have been at least a million people. The jungle that had invaded the city had been fertilized by all those rotting corpses.

Killing everyone only complicated the pirates' conquest: there was no one left to do any of the work, and a disease quarantine put the city's bounty out of immediate reach. Which led Mildred to believe that this had to have been an earlier deployment of the weapon, perhaps even the first deployment, before the pirates realized the full extent of what it could do, and how fast it could spread. Perhaps the citizens of Panama City had successfully resisted the Matachìn incursions up to that point. Certainly they would have had the sheer numbers to turn back invaders.

For what it was worth, the birds, monkeys and jaguar seemed to be immune to the plague.

During the night they had spent on the waterfront, the Fire

Talker's ebullient mood, fueled by multiple doses of opiate, had turned suddenly darker. He began talking to himself like a man possessed, using the absurd voices of his absurd characters as they confronted his abusive and long-dead parents.

It made sleep impossible.

Doc had found this particularly irritating. "Have you any idea how grating your ridiculous monologues are becoming?" he demanded of the Fire Talker.

"You've got to be kidding me," Mildred remarked.

When Doc glared at her, she added, "What? What?"

She couldn't tell whether Doc had completely missed the irony or whether he was affronted by it.

Mildred turned her attention toward the Bertram's bow as the little whitecoats and one of the warriors escorted Krysty back to the bait well, this after a trip to the salon's head. While the women "scientists" reattached Krysty's manacles to the stainless-steel rub rail, the soldier held the muzzle of his submachine gun to the back of her skull. Resistance was impossible.

After their captors returned to the air-conditioned salon, Krysty spoke in hushed tones. "I think I know where they're taking us. I saw a nautical chart laid out on a table. The course was plotted on a plastic overlay. We're headed for an island called Coiba."

"The dictator Noriega used to torture his political prisoners there," Mildred said. "This was back in the 1980s, before he was overthrown by the U.S. invasion. It was a maximum security prison back then. A prison hidden deep in the jungle. An awful place, by all accounts. They called it the 'Devil's Island' of Panama."

"So they renamed it Xibalba?" Krysty said.

Mildred tried to recall the myths she'd read about the place so long ago. "I'm pretty sure Xibalba was supposed to be hidden somewhere in Guatemala," she told the others. "And it was supposed to be belowground, a vast cavern with apartments, palaces, a council place, and rooms with various harrowing trials for visitors. The Lords of Death were supposed to be *humanlike,* whatever that means."

"Perhaps it refers to bipedalism?" Doc remarked. "Stereoscopic color vision? Opposable thumbs?"

"Who knows?" Mildred said. "It's just a thousand-year-old folk tale."

"I know," Daniel asserted.

They all stared at the man in the net suit. He finally seemed to have stirred from his day-long stupor.

"You're going to fill us in, now?" J.B. said dubiously.

"Why not, we're almost there. That dark hump on the horizon is Xibalba."

"What do you know about it?" Krysty said.

"Before skydark I volunteered for an ultrasecret experiment," Daniel said. He enunciated his words carefully and slowly; it seemed to take considerable effort to fight off the effects of the opiates. "I didn't know where I was going or what I was getting into when I signed on. By the time I figured it out, it was too late. The experimentation on Coiba didn't go as planned. I was infected but I didn't die—I carried the plague in my blood. I was given a choice by the whitecoats—live out the rest of my life on the island, or go into cryostasis until a cure could be found. When I was reanimated, there was no cure and the Atapuls had been in command of the prison and in command of the Matachìn for close to a century."

"Who are the Atapuls?" Mildred said.

It took a moment for the sense of the question to sink past the opiate fog. Then Daniel said, "They're the offspring of convicts who escaped into the island bush. Criminal royalty whose lineage stretches back to before Armageddon. I was in a cryotank on nukeday when escaped prisoners returned from the jungle and took over the prison. I wasn't the first carrier they reanimated over the years, there were plenty of others to choose from. Like I said, the project was a disaster, start to finish."

"Why are they bringing you back here now?" Krysty said. "What do they want with the five of us?"

Daniel lowered his head. "I don't know, I don't know," he said.

"Tell us, you piece shit!" Jak snarled.

The Fire Talker began to sob weakly into his hands; the sobs rapidly grew further and further apart, until he appeared to slip back into a drugged sleep. There was no rousing him from it.

Mildred turned her attention to the island looming off the starboard bow. Looking at it, she felt no curiosity, no anger, only dread. Coiba was immense, and separated from the mainland by fifty shark-filled miles of ocean. As they got closer, she could make out the shoreline: convoluted blobs of black lava formed sheer cliffs that were crashed by white surf, and topped by a vast, seemingly impenetrable rain forest. There were dots of color scattered here and there among the branches and drooping vines: bright yellow flowers that could have been wild orchids.

A wall of heat hit them as the Bertram glided into a protected cove. Two other pleasure craft—a twenty-eight-foot Aquasport center console and a thirty-two-foot Pursuit—were moored in close to shore with no crews in sight; the water dropped off steeply from the curve of white sandy beach. The beach was on a finger of land, and on the far side of the land a sluggish green river flowed into the sea. Nibor and his men anchored the boat, then rowed the passengers the short distance ashore in an inflatable dinghy. It took several trips to transfer them all. Although doped to the gills, Daniel came to at the last moment. He had to be dragged screaming from the Bertram. One of the paramilitaries clubbed him into compliance before dumping him into the raft.

The warrior-priests brought their RPDs along with them, and some extra 100-round drum mags. Obviously they considered the intended route to Xibalba as dangerous as the journey across the isthmus.

The reasons for the show of force immediately became apparent. Crocodiles sunned themselves on the riverside of the beach, not thirty yards from their landing site. These creatures were fifteen feet long, and more than a yard across the widest part of their rib cages. The saltwater crocs didn't seem interested in the visitors. Or perhaps they weren't within easy enough eating distance.

Nibor and his crew ignored them in return.

With three warrior-priests on point, followed by the companions, the whitecoats, Daniel and a two-man rear guard, they followed the sliver of land to the edge of the forest, then ducked under the rain-forest canopy.

It was smotheringly hot in the deep shade, like a bake oven. The trail was narrow and winding, they had to walk single file. Visibility was no more than ten feet ahead. The jungle off the trail was so thick that escape to either side was impossible. There was nowhere to run.

Dog-face and his crew immediately unsheathed their machetes.

Snakes, Mildred knew, were dispatched with machetes more easily than machine guns, especially in this kind of close quarter.

Even if there weren't any muties lurking in the deep shadows, there were a thousand other ways to die in this place, all of them excruciating. From the way the warrior-priests clutched their weapons, they felt ambush or attack was likely at any moment.

After they had trekked in about two miles, up and down the sides of steep ravines, waded shallow creeks, and were drenched in sweat, Nibor stopped the advance with a hand signal. The jungle sounds that had surrounded them for more than an hour—the bellows of the howler monkeys and the screeches of the toucans and macaws—had gone suddenly silent. He listened for a moment, then announced to all, *"Los perros vienen."*

The dogs are coming.

What dogs? Mildred thought.

The news sent the whitecoat women into a wide-eyed panic. They clutched each other's hands and hung on for dear life. For his part, Dr. Montejo looked like he was about to swallow his own tongue.

A minute later Mildred heard the distant baying. Dogs, indeed. Dogs, aplenty.

The warrior-priests in the lead took off running; the pair at the rear drove the middle of the file onward, shouting and cursing to try to make them go faster.

Another two hundred yards up the path, and they had to hop over and around body parts strewed along thirty yards of trail. Clods of meat sprouted bristly tufts of hair. Uncoiled gray intestines festooned the low branches. Bloody shattered bones lay everywhere. To Mildred, it looked like the remains of a boar or wild pig, recently torn to shreds, dismembered, gutted and left there to rot.

Farther on, the decapitated head lay on its cheek at the edge of the trail, the head of a huge boar, with up-curving yellow tusks the size of Bowie knives. Anything that could rip apart something of that size was big trouble, even with machine guns.

The baying had grown louder and louder. It was coming at them from all sides now. Encirclement, and the horror that entailed, was clearly a possibility. And the column was losing ground to the pursuit, its speed slowed by the captives and their ankle manacles, but there was no time to stop to remove them.

Nibor quickly took measure of the problem and in a stunning bit of command-decision nastiness, he whipped his machine gun around on its shoulder sling and fired a single round, shooting one of his own men through the thigh. The wounded man let out a yelp and dropped to the ground, clutching his leg as he writhed in pain. They ran on, leaving him behind to occupy and slow the dog pack. He had the misfortune of being the least valuable member of the group, therefore the obvious choice for sacrifice.

A few minutes later awful sounds erupted from behind them, snarling, barking, shrill screams all mixed together. It sounded like a hundred animals had descended on the helpless prey.

Nibor's act of betrayal had bought them a little time, just enough time as it turned out.

The trail ended at the old prison gates and a perimeter of rusting hurricane fence topped by razor wire. On the far side of the entrance, the rain-forest canopy had been cleared to the bare ground in an acres-wide circle. Sunlight streamed in, unfiltered.

Mildred had visited the Mayan ruins at Palenque and Tikal, and she had always imagined Xibalba as being something architecturally similar—steep-sided, white-limestone pyramids with unbroken rows of stone steps, and broad, cobblestone thoroughfares to accommodate religious festivals and parades. Massive sculpted stone faces and elaborate hieroglyphs for decoration, maybe a road of crushed white rock or shell leading in. This Xibalba was none of those.

Beyond the gates, in the center of the expanse of flat ground, was a densely packed complex of one- and two-story, windowless concrete buildings—modern, purely functional buildings. The site seemed to be unchanged from what it had been more than a century ago: it still looked like a maximum security prison. At one time the concrete had probably been painted a warm gold, now that color could barely be seen between the streaks of black mildew that striped all the walls. One of the low buildings looked newer; at least it was slightly more beige than mildewed.

Protecting the cluster of prison buildings was a second, razor wire–topped hurricane fence. It formed a twelve-foot-high hexagon around the compound, and at each of the six points there was a twenty-foot-tall guard tower with a spotlight. From where Mildred stood it didn't appear that any of the towers were manned.

The warrior-priests shut and bolted the entry gates behind them, then urged them on, toward Xibalba proper.

Mildred could make out the hum of diesel-powered generators as they approached the second, much smaller gate.

Between the barrier fence and the mildewed buildings there were about two hundred people. Some were performing menial tasks—tending gardens or animals, moving materials in wheelbarrows, digging ditches, and the like—but most were just milling around aimlessly. It reminded Mildred of a squalid Third World farmer's market, or perhaps a Renaissance Fair in hell.

Greasy smoke from a row of roasting meats wafted over them. The skinned and gutted carcasses of some very large animals were being turned on spits over beds of heaped coals. Crocodile? Deer? Wild boar? Brown women naked to the waist basted the crisping haunches with rag mops. To Mildred, the joy on their faces seemed excessive and patently false— as in *look* extrahappy or *die* extrahorribly.

Then she realized with a shock that the broad grins they wore had been surgically installed, the muscles of their cheeks trimmed and then pinned to bone, the corners of their mouths permanently upturned with the tip of a scalpel.

Nibor led them toward a two-story building with a single row of narrow, wire-glassed windows just below the edge of the roof. To reach the structure they had to run a gauntlet of perpetually smiling supplicants lined up on either side of the path. Some of them were plastic surgery catastrophes, their faces and bodies horribly mutilated. Attempts to join plastic, metal and bone had gone awry, and massive infection had resulted.

So much pus, so much happiness.

What were they lined up for? Mildred asked herself. Not food, surely; food was everywhere and apparently free for the taking. Not clothing because they had clothes, and it was too hot to wear much of it, anyway. For payment of some kind?

For some special entertainment? Neither of those seemed likely, either. Then the truth struck Mildred: these grinning bootlickers and insignificant demons were waiting patiently for audiences with the Lords of Death.

Mildred had a sudden, and under the circumstances, jarringly incongruous flashback. The closed double doors that loomed in front of them reminded her of high school gym class.

Nibor and the warrior-priests ushered the chained companions into the old prison's basketball stadium.

This is their Ball Court? Mildred thought. She didn't know whether to laugh out loud or scream foul. The details of her reading on the ancient Maya came back to her in a rush. A central feature of the myths of Xibalba was how much the Lords of Death loved their ball game, which they played with a razor-studded ball and a horizontal, stone hoop. The basketball backboards from the Noriega days were long gone, but Mildred could still make out the remnants of the free throw line on the concrete floor.

Across the court, in the top two rows of the bleachers, the Lords of Death awaited. Mildred did a quick count. There were thirty-six of them. Three times as many as there should have been. They sat as still as statues, in full head masks. The masks were garishly painted; they had the same stylized animal maws, pop-eyes and lolling tongues as the papier-mâché heads on sticks in Veracruz. Mildred was too far away to see eyes glittering behind the eyeholes. The Lords wore loose, flowing robes and sandals, like pharoahs or Roman senators. She couldn't recognize any of the masks from the banners and models she'd seen in Mexico; she'd been too distracted at the time to take proper note.

Stationed along the narrow end of the court to her left were at least fifty more of the jungle-camouflaged paramilitaries. The sec men for the Lords of Death all had shaved heads; most were ritually scarred like Dog-face. They carried light automatic weapons, the same stubby, 9 mm submachine guns as their Matachìn brethren. Their position gave them clear firing lanes down the length of the court. If there was trouble in Xibalba, they could sweep it away in an instant with sustained bursts of autofire.

Mildred noted the chest-high clusters of bullet holes in the concrete of the opposite wall. It looked like a firing squad backstop.

The only game played on this court was stand-still-while-I-shoot-you.

Dr. Montejo and his assistants hurried over to greet the six other whitecoats gathered at the foot of the bleachers. One of the men, much younger and shorter than Montejo, with sweeping wings of black hair parted in the middle, shoved a stiffened finger in his face as he angrily berated him. Mildred couldn't hear what was being said, but the younger man appeared to be Montejo's superior and he was most agitated. As the wild-eyed young whitecoat took Montejo to task, he swept the plaits of hair out of his eyes with both hands. This was a gesture he repeated every few seconds, a nervous tic to be sure.

Then a voice boomed down on the court from above. Because of the echoes in the cavernous room it was impossible to tell which, if any, of the thirty-six seated Lords had spoken.

The voice itself sounded very strange to Mildred. Not muffled like Nibor because of bizarre facial surgery, but almost electronic, à la Stephen Hawking. The stilted absence of inflexion seemed surprising for a native speaker of Spanish.

One of Nibor's paramilitaries grabbed hold of the back of Mildred's neck and forced her to kneel on the floor and genuflect.

Then everyone in the room, save the sec men at the far end, were on knees, palms and noses.

For Mildred the sense of what had been said finally sank in.

Worship and tremble! I am Atapul the Tenth! First among the Lords of Death!

Nose pressed to the concrete, Mildred managed to turn her head and steal a peek as one of the masked figures, presumably the speaker, slowly stood. The rest of the Lords sat there like mannequins.

The mask worn by Atapul X was the stylized head of a jaguar, painted black with a headdress of a fan of red snakes, all poised to strike. The cat face had great long fangs and a lolling purple tongue. Even with the outsize mask on his head, Atapul X appeared to be an impressively wide-shouldered specimen. Mildred could see he was wearing some kind of tight-fitting, black body suit under his gold-trimmed white robes. The cuffs of the body suit came down to his massive wrists and down to his even more massive ankles.

The chief Lord of Death wore heavy rings on every finger and both thumbs. They were silver or stainless steel, and the centers of each were adorned not with gemstones, but with substantial, two-inch-long, steel points—miniature broadhead arrow tips. Together they made up a particularly wicked set of brass knuckles. With a straight punch or a raking slash, they could cut to the bone. Atapul X also had what looked like shiny, black-painted fingernails, and they were a half inch long and cut into sharp points. An odd and unsettling affectation, Mildred thought.

The bleacher seats creaked and groaned as Atapul X used them as steps to descend to the court floor. He was not a lightweight, by any means. On a leather thong around his right wrist, he carried a fearsome weapon. It was shaped like an oversize machete—heavy-bladed, single-edged, and thirty inches long. In the hands of a large, athletic person such a cleaver could make a head fly off a neck or an arm jump clear of a shoulder joint in one swipe.

The rows of unmoving, grotesquely masked Lords above, and this one lumbering down the bleachers like a bear in a Halloween suit was something out of a Grade-B horror movie.

The bear stopped in front of Nibor.

Dog-face immediately began to rattle off a list of the recent military successes in Tierra de la Muerte. And then he waxed poetic about the prospects for more victories, and the ease and speed with which they would come.

"This is all you brought me?" Atapul X demanded of the kneeling man, gesturing at the nose-down companions. "Five will not be nearly enough."

Again because of that almost computer-sim voice, the Spanish took Mildred a moment or two to puzzle out.

Nibor replied with his eyes closed and his breath fogging the concrete. He said that it was all his fault and begged for Atapul's mercy.

Mildred was surprised that Dog-face didn't try to pass the buck to Casacampo. But maybe he knew bringing up the name would only increase Atapul X's wrath, since the Matachìn commander wasn't there to be punished in the flesh.

The chief Lord of Death ignored his pleas and advanced out onto the middle of the ball court, stopping to loom over the prostrated and be-netted Daniel Desipio.

"Don't worry, you will have more brothers and sisters soon," Atapul X told the cowering freezie. "Dr. Yorte will see to that."

Daniel had to have understood the stilted Spanish because he muttered a baleful, "Oh, please no…"

"Creature, it is your privilege to supply the Lords of Death with what we demand," Atapul X said. "Your diseased bones will make the weapons to bring this world to its knees, and in return for your servitude, we will feed and clothe you and let you live."

The other Lords hissed down from the bleachers, hissed through the mouth holes in their masks. Not in disapproval; apparently the noise was their way of applauding. None of them moved so Mildred still couldn't tell which of the figures were real, and which were just dummies.

When Atapul X turned in her direction, she quickly shifted her gaze to the floor under her nose. She had a bad feeling in her gut. By "brothers and sisters" did Atapul X mean this Dr. Yorte was going to thaw out more carriers from the cryo tanks? Or did he mean Dr. Yorte was going to *make* some more carriers, using Daniel's donor marrow?

Mildred was having trouble swallowing the whole thawing business. It was chock full of logical problems, and the timeline didn't make any sense, either. Successful thawing from cryogenesis was a complicated procedure even when automated because there were so many variables to monitor and compensate for. Relative tissue densities. Differential trehalose absorption—trehalose was the natural sugar that kept the internal components of living cells from freezing solid and cell walls from being ruptured by expanding ice—and variable antifreeze concentrations in organs and bones.

Critical hydration and nutrient loss to specific tissues during the stresses of reanimation. The list went on and on. The convicts who first took over the prison were likely uneducated and mentally ill, if not completely deranged. How could *they* figure out how to unfreeze the carriers?

Furthermore, how could the eighth generation of offspring of the convicted murderers figure it out? Long before the Fire Talker was revived there were no whitecoats left to demonstrate or oversee the procedure. The convicts could have been trained by whitecoats from Day One and the training then passed down through the years, but for that to have happened, the Coiba prisoners would have had to anticipate that circumstances would demand deployment of the bioweapon at some point in the future. It was hard to believe that the convicts could have had that kind of foresight, or that amount of patience. Or the willingness to tempt fate, having seen firsthand what the whitecoats' "failures" had suffered. Yet the necessary information and skills had been transferred or Daniel would never have been revived.

According to the Fire Talker, when he woke up the Atapuls were already *in situ* here, and had been for more than a century. He had accepted what he was told, that the Lords of Death were part of the bloodline of the original convicts, and that the pirates had turned themselves into gods using *enanos* as their instruments.

There was no way of testing either of those hypotheses.

The total annihilation of the population of Panama City, which ran counter to Matachìn self-interest, seemed to reflect unfamiliarity with the weaponized disease. Apparently the Atapuls had no idea how deadly the plague was until they used it the first time.

And then there was the hellhole factor.

The Lords of Death and their groveling subjects all seemed blind or oblivious to the squalor they inhabited. It was like they were living in a dreamworld far, far from this wretched place. Xibalba was the seat of the Lords' authority and their supposed spiritual power, but it was a shit pit.

The more Mildred considered all this, the more puzzling it became.

Then Atapul X stepped up right beside her and every other thought vanished from her mind. The chief Lord gave off a distinctly unpleasant odor. It was fusty and sour. It reminded her of something she couldn't quite place, but she found the vague memory disturbing, nonetheless. The toes sticking out of the sandals were webbed, and the nails, crescent moons of ebony, looked like talons. Were they the product of plastic surgery? Some kind of synthetic implants?

Then Atapul X touched the bare back of her neck and she felt the points of those thick black fingernails drag across her skin.

Despite herself, Mildred shuddered, squeezed her eyes shut and pressed her nose into the concrete. She, who had traveled through time, who had already died once, who had shot and stabbed her way across a ruined continent, hadn't been this terrified since she was a little girl.

It was more than just the smell, the sight, the touch of this creature. Mildred sensed there was no humanity there. No semblance of humanity. Human evil had its own limits, its comprehensible limits. Like every other *homo sapien,* Mildred could envision the range of harm that could be done to other people; like everyone else she could *imagine* doing most of it, herself, even if she never intended to and never would. This creature was not limited by those natural boundaries. Whatever boundaries Atapul X had, if he had any, they were inscrutable.

"Take them away," Atapul X ordered Nibor as he turned back for the bleachers.

Mildred and the others were summarily hauled to their feet and quick-marched out the same gymnasium doors they'd entered, this time with all the whitecoats marching in front of them. The warrior-priests pushed them into a sally port, a hurricane-fenced corridor that had originally kept prisoners from wandering around the yard. Evening was closing in. The sky above the clearing was shot with salmon pink and turquoise. Mildred was very relieved to be out in the open air.

"That went well," Doc said.

Behind them, Daniel Desipio had gone limp. Two of Nibor's sec men were lugging him along by the armpits, dragging the toes of his boots in the dirt.

"Wherever he's going, it doesn't look like fun," Krysty said.

The whitecoats veered off toward the more recent-looking structure. Unlike the prison block that loomed to their left, this building had windows and once it had plate-glass doors, which had been broken out and replaced with plywood scrap. Daniel and his bearers veered off, as well. One of the whitecoats held a door open, and the Fire Talker was dragged inside.

"*Casa de la Navaja,*" Nibor announced, having noticed their interest. He then indicated his disfigured face with a sweep of his hand, and obvious pride.

"What'd he say?" J.B. asked.

"Razor House," Mildred translated. "That building's called Razor House. It's a reference taken from the ancient Mayan legends. In the Xibalban creation myths, it was supposedly filled with sentient knives that could fly. In this incarnation it's the whitecoat surgical center."

Dog-face indicated a doorway to their left, in the single-storey arm of the L-shaped prison block. *"Casa de Frio,"* he said.

"That would be Cold or Rattling House," Mildred told the others. As they passed the doorway, she could hear the steady hum of generators. "Where they store the bioweap freezies, no doubt."

A second separate structure looked like it had once been a maintenance shed. As they walked past, from inside came the sounds of snarling and growling.

"Casa de Balam," Nibor said.

"Jaguar House," Mildred translated.

"Since when do jaguars bark?" Krysty said.

"They've substituted wild dogs for the jaguars in the myth," Mildred said. "It's understandable. Jaguars are probably few and far between on this island."

"What's the point of all these 'houses,' anyway?" J.B. said.

"According to the legends," Mildred replied, "they provided tests that would either kill or humiliate visitors to Xibalba. The goal was to outwit the test and survive—only to be confronted by the next test. And the next. They got worse as they went along."

"Must have cut down on tourism," Doc said.

"Xibalba was supposed to be Hell for regular folks," Mildred said. "Whoever applied the myths to this place doesn't have a clue what they were really about."

Nibor opened a heavy, riveted-metal door in the window-less wall ahead of them. As the door swung back, Mildred could see the faint glow of electric lights. The bulbs throbbed in time with the generators. Then, out of the doorway, there came a rush of leathery wings just over their heads. All of the companions ducked reflexively.

"Don't tell me," J.B. said, "it's Bat House."

The prison's interior was in no better shape than the outside. The corridor between the two-story-high tiers of cells was gritty, littered with refuse, mildewed and dank. The cells' steel bars looked rusted, but they were two inches in diameter, still plenty thick enough to do the job.

All five companions were shoved into the same narrow, low-ceilinged cell. It only had four bunks. There were no mattresses, just metal bed frames suspended by chains eye-bolted into the concrete. There was a bucket for a toilet, and a bucket for water; they sat side by side. The toilet hadn't been emptied in a while.

Across the corridor, in the cell opposite, another prisoner dozed on a top bunk in a sitting position, leaning with his back against the concrete wall. The sound of the cell door clanging shut didn't wake him up. In the dim light it looked like his holed-out, yellow sweat-stained T-shirt had been fitted with a pair of shiny black epaulettes. Slurpy, sucking sounds were coming from the cell. Then the epaulettes fluttered their pointy wings and changed attack angles.

Not just any bats, as it turned out.

Blood from open wounds spilled down the prisoner's chest.

Maybe he was already dead.

Bats in droves were shooting back and forth down the hallway, darting and diving between the bars, into the occupied cells. When their own cell was trespassed, Jak jumped up like a cat. He caught the flying vampire in his bare hands and then broke it in two like a fortune cookie.

A fortune cookie with blood and guts.

"We'd best take turns sleeping," Doc said.

"Who the hell's going to sleep?" Mildred said.

Chapter Twenty

Ryan gave up trying to sleep. It wasn't the snoring of Tom and Chucho that kept him awake. It wasn't the stink of the Matachìn commander tied to a chair five feet away. It wasn't the eight dead men he was sharing the room with. He was thinking about his friends, about what they had to be suffering, about what kind of a lead their captors had, and he was chomping at the bit to be off after them.

But outside the Panama City yacht club it was still pitch-dark. There was no way to pick up the pursuit before dawn. Not across more than a couple hundred miles of unfamiliar waters in an unfamiliar ship.

The previous evening the four of them, Tom, Chucho, Casacampo and Ryan had arrived on horseback; this after three full days in the saddle. Riding along the city's deserted, bay-front avenue, on the other side of the harbor they had seen the boats tied up off the old yacht club.

They had also seen the ancient plague warning signs along the road.

Both Tom and Ryan had demanded that Casacampo tell them the story of what happened. The commander obliged, and Chucho did the translating as they rounded the shore of the bay. Casacampo was wearing pants, and had been since the first night in Colón. Chucho had relented on the no-clothes issue, but it wasn't because he felt sympathy for the bastard. He just didn't want him to get saddle sores on his bare ass and be unable to walk, which would have slowed them.

The commander had assured them there was no plague anymore. But there were no people left in the city, either. They had all been killed. He said it had happened thirty years before he was born.

"The Matachìn did it?" Tom had asked.

"I only know what I've been told since I was a little boy," Casacampo replied. "Way back when, Panama City was prime for the picking. Richer than Veracruz or any of the cities on the Atlantic. When the Matachìn attempted to take over the city there was concerted resistance. The people fought back hard when pirates attacked and managed to drive them off the beach. Afterward the people here realized the threat was not going to go away, that the enemy would keep coming back, so they organized an assault force to root them out and destroy them. Many ships, many guns, many fighters. They were about to send their fleet north to attack Xibalba and kill the Matachìn down to the last man. But the Matachìn got wind of their plan and struck first."

Ryan had gestured at the vast city overwhelmed by jungle, groves of mango trees growing up through the asphalt, sky-scrapers draped in greenery. "So what went wrong?" he asked.

"As it turned out the job was much easier than the Lords of Death thought," Casacampo said. "They sent in too many of their *enanos*. They didn't know how many they'd need to bring a city of this size to its knees. And once the disease carriers were released and the plague started to spread, they couldn't stop it. It burned like wildfire through every neighborhood and out into the countryside, too. In two weeks

almost everyone in the city was dead. The streets were heaped
with unburied bodies. The houses and apartments were full of
them. Those who didn't die from the plague killed themselves
in despair. Many of them jumped out of the skyscrapers.

"Only in the last ten years have we started to explore the
edges of the city. There is much booty inside. And not enough
Matachìn manpower to carry it out, or even to do a thorough
search. Cutting back the jungle after all these years, and keeping
it cut back would take ten thousand slaves, maybe more."

Ryan rose to his feet, stepped over the sprawled bodies of
the warrior-priests and walked to the picture window. He
could just make out the broad, glassy bay in the starlight. The
four of them had spent two nights under even worse conditions in the pirates' hillside bunkers as they worked their way
across the isthmus. As the evenings approached, he and Tom
had noticed a change in Chucho and Casacampo's demeanor.
A nervousness gripped them both.

An urgency.

When Ryan had remarked on it, Chucho said, "As long as
we ride quickly and reach the shelter before nightfall, there
will be no problems. The jungle is very thick and the road is
narrow. Many bad things come out after dark."

"You mean, animals?" Tom said. "Or men?"

"No one knows what they are," Chucho replied. "Things
happen, though. People disappear along this trail without a
trace. Entire mule trains just vanish. The forest is too thick to
try to track them. It isn't like it used to be."

"What do you mean?" Ryan said.

"It is much more dangerous in these parts than it was
before nukeday. There are things here now that didn't used to
be here. No one knows why. No one knows where they came

from. No one has ever seen them and lived to tell about it. These things do not show themselves until it is too late."

Ryan had seen nothing and heard nothing as dusk gathered around them, but he respected Chucho's word. Even though he had wanted to push on, riding into the night to gain more ground on the companions, he hadn't press the issue. Before dark, they were bolted in behind the bunker doors.

Taking the yacht club from the warrior-priests had been less of a challenge than the three-day ride. When push came to shove, and when Chucho was doing the pushing, Casacampo cared more about living than he cared about his fellow Matachìn. He didn't like it, but he went along with it.

After dark, they had forced High Pile, now Low Pile, to pound on the clubhouse door with his fists and call out to the men inside, demanding shelter.

The bad things out at night didn't knock.

And they didn't ask for help.

When the door opened, Ryan, Tom and Chucho had pushed the commander through it in front of them.

The room beyond was a lounge of sorts. It was furnished with low tables, couches, armchairs, all lit by three white gas lanterns. There was a full bar along the back wall. Two Matachìn had come to answer the knock on the door, both carrying semi-auto handguns. Casacampo's flying entrance knocked them aside and off balance. Before they could recover, Ryan rammed the muzzle of his silenced H&K subgun into the chest of the man on the right, and fired a triburst straight into his heart. The blast of lead sent the pirate flying backward. He crashed onto his butt, then went spread-eagle on the floor.

Chucho likewise dispatched the man on the left, blowing

him off his feet with nine millis, blowing chunks out of the middle of his back.

The other pirates were in the middle of a card game, drinking white liquor from quart bottles, smoking cigars. Their weapons were out of easy reach.

They were caught dead in the water.

And from the looks on their faces, they knew it.

Casacampo had hit the deck in front of Ryan as he, Tom and Chucho had all cut loose with their submachine guns. Bullets stitched across the couches and chairs, across the heads and chests of the seated bodies. The Matachìn died where they sat, and in their death throes they kicked over the table, the loose cards fluttered down along with tufts of couch stuffing, and the game's jackpot, which was consisted of a pile of gold teeth, skittered across the tile floor.

One of the pirates somehow managed to avoid being hit and vaulted off the end of the couch. He scrambled on all fours behind it, trying desperately to reach the bar and room's rear doorway. Tom and Ryan shifted their aim points to take him out.

"Don't shoot him!" Chucho had cried. Then he crossed the room in a blur. He cut off the man's retreat, and nipped any further resistance in the bud by pressing his red-hot gun muzzle against the man's shaved skull.

When the Matachìn looked up and saw the eye patch and the long hair, his jaw dropped open. "Are you really *him?*" he moaned. "Are you really Chucho?"

"They know your legend down here, too?" Tom had said, obviously impressed.

"Wherever these bastards are, I give them nightmares."

Ryan had noted the surgical alterations on the new prisoner's face. Shiny scalloped weals of scar tissue divided both his cheeks. The scars were too precise, too complex, and too symmetrical to be the result of an accident or combat. Some of the dead men had similar markings. Minor league Fright Masks. Perhaps if they were really, really bad they got the full treatment.

As Casacampo slowly got to his feet, Tom had asked him whether *this* was the extent of the garrison in Panama City.

The commander grimaced at the bodies that littered the couch and the floor. Then he said, "There are only ghosts here. This is all the garrison that's needed."

They had made Casacampo and the other prisoner drag the corpses out of the way. There was no choice; they had to spend the night. They needed daylight to continue the chase.

Unable to sleep, and not wanting to disturb Tom or Chucho, Ryan turned away from the window. He picked up a lantern and poked around the rest of the yacht club. In a back room closet, he discovered five Soviet RPD light machine guns and extra drum mags of 7.62 mm rounds. He field-stripped and checked the weapons and found them to be well oiled and in shooting shape. He had them lined up and ready by the front door when, just before dawn, Tom woke up.

"Slept like the dead," the trader said as he stretched. Then he looked over at the heap in the corner and corrected himself. "Well, on second thought, maybe not. Couch sure beats a horse blanket on the ground, though."

After waking Chucho, Casacampo and the prisoner, they lugged the backpacks of C-4 and detonators, their submachine guns, and the RPDs and ammo outside. Dawn was just breaking behind them; in front of them, the pirates' commandeered navy sat peacefully at anchor.

"We need better than a five-hundred-mile range," Tom

said. "There may not be any way to refuel once we get there. We have to be able to make it back on whatever's in the tanks."

Then he made the scarred Matachìn point out the boat with the most fuel on board and the most range. Without hesitation, the prisoner indicated a yellowing, forty-five-foot Hatteras with flybridge.

They loaded a rowboat tied to the yacht club dock and made Casacampo and the prisoner row them over to the stern of the sportfisher. Tom boarded ship first. He scampered up the stainless-steel ladder aft of the main cabin, and cranked over the engines using the flybridge auxiliary controls. The diesels roared to life, and a huge plume of black smoke erupted from the exhausts. After a little feathering of the throttles the smoke belching aft turned white, then became invisible.

"Oh, yeah!" he shouted from the bridge. "This will do just fine."

Ryan climbed aboard and helped Casacampo through the transom gate. "On your belly on the deck," he told him, pointing. After the commander got the meaning and complied, Chucho started passing up the guns and explosives.

Tom let the engines idle while he descended the flybridge, ran for the bow and started winching up the anchor.

When all the matériel was transferred from the rowboat, Ryan looked at the prisoner at the oars, then at Chucho. "What about him?" he said. "Are you going to shoot him, or should I?"

"What's he going to do here by himself?" Chucho said. "Besides, someone has to live to tell the tale, right?"

Ryan shrugged. He didn't care one way or another. "Swim, you lucky asshole," he told the Matachìn.

The pirate gave him a blank, helpless look.

When Chucho repeated the order in Spanish, the man's face brightened. Without a word, he dived over the side and started stroking hard for shore.

After shifting the guns and C-4 to the salon, they tied Casacampo securely to the stern scupper, then joined Tom up on the flybridge.

"If we follow the coastline, we can't miss Coiba," Tom told them. "It's eight or nine hours away, depending on how much speed I can squeeze out of this boat."

The trader pushed down the twin throttles and the Hatteras responded, surging forward, splitting the mirror surface of the bay.

The sun was only half an hour up and it already was getting hot.

Chapter Twenty-One

Dressed in a pale blue, paper hospital gown Daniel Desipio sat manacled to a wheelchair in the hallway outside the office of Dr. Dolan Yorte, awaiting a surgical procedure he was all too familiar with.

If Daniel could've touched the floor with his tiptoes, he would've tried to toe-tap the wheelchair out of the building. If he could've reached his wrists with his teeth, he would have tried to gnaw through them. But due to the head and ankle restraints, he could do neither, so he was forced to simply sit and wait for the horrible inevitable.

The whitecoat building had been added to the prison after the secret deal was struck for use of the site and the convicts as guinea pigs. The cost came out of the black box budget of Project Persephone. Construction materials and laboratory equipment had been choppered in from a U.S. Army base on the mainland, and they'd been assembled by a company of Army engineers. Over a century of hard use, the original white acrylic tiles had turned dingy yellow, and here and there had curled up from the subfloor like oversize tortilla chips. There were rust stains on the acoustic drop ceiling, and deep scrape marks along the white-enameled walls where countless gurneys had grazed them.

As the door to Yorte's office was open, the Fire Talker

could see inside. The far wall was covered from floor-to-ceiling with sketches of demons on scraps of paper of various sizes, wild renderings by the head whitecoat and chief surgeon of Hell himself, in thick strokes of black marker with bold highlights of red. The doctor first dreamed the hideous faces he constructed, or so he claimed, after drinking enormous quantities of mescal. He claimed that the Lords of Death visited him with visions of their progeny when he was in an advanced intoxicated state. And that they gave him detailed instructions on how to make the visions real. Cut this. Sew that. Insert plastic chin here.

It was a revelation that had always puzzled Daniel. But so much of what surrounded him in this place was difficult to make sense of, and not worth the trouble of trying, since he was at best a pawn in whatever his masters were about, at worst a lab rat.

Yorte came into view in the doorway, his lab coat stained with drops of blood or perhaps hot sauce. Pushing his hair back from his eyes with both hands, he let out a howl of frustration. Then he laid into the room's other occupants, Dr. Montejo and his two assistants, some more. From what Daniel could gather he was unhappy about the number and the quality of would-be plague vectors he'd been given to work with. He seemed particularly upset by the choice of the geezer with the perfect teeth and the albino. Daniel knew that Montejo had washed-out as a Xibalban plastic surgeon, although many of his attempts were still lurching around the prison yard. He had been relegated to *enano* babysitting duties and light defrostings. Things he couldn't screw up.

After a few more minutes of yelling, Dr. Yorte stormed out of his office and confronted his wheelchair-bound patient.

The only thing that kept the surgeon's colossal ego in check was fear.

Fear of the Lords of Death.

Yorte pushed back his flyaway hair and said, "Well, *enano*, how about I remake you on the outside while I'm at it? I can make it match the inside. Maybe you'll wake up with a face like a monkey's anus?"

Quite a card, that Yorte.

Daniel knew better than to banter with the man when he was in a friable mood and about to begin surgery. He kept his lip zipped.

Montejo and the *brujas* wheeled him down the hall to the surgical suite, a trip he had relived in nightmares countless times. This was his fifth excursion into the realm of pain-beyond-belief.

Because he was already semisedated, the trio had little trouble shifting him from the chair to the crucifixion table. They pinioned his wrists, chest, waist and ankles with heavy leather belts, pulling them so tight he couldn't move and could hardly breathe.

One of the assistants put an IV line into his forearm, hung a saline bag and then used a syringe to inject him with something.

Dope.

Although it hit him between the eyes like a two-by-four, he remained fully conscious. He wanted to ask the grinning bitch to give him more, but he knew there wasn't enough dope in the world to dull the agony of marrow harvesting. Besides, he couldn't make his mouth move. That, he decided, was the real purpose of the narcotic: to keep him quiet while they mined his very bones.

Dr. Yorte pushed a stainless-steel tray on wheels beside the table. From a towel he picked up a hypodermic needle of impressive length and unholy diameter. At the end opposite the point, it had a kind of bolt head, with six faceted sides. A *bruja* pulled Daniel's gown away from his hip, daubed it with Betadine, then Yorte rammed the needle into his pelvis hard enough to seat its hollow tip in the bone.

Now that hurt, no denying. A steady stinging pain that shot up and down his leg. But it was nothing compared to what came next.

Dr. Yorte snatched a crescent wrench from the instrument tray, fitted it to the bolt head, then made a quick adjustment of the gap. Jaws nice and tight, he used the wrench's leverage to turn the needle and drive the point into the marrow.

Supposedly one of the litmus tests for whether a bone was broken or not was the person's reaction to the shock. If he or she passed out or puked from the pain, the bone was probably broken.

Daniel's bone wasn't broken, but he turned his head and puked anyway, over the side of the table, forcing Yorte to take a quick step to avoid having his shoes splattered.

Screwing the needle deep enough was slow, difficult work for the corer.

And excruciating agony for the core-ee.

Was it worse than he had remembered it? Or was it that something that bad couldn't be remembered? It could only be reexperienced.

As he writhed against the restraints, Daniel tried to recall what it was like being an ice cube for a hundred years. He was desperately searching for happy thoughts.

When the needle had been augered in to sufficient depth, the pain was constant and unrelenting; his entire body vibrated from it. Yorte then fitted a plastic tube to the back end of the needle and used a squeeze bulb—like a turkey baster's—to suck out the marrow. The cells were a brilliant red as he spritzed them from the baster into a stainless-steel basin. Then the good doctor went back for more.

In the midst of his delirium of pain, Daniel started to hallucinate. Suddenly it wasn't Dolan Yorte working the rubber bulb, but the five-foot-two-inch publisher of *SR,* this while he puffed away on a foot-long cigar.

Behind the homunculus, in the hard glare of the surgical lights, Daniel saw the familiar outlines of his heroes. They, too, had gathered around his bed of pain. There was pushing and shoving between them, and the usual hurling of threats.

"Use your broadsword, Ragnar!" the author beseeched his character. "Cut off the motherfucker's head!"

The red-pigtailed Norseman made no move to draw his weapon.

"Liv Nacim, your rapier! Skewer his guts!"

The patriarch of the celery people wouldn't be interrupted. He was caught up delivering an overlong insult to Ragnar.

Daniel didn't even bother with the Princess. She was applying fresh dabs of rose-pink to the centers of her buckskin-hued cheeks.

"You ungrateful bastards!" Daniel cried. "I breathed life into you! And this is what I get in return?"

The heroes of *SR* blinked at him for a moment, then returned to whatever it was they were doing.

As the needle was slowly rotated out of his hip with the wrench, Daniel nearly passed out.

In the middle of the exit procedure, Dr. Yorte paused to address Montejo and the *brujas.* He tapped the stainless-steel basin with the jaws of the crescent and said, "Not so much yield from his pelvis. Maybe we have finally drained him dry? Maybe we should suck the cells from his spine. Oh, no, wait a minute. I forgot, he doesn't have one. Heh-heh-heh-heh."

Then it was time for the other hip to give up its treasure.

The big-bore needle pierced flesh and penetrated a quarter-inch into the bone. The crescent wrench clanked hard against the bolt head, sending undulations of agony down Daniel's leg. Then the needle corkscrewed into him again, 'round and 'round, with Yorte leaning on the wrench and grunting from the effort.

Oh mommy.

Chapter Twenty-Two

Doc Tanner was awakened from a dreamless sleep by a hard shaking and a familiar voice urging, "Get up, damn it."

When he opened his eyes he saw that Mildred had already roused everyone else in the cell. Doc swung his long legs over the edge of the steel platform that served as a bed. "What is it?" he asked. "What's so important?"

"They're going to infect us with Daniel's disease," Mildred told him. "I figured it out."

"You mean, we're going to start writing bad science fiction?" Doc said. "And then have the audacity to defend it?"

"No, you idiot," Mildred snapped. "They're going to give us what killed the people of Padre. They're going to try to make us into carriers, like Desipio."

"Nukin' hell they are," J.B. said.

"If we cannot stop them from doing that," Doc said, "I for one do not intend to live a second so sullied. I will find a way to end the wretchedness forthwith. Even if I have to dash my own brains out against the nearest wall."

"Our only chance is when the guards come to take us away," Krysty said. "We've got to jump them when they open the cell."

"This is hold-back-nothing time," J.B. said. "If we can get out of here, mebbe we can snatch some blasters, turn this dump upside down."

The plan was just simple enough to work, Doc thought as he listened for the sound of the guards' footsteps on the concrete. They would rush the open door all at once, using the mass of their bodies to overwhelm and pull down the closest Matachìn, then to block the closing of the cell. With the door wedged open, they would take out the other guards with a human wave before they could cry for help or respond with deadly force. Once they were out of commission, keys for the cuffs and weapons could be confiscated.

A good plan, but it didn't take into account one thing.

The firehose.

When the cell door opened, the companions rushed it in unison. Doc managed to get hold of the guard's arm, and that fraction of a second delay allowed the others to pile on. From out of nowhere, a stream of high-pressure water slammed them through the bars. It was like being kicked in the chest by a mule. The force of the impact lifted Doc off his feet and slammed him against the back of the cell.

"By the Three Kennedys!" he growled, lowering his head and throwing himself toward the exit, only to be driven back again.

It wasn't just the power of the water that kept him from reaching the open door, it was also the effect it had on the concrete floor—turning it as slippery as ice.

Doc couldn't breathe. He couldn't get up. And neither could anyone else. The hose pressure knocked them down and held them down.

Over the roaring hiss, Doc could hear the Matachìn laughing.

The guards hosed them down until they stopped struggling, until they had exhausted trying to fight the force of the water.

Then the companions were dragged out one by one, like drowned rats.

They had tried, but in the end all it had added up to was a soapless shower, fully clothed.

When his turn came, Doc was dragged out of the cell block, down the sally port, and through the front door of the Razor House. Inside, he was plopped down in a wheelchair and rolled into an examination room. Where the others had been taken, he had no clue; there was no sign of them, but there were other closed doors along the corridor.

The sights and odors of the medical unit made him flashback to his first time trawl and his first interaction with whitecoats.

Helpless in the hands of idiots.

Perverse idiots, at that.

A case in point was Dr. Dolan Yorte, who breezed into the room, brushed back his overlong hair with a precise two-handed sweep, snapped some orders to the little female white-coat in attendance, brushed back his hair a second time, then breezed out, slamming the door after him. In those brief moments Theophilus Tanner took what he believed was the full measure of the man. Yorte's insecurities, both professional and personal, were vast, perhaps bottomless. And they were coupled with and confounded by a manic energy, an excess of narcissism and uncrackable pigheadedness.

The whitecoat poster boy.

"Let me help you out of those wet clothes," the little white-coat said, speaking slowly so he could understand her Spanish.

"I think not, madam," he said resolutely.

"There are things I must do before we can proceed," she went on. "I must conduct a thorough physical examination to identify any health problems that need to be treated. I must draw some of your blood for testing."

"What is the ultimate goal of this exercise?"

"You are to be given the *mujera*'s sickness, of course. In the hope that you will survive the disease as a carrier and thereby replace the *enanos* who were lost in the campaign in Tierra de la Muerte."

"*Mujera?* I don't know that word."

"*La mujera.* The man who whines and fusses like a little woman."

"Oh, you mean the Fire Talker, Daniel."

"The sickness is very, very bad." The whitecoat made a serious face, complete with brow furrows and pouted lips.

"I know, I have seen it."

"Doctors Yorte and Montejo will make sure you catch it. And when you do there will be fever, vomiting, diarrhea, delirium. And the red boils all over the skin. You will be sick for a very long time. If you live through it, you will serve the Lords of Death, like Daniel."

"If not, I will be dog food."

The *bruja* nodded, her eyes glittering merrily.

"Why do you not take off my shackles?" Doc suggested.

"Why would I do that?"

"Because I like you very much."

Her eyes grew wide in surprise, but she smiled.

"You and I could go off into the jungle and be very happy together," Doc continued. "We could make large numbers of little Docs and *brujas*. We could raise spotted pigs. And eat papaya and guanabana every day. This place is a hellhole. You deserve so much better."

"No, can't you see I am a serious professional. I have a career to think of."

"Where exactly did you get your training?"

"*Los CDs.*"

"I beg your pardon."

"Oh, wait, it's too hard to explain. I'll show you."

The little woman disappeared, then came back with a handful of flat, black plastic cases. "*Los CDs,*" she repeated.

The covers had no pictures or photos to identify their contents, just slips of paper on which were printed multisyllabic words in Spanish. The titles were uniformly uninspired: *Implantation surgery, Facial Reconstruction Techniques, Viral Load Management, Cryogenic Reanimation, Recovery, Relapse and Morbidity.* The discs looked homemade, or at least home copied, and they appeared to cover the specific tasks required of Xibalban whitecoats. Which was very convenient. Perhaps the last real whitecoat standing had made them? Or perhaps they were the products of the Lords of Death?

"I do not know what these are," he told her as he handed them back.

"If you live through the sickness, we will watch them together, perhaps. You will need to wear protection, though."

"Do you mean a condom?"

The *bruja* giggled, then play-slapped him on the shoulder. "You don't understand. After the procedure you will be an *enano*. You won't be allowed out without a net suit. Otherwise you might kill everyone. One little mosquito, you know…unless you are the Lords of Death."

"What do you mean?"

"Mosquitoes don't ever bite them. Don't like their smell, some people say."

"I like your smell."

The bruja giggled some more.

Doc thought he was making some headway. Sex was not

the primary thing on his mind; it was a means to an end. The end being getting free of his shackles, and then freeing his companions from theirs.

"If you and I do not consummate our relationship post-haste, we never will," Doc said, pressing on with all the ardent enthusiasm he could muster. "Once I am infected with the disease, romantic love will be impossible for me. This is our only chance, my dear. Come on, you have me at a disadvantage. I cannot move my arms or legs. You could have your way with me and I could not stop you."

"Is tempting."

"It has been a long time since I've enjoyed the company of a beautiful and willing woman, and if what you say is true, I will not be able to do so ever again without killing her. How can you deny me a last taste of passion?" He glanced down at his crotch. "I am not a small man."

His nurse was looking at his crotch, too.

"Is very tempting. Tee-hee."

"Well?"

The *bruja* bit her lower lip as she carefully mulled over the offer. Doc imagined that he could hear the gears of her mind ticking over. They ticked very, very slowly.

Finally she shook her head and said, "No, I'm sorry, I can't do it. You are an attractive man, and you are very charming, but there is too much for me to lose. If the Lords of Death found out, they would throw me to the dogs."

Chapter Twenty-Three

The Hatteras was a big target. Not only was it white, or once white, and two-stories high, it threw a big bow wave. Even though they were running with the sun at their backs, Ryan knew they could be seen from a long way off.

"Someone could be waiting for us on the beach," he said to Chucho as the dark island grew ever larger. The Hero Twin passed on his concern in Spanish to the Matachìn commander who had been tied to the stern for the entire nine-hour trip.

"No one will be watching in the heat of the day," Casacampo assured him. "Besides, boats come and go from the island all the time, bringing in supplies. No one pays much attention."

Ryan listened to the translation. Low Pile might have been trying to pull something on them, but he doubted it. Not with Chucho so close.

"Just in case," Ryan said, "mebbe we'd better break out the RPDs to handle any beach crowd."

The Matachìn commander rattled off more Spanish.

"He says there's more than one landing place," Chucho told Ryan. "On the north side of the island there's a rocky point with caves at the foot of the cliffs. He says we can follow them up into the rain forest. Keep out of sight the whole time."

"What about the ship?" Ryan said.

After a brief exchange with Low Pile, Chucho added, "He says there's a cove, a natural harbor with a lava breakwater. He says the Hatteras should make it over the bar. It's been in there before. Inside the protected cove, it's plenty deep."

"Think it's bullshit?" Ryan said.

"He's too scared to lie to us," Chucho replied. "If he's looking to make his move, it wouldn't be something this easy to see through."

"I'll tell Tom," Ryan said, then he started up the flybridge ladder.

The north side of the island was in the wind's lee, and because of that it was a good ten degrees hotter. The coastline along the point was made up of cliffs of volcanic rock. They looked like piles of giant, ossified black turds, segmented, some with twisty-twirly tops. The walls of lava soaked up the sun's heat and radiated it back like a bake oven.

Tom negotiated the passage between the tip of the natural breakwater and the head of land. Inside the cove the water was pale turquoise and very clear. Ryan could see the white, sandy bottom fifty feet down.

Casacampo made a comment from the stern.

"He says in the olden days escaped prisoners sometimes got this far," Chucho said. "Then they tried to swim or raft across the water to the mainland. There were huge sharks waiting for them. He says the prison guards used to watch from cliffs with binoculars and make bets on which convict the sharks would eat first."

After the Hatteras was anchored, they launched the ship's dinghy. Tom and Ryan waded ashore carrying twenty-five pounds of C-4 each, in pre-rigged, one-pound chunks, plus two loaded RPDs and a pair of H&K MP-5 SD-1s and machetes. Chucho carried a silenced submachine gun, a backpack with extra drum mags for the Soviet machine guns and a machete. Casacampo had all their canteens over his shoulder; Chucho held him with a leash around his neck. His hands were bound at the wrists in front of him.

At the foot of the cliff, white sand met black rock. There was more than one cave entrance. It was impossible to tell which were dead-end tunnels.

"Which one is it?" Ryan asked Casacampo.

Even though the question was in English, Low Pile understood it. He pointed at a vertical gash in the bedrock.

After putting on their headlamps, they entered the cave, which reeked of rotting seaweed and bat shit. The sand floor quickly gave way to rock as the cavern up-angled. Runoff from the forest above had cut the steep-sided crevice down to the sea.

The confined space, the fact that they were using headlamps, would make for a prime ambush, Ryan knew. They'd never know what hit them.

"Keep the pirate close," he reminded Chucho.

They climbed steadily up through the pitch-darkness with silenced weapons at the ready. After a short distance the cave widened into a low-ceilinged gallery and the floor angle flattened.

There was a different odor. A carrion odor.

Then Ryan's headlamp reflected in pair of eyes. Lots of eyes, low to the ground.

Then the growling started.

Three headlamps swept over the crouching forms.

"Nice doggies," Tom said hopefully.

Yeah, right, Ryan thought, gripping his H&K. The dogs

looked wet to the skin. They were big, rangy animals, 70 to 120 pounds. They were slathering mad. And they had just cause. Their turf had been invaded by strangers.

Edible strangers.

A particularly large specimen rose from its haunches and edged toward them, low to the floor, every muscle tensed. Its body language said attack was imminent. Behind it, a dozen pairs of red eyes followed.

Ryan let the H&K fall to lanyard around his neck. He reached for the butt of the RPD and swung it around on its sling. As he brought the muzzle to bear, the lead dog charged them and the others followed suit. Tom cut loose with his submachine gun, but the silenced burst of 9 mm rounds didn't even slow the animal down.

Not enough knockdown power.

The noise didn't matter. Ryan had to use the RPD or be torn apart. He focused on the center of the pack, firing from the hip. The MG roared in the confined space. It was so loud that it buried the sounds of bullets slapping flesh. In his headlamp's glare Ryan saw explosions of gore and slobber, and bright sparks as ricochets zinged off the cave's floor and walls.

The meat-grinder effect of all that compressed firepower aerosolized flesh and bone. Ryan fired fifty or sixty rounds, filling the cavern with a haze of gunsmoke.

After the haze lifted, Tom pointed over at the cave wall. "Lookee there," he said. "We got one more and she's nursing her pups. They don't even have their eyes open yet."

"Mebbe we're gonna have to deal with her on the way out," Tom said. "Mebbe we should just chill them all now."

"Go ahead, be my guest," Chucho said.

Tom shook his head, making the light from his headlamp dance across the wall. "Bitch with puppies, that's bad juju."

"They're feral dogs," Ryan said. "Just leave them be. They can eat any Matachìn we don't manage to chill."

"Perros locos," Chucho said. "There are many more. They run in much bigger packs than this. Pray they don't find us before we're done here."

Ryan walked past the carnage he'd created. Nukin' hell, he thought, those were some big-ass dogs. The bigger ones survived because they were strong enough to pull down deer and boar. Damned hard for a dog to catch a howler monkey or a macaw. That's what Mildred called natural selection.

The cave exit opened onto a jungle trail. It was very hot under the canopy and dark, but not dark enough to need the headlamps.

"How far is it?" Tom asked Casacampo in Spanish.

The answer was six miles.

A ways to hump in 100-degree heat and humidity.

The trail looked like it had been made by game. It was less than three feet wide and weaved back and forth around the bases of the massive trees.

"Too tight quarters for blasters," Ryan said, shoulder-slinging the RPD and unsheathing his machete as he took point.

Tom and Chucho did the same.

The fer-de-lance is a reddish-brown, white and black venomous snake; its coloring makes it easy to hide in the litter on the rain-forest floor. The one that reared up to strike Ryan was impossible to miss. It was more than ten feet long and its back was bigger across than his bicep.

Ryan neatly stunned it with a backhanded blow of the side of his machete, then he forehanded and just as neatly clipped off its head. He kicked the still-writhing body into the brush.

"Eyes skinned," he reminded the others.

To hike the six miles along the winding game trail, with all the ups and downs, the ravines to scale and the creeks to jump, with occasional water breaks to keep from getting too dehydrated, it took a little over two-and-a-half hours.

They heard the hum of the generators long before they reached the prison's outer fence.

Through the branches they could see the bright clearing.

"Tell the pirate if he makes a sound, he dies," Ryan said to Chucho.

Casacampo nodded that he understood the price of betrayal.

Understanding it and being willing to pay it were two different things. Ryan sensed the man's tension and guessed that he was considering the odds. If he could break free and alert his pals, he might get out alive and end up being a hero. Ryan wasn't going to let him do that. Under other circumstances, he would have chilled the bastard at once. Under these circumstances there was still vital information to be had because Casacampo had visited the compound before.

They crawled forward to the edge of the forest and gazed upon Xibalba, the mythical home of the all-powerful Lords of Death.

Not much to recommend it, Ryan thought. It looked like a shit-hole jungle prison. Double high-wire fence with guard towers along the inside perimeter. Mildewed, windowless, concrete buildings on a roughly circular plain of dirt and scrub grass. People wandering around or stretched out in the shade.

"Ask him where my friends are," Ryan said to Chucho. "Ask him which building they're being held in."

The Matachìn indicated the corner of a single-story struc-

ure that was just visible around the corner of the two-story
ell block.

"He says it's probably that one," Chucho said. "Razor
House. He says it's where the whitecoats saw people up."

"Do you believe him?" Tom asked Ryan.

"If he lies, he dies," Ryan said. "We won't make it to the
nner wire if those two guard towers are still manned come
unset. They've got a clear, overlapping kill zone between the
wo fences. We have to take them out nice and quiet so we
an cut the wire and make our entry from the rear."

Getting through the wire was no problem because Tom had
rought a pair of cutters in his pack. Getting out the same way
night be more difficult, depending on how many enemy were
till alive when the time came. The plan was to wait for the
ading light of evening, snipe the tower gunners with the
ilenced SMGs, free the companions, chill as many Matachìn
nd Lords of Death as they could, then blow the whole place
o rubble and beat feet back to the ship.

A tall order, Ryan knew. There were an uncounted number
f ways the whole scheme could implode. Every step was a po-
:ntial stumbling block or dead end. But there was no going back.

Suddenly, the order got even taller.

In the jungle behind them, dogs started baying.

"Shit, they've picked up our scent," Tom said.

Chapter Twenty-Four

The tall and lanky Dr. Montejo had the diminutive *bruj*
pressed up against the wall of the inoculation room, his hip
driving while she clung around his neck, her legs wrappe
around the small of his back.

This while they made grunting, monkey sounds.

Both of them kept glancing over at Krysty every few
seconds to see if she was watching. If she was, they ratchete
up the frenzy of their rutting.

Krysty, who lay strapped to a crucifixion table, a captiv
audience of one, viewed the recreational in-out with disdair

The *bruja* was a spinner.

Her boyfriend was a whimperer.

Which made for a very unpleasant spectacle.

Krysty couldn't decide if they were indulging in celebra
tory sex, or if this was their usual pastime come evening. It wa
however, the first time she saw Dr. Montejo break a sweat.

"Pul-eeeze!" she exclaimed. "I hate to break it to you tw
but you're not much to look at and you're not that good at wh;
you're up to."

The comment, rendered in a foreign, and therefore unir
telligible language, made Montejo hump harder and faste
and the *bruja*'s eyes rolled up in her head so Krysty could se
only whites. After that, Krysty decided to just ignore them

When, some ten minutes later, they finally finished, the lab assistant pulled her bunched-up whitecoat skirt down over her somewhat wobbly, brown bandy legs. She licked her finger, then used it to smooth her eyebrow.

Very classy.

Aside from Mildred, who was by all accounts a special case, the whitecoats Krysty had seen had never impressed her all that much. This pair impressed her the least of any, and it wasn't just their lame sexual technique or penchant for exhibitionism. Their attire notwithstanding, they appeared to be dumb as frigging fence posts.

While Krysty watched, the doctor and his assistant began pulling on protective gear. They both donned latex gloves and some kind of heavy-duty antiviral masks with twin filtration canisters sticking out the sides of the mouthpiece. They also put on plastic goggles.

From a countertop, Montejo picked up a clear plastic basin with a tight-fitting lid and carried it gingerly over to the rolling tray beside the crucifixion table. He opened the lid and took out a hypodermic syringe, moving in slow motion. The way he handled it, the thing might well have contained nitro.

The fluid inside was the color of diluted blood.

Or strawberry juice.

About ten cc's.

It was an "Uh-oh" moment for Krysty. Accordingly, her prehensile hair drew up in tight ringlets of alarm. For the hundredth time, she tested the flex in her restraints. They didn't give so much as a millimeter. Even though her wrist and ankle manacles had been removed, she was pinioned to the table, all except her neck and head.

She knew that the strawberry fluid had been taken from

Daniel, that his filthy spew was about to be put inside her an
there was nothing she could do about it. It was as bad as rape
Mebbe even worse, because of what it was going to do to he
once it was inside her veins.

Krysty remembered all too well what the dying at Padr
had looked like. People lying helpless in their own shit an
piss and puke, waiting for the end. Could she be forced to b
another Daniel, to become the knowing cause of somethin
like that? Used to spread that kind of horror across the hell
scape, leaving nothing behind but piles of corpses?

She had no illusions on the subject. The spread of thi
disease, this plague, would end Deathlands, and the faint, bu
lingering promise of a resurrected nation would be torn ou
by the roots.

Where were the others? she thought desperately. Were the
already infected? How much serum from Daniel's bones wa
needed? Could they make enough of it to dose them all at once
Only Mildred would know the answers, and she wasn't here

Part of her was glad Ryan wasn't with her, either. She wa
glad that he hadn't lived long enough to be put through thi
obscenity.

Even though she knew they couldn't understand her, sh
addressed the whitecoats, anyway.

"You can give me the rad-blasted disease," she said, "bu
you'd better pray it kills me, because if I survive I will b
coming after you both. And what I will do to you smirking
self-satisfied, murderous shit hooks, you can't even begin t
imagine."

The little *bruja* made animalistic "There, there" noises a
Krysty twisted and fought against the restraints.

Montejo's bedside manner lacked even that subtlety.

"Calma, por favor," he said, putting his free hand on her breast.

She was about to call on her Gaia powers, hoping that the Earth Mother would grant her enough strength to not only break her bonds, but to chill these two wastes of breath, when blasterfire erupted from outside the building.

Dr. Montejo hesitated, plague hypo in one hand, Krysty in the other.

Chapter Twenty-Five

The baying sounds of the feral dogs rapidly grew louder and more frenzied. They seemed to be coming from three sides as the pack filtered through the jungle, closing in for the kill.

"We can't wait for sundown," Ryan said, rising to his feet. "In another five minutes the dogs will have us pinned against the fence. That will alert the Matachìn and then we'll be attacked front and rear, with no way out. Tom, cut the outside wire here. I'll take the tower gunner on the right, Chucho you take the other one. Tom, get through the wire as quick as you can. Once the gun towers are dealt with, cross the no-man's-land and cut us a hole in the inside fence."

"With the exception of your friends of course," Chucho said, "everyone inside the compound has earned death. The so-called gods. Their pirate criminals. The whitecoats and dwarves who spread the plague, and the miscellaneous underlings and bootlicks that keep this place running. These creatures have sucked the blood of my people for decades. For that they must pay. And they must never be allowed to rise up again."

"But we can't possibly kill them all," Tom said as he took out the wire cutters. "We can't cover all the ways out of here. Once we start shooting, they can scatter out the main gate or scale the fence and hightail it off into the jungle."

"Let them," Ryan said. "If the dogs don't run them down

ey will have nothing to come back to here. We'll make sure
f that."

"We will sink all their boats so they can't escape from this
lace," Chucho added. "Let them try to swim to the mainland
r make rafts from the trees. When the first few are eaten by
harks, there will be no more swimmers or rafters, I guaran-
e you. Once again there will be prisoners for life on this hell
land."

Casacampo stood as if to join them in the next phase of the
peration.

"Not you," Chucho told him.

The commander's face dropped.

"You die here and now. Before you can betray us."

"But…"

Chucho's H&K coughed once in a summary execution.
ragments of Casacampo's skull and brains splattered the
aves and branches behind them. The body flopped to the
round on its back, arms and legs twitching.

"Shit," Ryan muttered. He knew the scent of the gore
ould be a beacon for the dogs. And it would lead them right
p to the hole in the fence. But he said nothing about it. It was
o late to undo what had been done. The bastard deserved
illing, anyway, no matter whose hand did the deed.

And time was running out.

Ryan hurried away, concealed just inside the edge of the
orest, moving parallel to the wire. When he arrived at a
oint opposite the gun tower, he peered through the dense
oliage. The Matachìn in the tower wasn't looking his way.
nder the shade of the tower's peaked metal roof, he had his
ack to the perimeter and he was staring down at the goings-
n inside the compound.

Ryan crawled to the wire, then bellied down in front of it He lined up the shot, bracing the silencer's fat barrel agains the mesh. The distance was no more than seventy-five yards He flipped the fire selector switch to triburst, snugged up th buttstock and acquired the target.

When the tower guard turned his way, Ryan tightene down on the trigger until it broke. The H&K coughed 3-round stutter and pushed back hard against his shoulde Downrange, the slap of metal on meat was lost in the stead throb of Xibalba's generators. The man in the tower threw u his hands.

Not in surprise.

Not in celebration.

In the ultimate surrender.

His body dropped out of sight behind the tower's front wall

Ryan scooted back to the forest. No longer concerne about being observed, he sprinted to the gaping cut in the wire He got there just as Chucho arrived. Both towers were no unmanned. The way in was clear. They slipped through th break in the fence and crossed the stretch of open ground o a dead run.

Tom was ahead of them, already kneeling at the secon fence, working like a madman with the cutters. When the reached him, the trader held open the hole he'd made so the could enter.

So far, so good, Ryan thought. Even though it was broa daylight, no one had noticed their penetration. He knew tha wouldn't last.

As the three of them cut across the swathe of open groun toward the two-story cell blocks, someone started shoutin at them.

Still there was no armed response. Perhaps because this incursion into the heart of Xibalba was entirely unexpected and unprecedented.

That all changed when four bald-headed pirates suddenly rounded the corner of the cell block, running with weapons up. Chucho and Ryan fired first, at a distance of about eight yards, aiming center chest. The silenced, full-auto bursts blasted the Matachìn off their feet. As they were flung aside, they fired their submachine guns into the air and the ground in front of them.

So much for surprise.

The Xibalban bystanders scattered as Ryan, Chucho and Tom charged around the corner, heading for the rear of the whitecoat building. They didn't have enough time or enough ammo to take out everyone in sight. Just the combatants. The ones who stood in their way.

Ryan hit the doors first. He burst into a foyer that opened onto a low-ceilinged reception area. A handful of whitecoats stood there, stunned for an instant, then they all dived for cover.

"Krysty, Mildred!" Ryan bellowed down the corridor. "J.B., Doc, Jak! Where are you?"

When there was no answer, he growled at Tom and Chucho, "Let's start kicking in some doors."

Ryan found Jak in the second room he tried. The albino was strapped and gagged on a table. Released, he was spitting mad. Not a pretty sight with those bloodred eyes and deathly pale face and hair. He looked like a demon ghost.

Ryan handed him the submachine gun and swung the big Russian MG around on its shoulder sling.

"Fuck 'em up!" Jak snarled. "Let's fuck 'em up!"

Out in the hallway, Tom and Chucho had found and freed

the others. When Krysty saw Ryan she ran toward him full-tilt, threw herself into his open arms and squeezed him tight. Her emerald eyes shining with tears, she said, "Oh, lover! Oh, Gaia, thank you, thank you!"

"You are a sight for sore eyes, my dear Ryan," Doc said as he stepped up.

"And we're seeing double," Mildred added, nodding at Chucho.

There was no time to get acquainted, or reacquainted. And definitely no time for explanations.

Harmonica Tom opened Ryan's backpack, reached in and took out a pre-rigged block of C-4. "Where is this going to do the most damage?" he said, hefting the oblong parcel in his hand.

Mildred pointed toward the quarantine section. "That's where they keep the *enanos* and the plague serum," she told him. "It's a triple layer of containment, pressure sealed so the disease can't accidentally get out. Once that's gone they'll never be able to rebuild it. Or make more plague carriers."

"If we blow it up, won't we be releasing it?" Krysty said.

"The heat of the explosion will probably destroy it," Mildred said.

"And even if it doesn't," Ryan added, "it'll be contained on the island. We're fifty miles from the mainland. When we leave, we're turning the lights out."

Ryan took Tom's H&K and handed it to J.B. There weren't enough extra weapons to go around. After Tom planted the charge, Ryan said, "Now, let's go pay a visit to the Lords of Death."

"They're probably all holed up in the gym building. Its their council place," Mildred said. "It's where they hold audiences with their toadies. They've got big-time backup in there."

As they exited the research center, bullets slammed into the concrete facade and skipped off the concrete walkway. They were moving too quickly to see where the blasterfire was coming from, and it didn't matter at that point; their goal was to reach the next bit of solid cover, which was the near wall of the gymnasium.

They ran past assorted sniveling wretches and pus bags who although still smiling to beat the band were wandering around in a daze, not understanding what had happened, or what was about to happen.

"Doors in, doors out?" Ryan asked Mildred.

"Two doors, one at either end," she said. "There are no other ways out."

"If they're in there, we've got 'em," Tom said.

Ryan sent Jak off to the right with extra mags for the H&K, to cover the gym's rear exit and forestall a retreat in that direction. Then he and the others ran for the building's main entrance. As they came around the corner, they took fire from the gun tower opposite. Slugs whined overhead, way too close for comfort.

Ryan shouldered the Soviet RPD. "Kick in the doors!" he growled at Chucho and Tom.

When the MG thundered, the recoil set Ryan back on his heels. The 10-round burst punched holes in the wall of the tower, raising a cloud of dust. The gunner disappeared from view.

Behind him, as Chucho and Tom approached the gym's entrance, a fusillade of blasterfire roared from within, and a ravening volley of bullets came flying through the closed doors.

Chapter Twenty-Six

The rain of outgoing slugs rattled the gym doors in their frames, the ragged, random exit holes making them look like giant cheese graters. Ryan moved closer to the building's front wall, out of the path of the ricochets. There was no telling how many blasters were cutting loose from the other side, but anyone standing in the doorway or the kill zone beyond it would have been chopped to pieces.

"Let's give 'em something to think about," Tom said to Chucho, stepping away from the wall and swinging his RPD up from the hip.

Chucho jumped to his side, then they both let it rip with their machine guns, firing back through the already holed-out doors. Teeth bared, muscular arms shuddering from the sustained buffeting of recoil, they moved to the left as they shot, edging into the killzone, sweeping the interior of the gym with a withering counterfire of 700 steel-jacketed rounds per minute. Spent brass arced from the blasters' ejector ports, smoke and flame billowed from the muzzles, and the steel-clad doors buckled in the middle and spread apart under the hellacious, close-range barrage.

The last of the two hundred smoking cases clinked to the concrete, and the ear-splitting clatter of the autofire echoed off in the jungle.

There was no return fire.

Ryan and J.B. stepped up and simultaneously booted the crumpled doors, and they crashed inward to the floor.

While Tom and Chucho reloaded their RPDs with fresh drum mags, Ryan and J.B. burst through the doorway with their autoweapons at hip level. Wreaths of gunsmoke hung over the middle of the court. The floor between the old free throw lines was littered with bodies and blood. The Xibalba hangers-on and minor demons had taken the brunt of the exchange of firepower. Some of them still stirred, albeit feebly. It was impossible to tell which side had fired the bullets that cut them down.

At opposite end of room, the exit doors slammed back, and bald Matachìn put up scattered covering fire as they retreated.

J.B. and Ryan fanned out, firing as they advanced. Ryan ran for the end of the bleachers. He could see the top two rows were occupied—large figures in white robes with hideous head masks—but the spectators weren't moving and they weren't armed. For the moment they could be ignored.

There were other fish to fry.

Unmanacled for the first time in a month, and now fully armed, J.B. was all about getting payback—with interest. Fearless in his fury, J.B. charged the exit, spraying it with 9 mm slugs. He took down three of the pirates before they could clear the doors, sending them sprawling to the floor. A fourth Matachìn tried to return fire and cover his own escape, and for his trouble, he took two rounds through the throat. He dropped his weapon and clutched his spurting neck in both hands as he slipped to his knees.

Ryan braced his RPD against the edge of a bleacher seat and punched out a stream of hot lead at the last three pirates who raced for the exit. The torrent of 7.62 mm rounds were like a flyswatter to flies. They lifted and slammed the running men into the concrete block, and as their bodies slumped to the floor they revealed big splotches of red splatter on the wall behind.

Shooting erupted from outside the gym. The retreating Matachìn had stumbled into Jak's ambush.

The battle sounded one-sided. Because Lauren's weapon was silenced, only the pirate return fire could be heard.

Then the shooting abruptly stopped.

The pirates had either chilled Jak, or they were all dead. Knowing the albino teen as he did, Ryan was guessing it was the latter. He turned his attention and the sights of his weapon on the two rows of spectators above.

"Get your hands up!" he shouted, forgetting in the heat of the moment that there might be a language barrier.

Chucho repeated the order in Spanish.

None of the seated figures moved a muscle.

"Those are the Lords of Death," Mildred said as she, Doc and Krysty joined them at the foot of the stands. "The rulers of Xibalba."

Ryan did a quick head count. Thirty of them. But there were holes in the ranks. Six places were empty.

"How come the masked assholes aren't moving?" J.B. asked as he slapped a fresh 9 mm mag into his submachine gun and flipped the actuator, chambering the first round. "Are they already dead? Or are they stuffed?"

"We should check to see if any of them are real," Mildred said.

"Yeah, I'll *check* them, all right," Chucho said, hoisting up the muzzle of his RPD. Without another word, he stitched steel-jacketed slugs across the top rows of bleachers, spraying the figures with autofire. The white-robed torsos jerked, then toppled over. Garish masks rolled off headless shoulders and bounced down the tiers of bleacher seats to the court below.

They were all dummies.

"Nukin' hell!" J.B. exclaimed. "The bastards got away!"

"Over here!" Jak shouted from the back door.

While Ryan, J.B., Chucho and Tom ran to join him, Doc, Mildred and Krysty took a moment to bend and pick up dropped submachine guns off the dead Matachìn. They immediately checked for full mags and made sure live rounds were chambered.

Everybody had a blaster.

Looking out the doorway, Ryan could see the bodies of half a dozen bushwhacked pirates caught by Jak's opening silenced burst.

"Pinned me quick, couldn't nail all," the albino said ruefully. He pointed at the entrance to the cell block on the other side of a narrow courtyard. "In there."

"How many?" Tom said.

"Ten, mebbe more."

"And the Lords of Death?" Ryan prompted. "Did you see them?"

"Already high-tailin', before camou fighters came out back door," Jak said. "Five, six motherfuckers in masks, run fast. Ryan, not see anyone *that* fast."

"They duck into the cell block, too?" J.B. asked.

"Nah, lit out for fence behind. Went through hole."

"Same fucking hole I cut!" Tom said.

"Out into the jungle by now," Ryan said. "Were they armed?"

"Nope. Empty hands."

"If they went out the way we came in they'll run right into the wild dogs," Chucho said. "That works for me."

"Me, too," Ryan said.

"Are you gonna blow up the council place?" Krysty asked Tom.

The trader eyed the structure dubiously. "Probably take most of the C-4 to bring it down," he said. "But it rains a lot here, doesn't it?"

Chucho nodded. "Rains like holy hell."

"Got enough extra C-4 to blow out a supporting wall and bring down the roof," Tom said. He quickly removed a pair of charges from Ryan's backpack and placed them at corners of the facing wall.

As he rejoined Ryan and the others, with a loud crack a single bullet zinged in from the direction of the cell blocks. It clipped the edge of the steel doorframe, sending sparks and bits of metal flying.

"Let's finish this job," Ryan said.

Chapter Twenty-Seven

Following Mildred out of the gym, Harmonica Tom had the rear guard on the file. Ryan was on point as they crossed the courtyard on a dead sprint, making for the cell block's doors. To their right was a low, windowless, shedlike building.

Another gun crack rang out and a slug from overhead kicked up the dirt. A narrow miss for Ryan, the bullet zipped over his shoulder and hit the ground beside Jak's left boot. Tom noted that the one-eyed warrior didn't even flinch. However, the sniper on the cell block roof forced them to change course to the right, moving up against the maintenance shed and under the eaves of its sloping roof.

As Tom was brushing past the shed's closed door, it jolted mightily in its frame. Heavy bodies hurled against the inside of the metal door, trying to break it down. Claws scraped its surface, trying to rip through it. This was accompanied by a chorus of baritone snarling.

"The Xibalbans call it Jaguar House," Mildred told him.

"Since when do jaguars bark and howl?" the trader remarked.

"Yeah, that's what I said. The truth is they've got a bunch of feral dogs trapped in there and they use them to torture their subjects, and to keep them in line. If you go in Jaguar House, you don't come out in one piece. You don't come out at all.

The smell of blood and the sound of gunfire has really got the dogs worked up."

"They smell dinner," Tom said.

Another single shot rang out from the roof and the bullet whizzed by Tom's left ear. The trader raised his machine gun to his shoulder, stepped out from beside the building and away from the narrow band of concealment its eaves provided. The others needed covering fire to cross the rest of the courtyard; aside from that, Tom didn't take kindly to slugs coming that close to his mustache. He touched off a rattling burst of autofire, aimed upward, at the edge of the roof. The lip of mildewed concrete disintegrated under the hail of lead, chunks fell away and dropped to the ground. Tom stopped shooting and waited, sights held steady on the roof line, while the others raced out from under cover for the front of the cell block. When the shooter peeked up with his weapon about five feet from where Tom thought he'd be, he shifted his aim to the target and pinned the trigger. The concrete was turned to dust by a dozen steel-jackets. The shooter fell back out of sight and his long blaster tumbled down the side of the building, crashing to the dirt below.

When Tom reached the front of the cell block, Ryan said, "We're going to have to blow the door. It's locked from the inside."

"No problem," Tom said. He unshouldered his backpack and from it took out a hunk of plastique already rigged with a blasting cap and a length of conventional fuze cord. He worked quickly, mashing the pliable explosive into the gap between the door hinges and frame, then he lit the fuze with a wooden match.

The others had spread out along the foot of the wall,

kneeling with their heads turned toward the building. Tom joined in the duck and cover.

The explosion rocked the ground and sent a plume of smoke and debris flying out into the courtyard.

Mebbe a bit too much C-4, Tom thought as he shook his head to clear it. The door frame was emptied but there were wide, branching cracks running up the side of the cell block's wall.

When Ryan led them inside, smoke was still pouring out the opening. The floor of the corridor was alive with small, flopping black things.

Bats.

Dying bats and already dead ones.

When Tom entered last, there were still some of the leaping critters to kick aside. He looked down the central corridor. In the light of electric bulbs, filtered through smoke, it was grim, gray, decaying. A different sort of prison than the ancient fort in Veracruz, more temporary, less eternal. Instead of an oppressively low, stone ceiling, the cell block had a towering, two-storey height. But the stink of death and damnation was the same. There were four metal stairways at each corner of the narrow rectangle, each leading up to the second tier of cells and a railed walkway that completely encircled it.

Nothing moved in front of them or above them.

But there were sounds coming out of the smoke and dust, moans of agony.

At Ryan's signal, they split up, four to a side of the first-floor cells.

Tom and Chucho held back a little, covering the second-tier walkway on the opposite side with their machine guns, while Mildred and Jak advanced ahead of them, checking the cells.

Across the corridor, Krysty, J.B., Doc and Ryan were doing the same, advancing with caution but with focused intent.

Tom could see the set to their jaws, the hard light in their eyes. It made him smile. All the evil that had been done by the Matachìn and their puppetmasters couldn't be undone, but it could be stopped, once and for all. This was his true element: blood and blastersmoke and a world of hurt for the coldheart bastards.

They passed cell doors ajar. Inside the barred cages directly opposite the doorway, prisoners or lackeys lay dead on the floor, either blown apart by the blast or chilled by flying shrap. Some of them had daggers of metal sticking out of their torsos and heads.

Then the live ones showed up. Dozens of minor demons and toadies burst from the cells in front of them and charged through the smoke. Waving their arms, male and female, half naked, their faces horror shows of botched surgeries and rictus grins, bleeding from eyes, ears and noses, they yelled and shrieked blue murder.

They were short of stature, carried no firearms, but they made up for that in sheer numbers and kill frenzy.

Tom and Chucho held their fire as a 9 mm crossfire from the others chewed up and spit out the attackers. The unsilenced weapons that Mildred, Doc and Krysty had commandeered clattered earsplittingly in the concrete box. Like the bats, the bootlicks flopped and thrashed around on the floor as they died. Unlike the bats, the blood volume their wounds released was fairly spectacular.

Tom unslung his backpack and pitched a few primed and prepped plastique charges into the empty cells. Across the corridor, Ryan was doing the same thing to the cages opposite.

Then both men reshouldered their packs and picked up their RPDs and continued on.

Down the row, J.B. chucked a spent mag on top of the still-twitching bodies and as he cracked in a fresh one he shouted up at the second tier, "Is that all you bedwetters have got?"

The challenge resounded through the prison.

Though they couldn't understand English, the Matachìn got the drift and took up the gauntlet at once.

Autofire rained down from the tier above, in the enclosed space the concentrated roar was mind-numbing. Slugs cratered the concrete floor, sending bits of lead and rubble in all directions.

The walkway offered no concealment and no protection for the shooters. It had holes in it for traction, which could be seen through. Behind the muzzle-flashes were bald-headed men who fired bursts over the railing, then ducked back.

Tom, Chucho and Ryan aimed their MGs at the undersides of the walkway, at the moving shadows, and returned fire.

Pirates above them crumpled, falling over the railing, cartwheeling and smashing into the corridor floor.

The survivors retreated down the rectangle of walkway, to the farthest end of the cell block.

The shooting petered out; the echoes died away.

"The way things stand, this isn't going to end well," Ryan said.

Tom had to agree. They were looking at a stalemate until one side or the other ran out of ammo. Chances were, the good guys would come up empty first.

"Chucho and I can take the rear stairways," Tom said. "We can rush them from both sides of the walkway. While we're keeping them busy, the rest of you can charge the stairs at the far end."

Ryan nodded. "We'll hold off until you open up."

When Tom and Chucho reached the back of the cell block, the spot where they had to part company, Chucho said, "I think we can get them all, but you've got to wait until I start shooting."

"Done," Tom said.

He went up one staircase and Chucho went up the other. Concealed from view, they moved low and fast along the walkway, close to the cells. Tom could see a wall behind the Matachìn position at the far end, and at the center, the top of a doorway. He saw movement, too. Seven or eight pirates crouched well back from the railing.

Across the open space, Chucho was in position on the opposite walkway, kneeling with his RPD shouldered.

Tom crept a little closer, then raised his weapon.

Whether the Matachìn sensed they were about to come under full frontal attack, or whether they just decided it was time to make their move to harder cover, they all straightened and turned for the door.

Someone spoke at that end of the hall, clear as a bell, in Spanish. The big bald-headed pirate in charge paused with his hand on the doorknob and looked back, puzzled.

Then Chucho popped up and let it rip.

Tom did the same, rising as he fired, and advancing on the targets.

The double stream of slugs chopped the Matachìn down in their tracks. Not one returned fire, not one made it through the door. They died on the walkway, a few feet from safety.

Ryan and the others started charging up the staircases, but it was all over.

"What happened?" Tom asked Chucho. "Why did they stop?"

Chucho's eyes glittered. "A little trick I picked up."

From behind Tom a familiar voice said in English, "Wait! It's a trap!"

Tom turned his head to look; he couldn't help it. When he turned back, Chucho was laughing. "Well, nuke me if that ain't a trick and a half," Tom said.

Ryan saw the partially open door and said, "Better check in there. Blasters up." He kicked the door back and entered with Tom right on his heels. The windowless room was deserted, but it wasn't empty.

There were beds, a sink, a flush toilet, countertops, and it was crammed with stuff. At one end of a table cluttered with other objects, on an open blanket lay an assortment of weapons. Familiar weapons.

A scoped longblaster.

A SIG-Sauer pistol.

A pump action 12-gauge.

Revolvers.

And an antique blaster.

Tanner made a beeline for his Civil War treasure. He pulled out the LeMat and checked the nipples and wadding. "Just the way I left it," he said, strapping the holstered weapon around his waist.

The others hurriedly reclaimed their hardware. Like Doc, they made sure everything was in good working order.

"What is this room?" J.B. asked.

"Mebbe a warden's or guards' quarters, back in the day," Ryan said.

"Have a look at this," Krysty said, waving the others over to the overloaded counter along one wall. In an array of covered plastic containers there were viscous-looking pastes: brown, green, golden-yellow. She popped one of the lids and sniffed. "Gaia!" she gasped, holding it at arm's length. "That is just awful."

"What is it?"

"I have no clue," Krysty said. "But if smells could kill…"

"This is interesting, too," Doc said, holding open a fat, spiral-bound notebook. "Perhaps you can make sense of it, Mildred. It is beyond me."

Tom looked over Mildred's shoulder as she scanned the open pages. He had never seen anything like it.

"Could be Sanskrit," Mildred said, flipping pages.

"Chicken scratching, you mean," Tom said.

Then she came to a series of hand-drawn diagrams or schematics.

"These look like chemical formulas," Mildred said. "But there are symbols here for elements that don't exist, or at least I've never heard of."

"Mebbe it's a kid's game," J.B. suggested.

"No kids here," Jak said.

"The symbology is too consistent for it to be something like that," Mildred went on. "Some of it almost makes sense, mathematically. If this is biochem, it's not like anything I ever learned."

"Where did it come from?" Krysty said.

Mildred shrugged. "Your guess is as good as mine."

"Who knows and who cares?" J.B. said with growing impatience. "If none of us can read it, it might as well be flies on dog shit."

He had a point.

After the room and the second tier were mined with C-4, Tom said, "I think we're ready to blow this dump to hell."

"Not quite yet," Mildred corrected him. "First we've got to destroy the freezies who haven't been reanimated. As long as they can be resurrected, so can the plague weapon."

"Blow them up, too," Tom said.

"Not necessary," Mildred told him. "All we have to do is pull the plugs on their cryo tanks and they'll start to thaw out. Without a computer regulating the defrosting, their bodies will turn to icy slunk and then rot in the heat."

Though the grounds were still crawling with terrified but smiling bootlicks, they found the entrance to the Cold House unguarded. Tom, the companions and Chucho just walked in and made themselves at home. Along the back wall was a row of stainless-steel cylinders, practically floor-to-ceiling high, and twice as wide as fifty-five-gallon drums, each with its own set of LCD readout monitors and massive, armored power conduits.

"I don't see any rad-blasted plugs to pull," J.B. said.

"Then how about this?" Mildred asked. She commenced to walk down the line of tanks, firing bursts from her 9 mm subgun point-blank into the front of each of them, emptying the 30-round, stick mag. Supercooled air jetted from the holes punched in the thin steel, and when it met the tropical heat it turned instantly to dense fog.

The clouds of condensing moisture were so thick they had to back out of the room, and they did so coughing. Before he backed out, Tom tossed down the last of the blocks of C-4.

J.B.'s spectacles looked like they'd been frosted. Scowling, he took them off and wiped them on the tail of his T-shirt.

"We need to put some distance between us and the C-4 before I detonate," Tom told them. "When this goes off, it's gonna be a big bang."

"We can't go out the way we came in," Ryan said. "That's where the dog packs are coming from. We've got to go out the front gate."

"Trouble is," Tom said, "the boat that brung us is the other way."

"The boats that brought us are tied up at the end of the path that leads to the front gate," Krysty said.

"Big enough to carry all of us?" Tom asked.

"Certainly," Doc said. "Big enough to carry us all in a modicum of comfort."

"Problem solved, then," Ryan said. "Let's get out of here."

Chapter Twenty-Eight

When the gunfire started outside, Daniel Desipio lay on his back on a gurney in the Razor House recovery room. Because he was still in terrible pain from the unanesthetized marrow-suck, the whitecoats hadn't bothered to strap him down. After all, he could hardly walk, so how could he run? And where would he run to?

He heard the sound of the main door being kicked open, then the tramp of boots and angry shouts booming down the hall outside. He recognized the voice at once and his blood ran cold. By now Ryan Cawdor should have been dead and wormy. Instead he was calling out to his friends. He had come to rescue them, and perhaps he was already too late. Holy fuck, he's going to find me, Daniel thought.

As doors banged back down the hallway, he managed to roll off the gurney, but in the process he knocked over a rolling tray of surgical instruments. When he hit the floor, white-hot pain exploded in his hips and he lost consciousness for a second. The shouting and footfalls woke him up. He had to assume that Cawdor and whoever was with him would search room to room, chilling the whitecoats as they went. He knew he'd get no mercy, either. From the sound of it, they were coming his way. Hand over hand, dragging his legs behind him, he crawled on his belly to the nearest cover, beneath the stainless-steel operating table.

When the door opened, it wasn't the one-eyed man who appeared, it was Dr. Yorte. The head whitecoat rushed in and quickly and quietly closed the door behind him. Leaning his back against it, he gasped for breath. His eyes were wide with fear as he swept his fingers through his thick black hair again and again.

Dr. Yorte was far too preoccupied to notice that his plague vector was gone from the gurney.

Daniel recalled the words spoken earlier, as he had writhed under the corkscrewing needle. "Maybe we should suck the cells from his spine. Oh, no, wait a minute. I forgot, he doesn't have one. Heh-heh-heh-heh."

Waves of pain shot down his legs and blurred his mind, jumbling the memories of his 135-year life. The distinction between the plastic surgeon and his predark publisher vanished. They became one and the same, a single object of hatred and loathing, a fixture of his existence.

Meanwhile, Dr. Yorte had crossed the room, and dropped to his hands and knees in front of a low cabinet built into the back wall. He opened the little cabinet door, pushed aside the contents, then squeezed himself inside and pulled the door shut behind him.

The shouts from the hallway faded, and after a pause more gunfire erupted from outside the building. Daniel lay there, listening with every muscle tensed, while the fighting escalated. There was one hell of a gun battle going on.

For the moment, he was safe.

He closed his eyes, and kept them closed for what seemed a very long time, until the shooting stopped.

Under his nose, amid the scattering of gleaming surgical tools, was a scalpel, its edge keen as a razor. Almost of its own accord, his hand moved to grab it. The feel of the steel handle against his palm was electrifying. A terrible energy animated his limbs, driving out the pain in his hips.

No spine? he thought, squeezing the scalpel so hard his knuckles turned white.

Then the epiphany hit. Before him was the opportunity he had been longing for: the time had finally come for him to write his own story.

Rising shakily to his feet, the Fire Talker approached the cabinet. "No spine, huh?" he growled down at the little door. He ripped open the cabinet, reached in and snatched hold of Dr. Yorte by the hair. As he hauled the whitecoat out of the hidey-hole, he rammed his right knee into the middle of his face and felt the nose cartilage crush. The impact made pain lance into his hip, but Daniel was past caring.

The worm had turned.

Yorte groaned at the stunning blow and went limp. Daniel dumped him onto his back, then straddled his chest, pinning his arms to the floor with his knees. Wielding the scalpel back and forth, back and forth in a frenzied attack, the Fire Talker slashed through white fabric and into the brown hairless skin. Quite literally, and in the span of a minute, he cut the man to ribbons, down to the bone from forehead to sternum. Because he was holding his breath the whole time, Daniel nearly passed out. With an effort, he lurched to his feet and stepped away from his handiwork.

Yorte, still horribly alive, was flapping his arms, smearing his blood, and making a red snow-angel on the white-tiled floor.

The smell of the gore turned Daniel's stomach. He projectile-vomited, splattering his victim and the floor at his feet.

Bloody scalpel in his bloody hand, the Fire Talker stumbled

from the room, down the hall, his paper hospital gown baring his ass to the world.

After two lifetimes of subjugation, of humiliation, he was finally victorious.

He had started his own story, at last. He had cast himself as the indomitable pulp hero. There were no pages of space-filling dialogue. No interminable backstory explanations that never quite made sense. This was the real deal. Daniel Desipio had become an avenging angel of the perpetually downtrodden, the victimized. And he wasn't done yet. There still had to be an ending, a shocking but appropriate climax. He owed that kind of finish to his audience, even if it was an audience of one.

Daniel staggered out of the building, then across the yard to the door of Jaguar House. Hounds of hell were baying inside, clawing at the door to be freed.

Imprisoned in the dark.

Starved.

Taunted.

Furious.

They would be the instruments of his vengeance on the criminal monsters still roaming the compound.

Having finally discovered his spine, Daniel found to his surprise that he couldn't undiscover it.

He knew he was just as much of a beast as those he was about to destroy. And his crimes were much more subtle than the machete chop and the shotgun blast. They were cowardly, backstabbing crimes of mass murder against the innocent and the helpless. He knew that for justice to be done he, too, had to be punished.

At last Daniel Desipio was the author of something truly

original, his lifelong dream come true. Throwing aside the scalpel, he hurled open the door to Jaguar House.

The dogs were on him in an instant, pulling him down onto the courtyard, biting into him as he screamed, shaking their massive heads, tearing out his flesh in great hunks.

Chapter Twenty-Nine

Ryan hustled the others out the prison's front gate ahead of him. He backed out of Xibalba looking down the sights of his RPD, covering the retreat. Figures were running around between the buildings, but no one was coming after them.

Harmonica Tom stopped fifty feet down the path, shrugged out of his pack and then dug around in it for the remote detonator. Holding it up for the others to see, he flipped off the safety switch and said, "Any last words for these bastards?"

"Fuck 'em," Jak said.

"My sentiments exactly," Doc said.

"Anybody else?" Tom asked.

"Do it," Ryan said.

"Fire in the hole," Tom said.

When he hit the button, the whole world jolted. Even in daylight, the flash through the trees was blinding, and the cluster of C-4 booms so tightly spaced they seemed almost simultaneous. It was the kind of explosion that nothing could survive. Debris began to rain down, falling through the forest canopy. Big chunks ripped off branches and released showers of green leaves.

"We're too close," Ryan said. "We need to move."

As they hurried down the path, he envisioned the destruction in his mind's eye. The site cratered, leveled, littered with pieces of concrete. When he turned his head, he saw Chucho was watching his expression and smiling like a proud pappy. The other Hero Twin was thinking the same thing he was.

Absolute nukin' wipe-out.

As they proceeded down the narrow trail, after the explosions' echoes faded, another sound rolled over them from the far side of the compound, the sound of the wild dog pack going crazy as it closed in for a kill.

Then came a terrible warbling scream.

So much for the gods of the underworld, Ryan thought.

As ATAPUL X CRASHED through the rain forest, his heavy footfalls jarred the mask that still covered his head. The terrible explosions at the heart of the prison were still echoing off the hillsides. Running away from the fight held no shame for him. He had nothing important vested in the effort, nor had any of the others. To creatures who lived as long as they did, the fictions of Xibalba and the Lords of Death were simply entertaining diversions while they waited for rescue.

The jungle felt like home to him; not because he had lived here for more than three-quarters of a century, but because it reminded him of his real home, far far away—the deep shade, the constant heat and humidity, the high oxygen content, the profusion of edibles from which dietary pastes could be made.

The EM pulse of nukeday had been the beacon that had lured Atapul X and his crew to Earth from deep space. During the planetary survey the unthinkable happened: the mother ship had malfunctioned, fallen out of orbit and crashed. Lucky for the surviving crew of the survey shuttle, they had been mapping the island as a possible habitation site for a future colonist base. It was easily defensible, with natural barriers to invasion.

The Lords of Death had never once left Xibalba because
not being human, they didn't recognize its squalor; they were
satisfied by the prison and the surrounding jungle. They
needed to be close to the shuttle when help finally arrived.

The initial takeover of the prison from the Matachìn had
been easy. The pirates were a superstitious and ignorant lot;
their leaders were deranged maniacs. The Mayan mythos
coupled with a show of advanced weaponry, quickly brought
them to heel. Atapul X and his crew understood the use of
plague weapons, and after the initial debacle in Panama
City, had designed a campaign of conquest around them. To
survive the centuries until their distress signal was
answered, they had to acquire a steady supply of goods and
services. In a nuke-blasted world, this required an empire
of sorts—cargo ships traveling back and forth from the
north, pack trains crossing the isthmus—a primitive extrac-
tive bureaucracy.

At the first sign of trouble that afternoon, he and the other
five members of his crew had scattered off into the jungle, according to plan, soon to regroup at their shuttle landing site.

Something moved on the trail ahead of him. Something
gray, slinking low and fast between the trees. Four legs. Atapul
X slowed to a walk. He could hear them moving in the bush,
creeping forward, then the snarling and howling began. Then
he could see them.

He stopped.

All around him, the feral dogs closed in, their coats wet,
their ears pinned back. He saw their eyes, their bared teeth,
their dripping maws. He saw their hot breath gusting out like
steam. There were dozens of them, none smaller than eighty
pounds, some half again that large. Creatures who loved to

kill, who killed each other out of boredom. Culling the weak was their recreation.

Atapul X was not weak.

He reached up and unfastened the clamps that held down his mask. When he removed it, the animals froze, either from the sight or the smell of him. Then he opened the hideous orifice that passed for a mouth and screamed with all his might.

The hell dogs whimpered in pain and dropped to their stomachs. As he strode past them, some rolled onto their backs and presented their bellies to him, the Alpha of Alphas; others slinked away into the jungle, tails between their legs.

There was no telling how much longer rescue would take, Atapul X thought as he refastened his mask. He resumed his jog to the rendezvous at the downed shuttle. With the plague weapon destroyed, Tierra de la Muerte was out of reach. Temporarily. He always enjoyed a challenge. It helped pass the time—and time was what he and the others had a surplus of.

Epilogue

The off-key music coming from the Bertram's flybridge made Ryan wince and look up. Tom was teaching Chucho how to play the harmonica as he closed in on the anchored forty-five-foot Hatteras.

It was a shame and a pity to destroy such a fine and rare ship, but the alternative—running it back to Panama City—was pointless. Ryan knew they'd just have to sink it there. They had already destroyed the boats at the island's other landing site. The idea was to cut it off from the mainland, permanently if possible.

Ryan figured that when word got back to Veracruz and the other Mexican city-states that there was no more threat of plague, and the Lords of Death were out of business, the red sashes and priests were going to be in big trouble.

Their empire would crumble in a matter of days. And it would be real heads on sticks leading the parades.

When Tom had the Bertram in position in the cove, Ryan and J.B. hefted RPDs and aimed close-range machine guns at the full length of the Hatteras's waterline. Two hundred rounds turned the fiberglass hull to splinters and made it leak like a sieve. The ship almost immediately began to list hard to port.

They watched until it settled to the bottom; the water

wasn't deep enough to entirely submerge it. The flybridge and radar mast were still visible above the surface.

Tom carefully backed the Bertram out of the cove, and Chucho tried another solo on the harmonica, tapping his foot. This time it didn't sound half-bad. Not so many off-key notes, and he had the rhythm down. He was catching on quick.

Doc was so moved by the serenade that he broke into an ungainly, impromptu jig on the stern deck. The scarecrow dance made Mildred, J.B. and Jak laugh out loud. They started to clap along, urging him on.

As Ryan turned to watch the time-traveler's perilous footwork, out of the corner of his eye he thought he saw something move on the beach near the cave mouth. Something white on two legs. With a big old head. But when he looked back the beach was empty.

"What is it, lover?" Krysty asked, noting the concern on his face.

"Nothing, it's nothing," he assured her as he slipped an arm around her narrow waist. "This rad-blasted place has got me seeing things."

TAKE 'EM FREE

2 action-packed novels plus a mystery bonus

NO RISK

NO OBLIGATION TO BUY